PAGAN

BABIES

Books by Elmore Leonard

The Bounty Hunters

The Law at Randado

Escape from Five
  Shadows

Last Stand at Saber River

Hombre

The Big Bounce

The Moonshine War

Valdez Is Coming

Forty Lashes Less One

Mr. Majestyk

Fifty-two Pickup

Swag

Unknown Man No. 89

The Hunted

The Switch

Gunsights

Gold Coast

City Primeval

Split Images

Cat Chaser

Stick

LaBrava

Glitz

Bandits

Touch

Freaky Deaky

Killshot

Get Shorty

Maximum Bob

Rum Punch

Pronto

Riding the Rap

Out of Sight

Cuba Libre

The Tonto Woman and
  Other Western Stories

Be Cool

Pagan Babies

ELMORE LEONARD

PAGAN BABIES

Delacorte Press

Published by
Delacorte Press
Random House, Inc.
1540 Broadway
New York, New York 10036

Delacorte Press® is a registered trademark of Random House, Inc., and the colophon is a trademark of Random House, Inc.

Library of Congress Cataloging-in-Publication Data

Leonard, Elmore, 1925–
p. cm.
ISBN 0-385-33392-7
1. Americans—Rwanda—Fiction.   2. Detroit (Mich.)—Fiction.
3. Criminals—Fiction.   4. Rwanda—Fiction.   I. Title.
PS3562.E55 P3 2000
813'.54—dc21   00-029506

Book design by Virginia Norey

Manufactured in the United States of America
Published simultaneously in Canada

September 2000

10 9 8 7 6 5 4 3 2 1

BVG

For Jackie Farber

PAGAN

BABIES

1
_____

THE CHURCH HAD BECOME a tomb where forty-seven bodies turned to leather and stains had been lying on the concrete floor the past five years, though not lying where they had been shot with Kalashnikovs or hacked to death with machetes. The benches had been removed and the bodies reassembled: men, women and small children laid in rows of skulls and spines, femurs, fragments of cloth stuck to mummified remains, many of the adults missing feet, all missing bones that had been carried off by scavenging dogs.

Since the living would no longer enter the church, Fr. Terry Dunn heard confessions in the yard of the rectory, in the shade of old pines and silver eucalyptus trees.

"Bless me, Fatha, for I have sin. It has been two months from the last time I come to Confession. Since then I am fornicating with a woman from Gisenyi three times only and this is all I have done."

They would seem to fill their mouths with the English words, pro-nounc-ing each one carefully, with an accent Terry believed was heard only in Africa. He gave fornicators ten Our Fathers and ten Hail Marys, murmured what passed for an absolution while the penitent said the Act of Contrition, and dismissed them with a reminder to love God and sin no more.

"Bless me, Fatha, for I have sin. Is a long time since I come here but is not my fault, you don't have Confession always when you say. The sin I did, I stole a goat from close by Nyundo for my family to eat. My wife cook it en brochette and also in a stew with potatoes and peppers."

"Last night at supper," Terry said, "I told my housekeeper I'd enjoy goat stew a lot more if it wasn't so goddamn bony."

The goat thief said, "Excuse me, Fatha?"

"Those little sharp bones you get in your mouth," Terry said, and gave the man ten Our Fathers and ten Hail Marys. He gave just about everyone ten Our Fathers and ten Hail Marys to say as their penance.

Some came seeking advice.

"Bless me, Fatha, I have not sin yet but I think of it. I see one of the men kill my family has come back. One of the Hutu *Interahamwe* militia, he come back from the Goma refugee camp and I like to kill him, but I don't want to go to prison and I don't want to go to Hell. Can you have God forgive me before I kill him?"

Terry said, "I don't think He'll go for it. The best you can do, report the guy to the *conseiller* at the sector office and promise to testify at the trial."

The man who hadn't killed anyone yet said, "Fatha, when is that happen? I read in *Imvaho* they have one hundred twenty-four thousand in prisons waiting for trials. In how many years will it be for this man that kill my family? *Imvaho* say two hundred years to try all of them."

Terry said, "Is the guy bigger than you are?"

"No, he's Hutu."

"Walk up to the guy," Terry said, "and hit him in the mouth as hard as you can, with a rock. You'll feel better. Now make a good Act of Contrition for anything you might've done and forgot about." Terry could offer temporary relief but nothing that would change their lives.

Penitents would kneel on a prie-dieu and see his profile through a framed square of cheesecloth mounted on the kneeler: Fr. Terry Dunn, a bearded young man in a white cassock, sitting in a wicker chair. Sideways to the screen he looked at the front yard full of brush and weeds and the road that came up past the church from the village of Arisimbi. He heard Confession usually once a week but said Mass, in the school, only a few times a year: Christmas Day, Easter Sunday and when someone died. The Rwandese Bishop of Nyundo, nine miles up the road, sent word for Fr. Dunn to come and give an account of himself.

He drove there in the yellow Volvo station wagon that had belonged to the priest before him and sat in the bishop's office among African sculptures and decorative baskets, antimacassars in bold star designs on the leather sofa and chairs, on the wall a print of the Last Supper and a photograph of the bishop taken with the pope. Terry had worn his cassock. The bishop, in a white sweater, asked him if he was attempting to start a new sect within the Church. Terry said no, he had a personal reason for not acting as a full-time priest, but would not say what it was. He did tell the bishop, "You can contact the order that runs the mission, the Missionary Fathers of St. Martin de Porres in Bay St. Louis, Mississippi, and ask to have me replaced; but if you do, good luck. Young guys today are not breaking down the door to get in the seminary."

This was several years ago. Terry left the bishop shaking his head and was still here on his own.

This afternoon the prie-dieu was placed beneath a roof of palm fronds and thatch that extended from the rectory into the yard. A voice raised against the hissing sound of the rain said, "Bless me, Fatha, for I have sin," and started right in. "I kill seven people that time I'm still a boy and we kill the *inyenzi,* the cockroaches. I kill four persons in the church the time you saying the Mass there and you see it happen. You know we kill five hundred in Nyundo before we come here and kill I think one hundred in this village before everybody run away."

Terry continued to stare at the yard that sloped down to the road, the clay hardpack turned dark in the rain.

"And we kill some more where we have the roadblock and stop all the drivers and look at the identity cards. The ones we want we take in the bush and kill them."

The man paused and Terry waited. The guy wasn't confessing his sins, he was bragging about what he did.

"You hear me, Fatha?"

Terry said, "Keep talking," wondering where the guy was going with it.

"I can tell you more will die very soon. How do I know this? I am a visionary, Fatha. I am told in visions of the Blessed Virgin saying to do it, to kill the *inyenzi.* I tell you this and you don't say nothing, do you?"

Terry didn't answer. The man's voice, at times shrill, sounded familiar.

"No, you can't," the voice said. "Oh, you can tell me not to do it, but you can't tell no other person, the RPA, the *conseiller,* nobody, because I tell you this in Confession and you have the rule say you can't talk about what you hear. You listen to me? We going to cut the feet off before we kill them. You know why we do it? You are here that time, so you understand. But you have no power, so you don't stop us. Listen, if we see you when we come, a tall one like you, we cut your feet off, too."

Terry sat in his wicker chair staring out at the rain, the pale sky, mist covering the far hills. The thing was, these guys could do it. They already had, so it wasn't just talk, the guy mouthing off.

He said, "You going to give me my penance to say?"

Terry didn't answer.

"All right, I finished."

The man rose from the kneeler and in a moment Terry watched him walking away, barefoot, skinny bare legs, a stick figure wearing a checkered green shirt and today in the rain a raggedy straw hat with the brim turned down. Terry didn't need to see the guy's face. He knew him the way he knew people in the village by the clothes they wore, the same clothes they put on every morning, if they didn't sleep in them. He had seen that green shirt recently, only a few days ago . . .

Among the stalls in the marketplace.

This one wearing the shirt and three of his friends drinking banana beer from a tin trough, the trough long enough for all four of them squatting around it to stick reed straws into the thick brew, lower their heads and suck it up warm, the beer giving them a glow that showed in dreamy eyes looking up at Terry walking past the open stall, Terry catching the look and the one in the green shirt commenting as the others laughed, his voice louder then, shrill, following Terry to a man who was roasting corn in a pan of hot coals. This was Thomas, wearing a yellow T-shirt Terry had given him some months before. He asked Thomas about the guy with the shrill voice and Thomas said, "Oh, the visionary, Bernard. He drinks banana beer and our Blessed Mother speaks to him. Some people believe him."

"What's he saying?"

"As you go by, 'Oh, here comes *umugabo wambaye ikanzu,*' calling you 'the man who wears a dress.' Then he say you come to buy the food your Tutsi whore cooks for you, the one you are fucking but don't want nobody to know it, you being a priest. Bernard say the Blessed Mother told him what you doing. Now he say he isn't afraid of you. *'Oli enyamaswa.'* You were sired by animals."

"I don't even know him. What's he up to?"

"He talks to dishonor you in front of the people here. He calls you *'injigi.'*" Thomas shrugged. "Telling everyone you stupid." Thomas raised his face in the sunlight as he listened again. On the front of his T-shirt were the words THE STONE COYOTES, and on the back, ROCK WITH A TWANG. "Now he tells everyone he saw you and you saw him, but you don't do nothing."

"When did I see him?"

"I think he means during the genocide time, when he's in the Hutu militia and can kill anybody he wants to. I wasn't here or I think I would be dead." Then Thomas said to Terry that day in the market, "But you, Fatha, you were here, hmmm? In the church when they come in there?"

"That was five years ago."

"Look," Thomas said, "the visionary is leaving. See how they all have machetes? They like to do it again, kill the Tutsis they miss the first time."

Terry watched the green shirt walking away.

Today he watched from the wicker chair, the green shirt on the stick figure walking toward the road in the rain, still in the yard when Terry called to him.

"Hey, Bernard?"

It stopped him.

"I have visions, too, man."

Francis Dunn heard from his brother no more than three or four times a year. Fran would wire funds to the Banque Commerciale du Rwanda, send a load of old clothes and T-shirts, a half-dozen rolls of film, and a month or so later Terry would write to thank him. He'd mention the weather, going into detail during the rainy season, and that would be it. He never sent pictures. Fran said to his wife, Mary Pat, "What's he do with all the film I send him?"

Mary Pat said, "He probably trades it for booze."

Terry hadn't said much about the situation over there since the time of the genocide, when the ones in control then, the Hutus, closed their borders and tried to wipe out the entire Tutsi population, murdering as many as eight hundred thousand in a period of three months: a full-scale attempt at genocide that barely made the six o'clock news. Terry didn't say much about his work at the mission, either, what he was actually doing. Fran liked to picture Terry in a white cassock and sandals gathering children around him, happy little native kids showing their white teeth.

Lately, Terry had opened up a little more, saying in a letter, "The tall guys and the short guys are still giving each other dirty looks, otherwise things seem to be back to what passes for normal here. I've learned what the essentials of life are. Nails, salt, matches, kerosene, charcoal, batteries, Fanta soda, rolling paper and Johnnie Walker red, the black label for a special occasion. Electricity is on in the village until about ten P.M. But there is still only one telephone. It rings in the sector office, occupied by the RPA, the Rwandese Patriotic Army, pretty good guys for a change acting as police."

There was even a second page to the latest letter. Fran said to Mary Pat, "Listen to this. He lists the different smells you become aware of in the village, like the essence of the place. Listen. He says, 'The smell of mildew, the smell of raw meat, cooking oil, charcoal-burning fires, the smell of pit latrines, the smell of powdered milk in the morning—people eating their gruel. The smell of coffee, overripe fruit, eucalyptus in the air. The smell of tobacco, unwashed bodies, and the smell of banana beer on the breath of a man confessing his sins.' "

Mary Pat said, "Gross."

"Yeah, but you know something," Fran said, "he's starting to sound like himself again."

Mary Pat said, "Is that good or bad?"

2

THE RPA OFFICER IN CHARGE took the call from the priest's brother in America, asking how he could be of service. He placed his hand over his ear away from the receiver as he listened. He said oh, he was very sorry to hear that. Said yes, of course, he would tell Fr. Dunn. What? . . . No, the sound was rain coming down on the roof, a metal roof. Yes, only rain. This month it rained every afternoon, sometimes all day. He said hmmmm, mmm-hmm, as he listened to the priest's brother repeat everything he had said before. Finally the RPA officer said yes, of course, he would go at once.

Then remembered something. "Oh, and a letter from you also came today."

The priest's brother said, "With some news he'll be very happy to hear. Unlike this call."

The officer's name was Laurent Kamweya.

He was Tutsi, born in Rwanda but had lived most of his life in Uganda, where the official language was English. Laurent had gone to university in Kampala, trained with guerrilla forces of the Rwandese Patriotic Front, and returned with the army to retake the government from the Hutu *génocidaires*. He had been here in Arisimbi less than a year as acting *conseiller*, the local government official. Laurent waited until the rain had worn itself out and the tea plantations on the hills to the east were again bright green, then waited a little more.

An hour before sunset, when the priest would be sitting outside with his bottle of Johnnie Walker, Laurent got behind the wheel of the RPA's Toyota Land Cruiser and started up the hill—maybe to learn more about this strange priest, though he would rather be going to Kigali, a place to meet smart-looking women in the hotel bars.

This was a primitive place where people drank banana beer and spent their lives as peasants hoeing the ground, digging, chopping, gathering, growing corn and beans, bananas, using all the ground here, the smallest plots, growing corn even in this road and up close to their dwellings, the houses made of mud bricks the same reddish color as the red-clay road Laurent followed, continuing up the slope to the school and the sweet potato field the children worked. Now the road switched back to come around above the school and Laurent was approaching the church, this old white basilica St. Martin de Porres, losing its paint, scars showing its mud bricks, swifts flying in and out of the belfry. A church full of ghosts, no longer of use to the living.

The road looped and switched back again above the church and now he was approaching the rectory, in the trees that grew along the crest of the hill.

There it was, set back from the road, a bungalow covered in vines, its whitewash chipped and peeling, the place uncared for, Laurent was told, since the old priest who was here most of his life had died.

And there was the priest who remained, Fr. Terry Dunn, in the shade of the thatched roof that extended from the side of the house like a room without walls, where he sat sometimes to hear Confession and in the evening with his Johnnie Walker. Laurent had heard he also smoked ganja his housekeeper obtained for him in Gisenyi, at the Café Tum Tum Bikini. The Scotch he purchased by the case in Kigali, on his trips to the capital.

You could see from his appearance, the shorts, the T-shirts that bore the names of rock bands or different events in America, he made no effort to look like a priest. The beard could indicate he was a foreign missionary, a look some of them affected. What did he do? He distributed clothes sent by his brother, he heard Confession when he felt like it, listened to people complain of their lives, people mourning the extinction of their families. He did play with the children, took pictures of them and read to them from the books of a Dr. Seuss. But most of the time, Laurent believed, he sat here on his hill with his friend Mr. Walker.

There, looking this way, the priest getting up from the table as he sees the Land Cruiser of the Rwandese Patriotic Army come to visit, turning into the yard, to stop behind the priest's yellow Volvo station wagon, an old one. Laurent switched off the engine and heard music, the sound coming from the house, not loud but a pleasing rhythm he believed was . . . Yes, it was reggae.

And there was the priest's housekeeper, Chantelle, coming from the bungalow with a bowl of ice and glasses on a round tray. Chantelle Nyamwase. She brought the bottle of Scotch under her arm—actually, pressed between her slender body in a white undershirt and the stump of her arm, the left one, that had been severed just above the elbow. Chantelle seldom covered the stump. She said it told who she was, though anyone could look at her figure and see she was Tutsi. There were people who said she had worked as a prostitute at the Hotel des Mille Collines in Kigali, but could no longer perform this service because of her mutilation. With the clean white under-shirt she wore a *pagne* smooth and tight about her hips, the skirt falling to her white tennis shoes, the material in a pattern of shades, blue and tan with streaks of white.

Once out of the Land Cruiser Laurent straightened the jacket of his combat fatigues and removed his beret. Approaching the yard he could identify the music now coming from the rectory, the voice of Ziggy Marley and the song "One Good Spliff," one you heard at Le Piano Bar of the Hotel Meridien in Kigali, Ziggy coming to the part, "Me and my younger sisters we take a ride." Chantelle now stood with the priest, the tray and the Johnnie Walker on the table that was without color from standing always in the yard, the bottle sealed, Laurent noted, before he said to the priest:

"Father, I am very sorry to tell you news from your brother. Your mother has died in hospital. Your brother said tell you the funeral is two days from now."

The priest wore a T-shirt that said NINE INCH NAILS—THE PERFECT DRUG across his chest. He nodded twice, very slow about it.

"I appreciate your coming, Laurent."

That was all he said. Now he was looking off at the church or the sky, or the hills across the way, a haze resting on the high meadows.

Laurent remembered something else the brother had told him. "Yes, and he said tell you your sister has permission to attend the fu-neral from . . . someplace where she is. I couldn't hear so good with the rain." Laurent waited.

This time the priest seemed engaged by his thoughts and wasn't listening. Or, didn't care about the sister.

Chantelle said, "His sister, Therese, is in a convent," and contin-ued in her language, Kinyarwanda, telling Laurent the sister was a member of the Carmelite order of nuns who were cloistered and had taken the vow of silence; so it appeared Therese had to be given permission to come out and attend the funeral. Laurent asked if the priest would also attend. Chantelle looked at the priest before saying she didn't know. Laurent told her his own mother had died in hospital, and began to tell how the *Interahamwe*, the Hutu thugs, came into the ward with spears made of bamboo—

Chantelle put her finger to her lips to silence him, then took the priest's arm to give him comfort, the touch of someone close.

Laurent heard her say, "Terry," her voice a murmur, "what can I do?"

Calling him by his Christian name—someone who must be more to him than a housekeeper. Who would hire a woman with only one arm to cook and clean? Chantelle was very smart-looking, even more attractive than the whores in the bar of the Mille Collines, women known for their beauty, many of them killed because of it.

Laurent told himself to be patient, Johnnie Walker wasn't going anywhere. Give the priest time to accept his mother's death, someone close to him but far away in America. He would be used to death close by, there in the church, less than one hundred meters away. Was he staring at the church, or in his mind staring at nothing? Or was he listening to Ziggy Marley and the Melody Makers now doing "Beautiful Day," Ziggy's Jamaican voice drifting over the hills of western Rwanda. Laurent became aware of his body moving oh so slightly and made himself stand still, before the priest or Chantelle would notice.

The priest was turning to walk away, but then stopped and looked back at Laurent.

"You know a young guy named Bernard? A Hutu, wears a green checkered shirt, sometimes a straw hat?"

It took Laurent by surprise, thinking the priest was grieving the death of his mother.

"I know of him, yes. He came back from Goma, the refugee camp. Those relief people, they don't know the good guys from the bad guys. The RPA comes, the Hutus run, and the relief people give them blankets and food. Yes, I know him."

"He tells everybody he took part in the genocide."

Laurent nodded. "So did most of the ones he tells."

"He admits he killed people. In the church."

"Yes, I hear that."

"Why don't you pick him up?"

"Arrest him? But who saw him kill people? The ones who were there are dead. Where is a witness to come before the court? Listen, RPA soldiers hear of a person like Bernard, they want to take him in the bush and shoot him. But if they do, they the ones are arrested. Two soldiers have been tried and executed for killing Hutu suspects. All we can do is keep our eyes on him."

"But if a man, not a soldier," the priest said, "sees the one who murdered his family and takes revenge . . ."

The priest waited and Laurent said, "I would sympathize with him."

"Would you arrest him?"

Laurent said, looking into the priest's eyes, "I would report I made a search and was not able to find him."

The priest, nodding his head, held Laurent's gaze, then turned and was walking away when Laurent remembered the letter. He said, "Father," bringing the letter from his pocket, "I have this, also from your brother." Chantelle took the envelope from him and brought it to the priest, again resting her hand on his arm, Laurent watching them: the priest looking at the envelope and then speaking to his housekeeper, his hand going to her shoulder, Laurent watching the familiar way they touched each other.

3

CHANTELLE RETURNED TO THE TABLE as the priest continued toward the house.

"He invites you please to have a drink."

"Is he coming back?"

"He didn't say."

She sounded tired.

"With ice," Laurent said, approaching the table. "He surprised me talking the way he did. I thought he was looking at the church, the death of his mother reminding him of the dead inside."

They used English now, Laurent's first language.

"He wants to bury them," Chantelle said, "but the *bourgmestre,* the same person who told the Hutu militia to go in and kill them, said no, it must stay the way it is, a memorial to the dead." She handed Laurent his drink. "Explain that to me if you can."

"He calls it a memorial," Laurent said, "and you think the

bourgmestre, Mr. Shiny Suit, is sorry now, look, he's showing remorse. But I think he keeps the dead in the church so he can say, 'Look what we did,' proud of it. You were here that time, in the church?"

"I tried to be here, but no, I was in Kigali," Chantelle said, "all day listening to the radio for news. The disc jockey tells the Hutus to perform their duty, go out in the streets and kill. He gives them such information as, 'Tutsis are in the Air Burundi office on Rue du Lac Nasho. Go and kill them. Tutsis are in the bank on Avenue de Rusumo.' Like the radio has eyes. I hear the disc jockey say militia are needed out in the country in different communes, and he names this one where my family lives."

"You must have been worried about them."

"Of course, but I didn't come here in time."

"What about the priest? Where was he?"

"Here," Chantelle said, pouring herself a drink over ice, "while you were in Uganda or you would be dead or missing part of you. Yes, Fr. Dunn was here, but earlier that day he was in Kigali visiting the old priest, Fr. Toreki, in the hospital, his heart failing him. In only two more weeks he's dead. Fr. Toreki was here forty years, half his life, when he died. This day Fr. Dunn is visiting they also hear the radio telling Hutu militia to go out to the communes. Fr. Toreki tells Fr. Dunn, go home and bring everyone he can find to the church, because the church has always been a place of safety. So now as many as sixty or seventy are inside, more frightened than ever in their lives. Fr. Dunn, on the altar, is at the most sacred part of the Mass, the Consecration, elevating the Host. At this moment they come in the church screaming 'Kill the cockroaches!' the *inyenzi,* and they begin killing everyone, even the babies, until no one is spared. The ones who try to run out have no chance. Some of the women they brought outside and raped, the butchers taking turns before killing them. Can you imagine it? Fr. Dunn, on the altar, watching his people being put to death."

Laurent said, "He didn't try to stop them?"

"How? What could he do? At Mokoto, the monastery, the priests walked away and a thousand were murdered."

Laurent would have to think about it. He held out his glass and she poured whiskey into it, Laurent saying that he thought it was here in the church she was mutilated.

"On the way here," Chantelle said, "worried to death for my mother and father, also my sister. They lived not in the village but on a farm in the hills where my father kept his herd of cows." Chantelle shook her head, her voice becoming quiet as she said, "No one has seen them or knows where their bodies are. They could be stuffed down a latrine or buried in a mass grave on the side of the road. I do believe my sister could be one of the dead still in the church. I look at the skull faces—is this Felicité or an old king of Egypt found in a tomb?"

"You were on your way here," Laurent said, prompting her.

"A friend drove me, a Hutu friend. He said there would be no problem, he would speak for me. But we came to cars stopped at a roadblock and everyone had to show their identity cards. If you were Tutsi you were ordered out of the car. There was nothing my friend could say to protect me. I was taken from his car into the forest where already people from other cars were waiting, some with their children clinging to them." Chantelle paused, she cleared her throat. "The Hutus, most of them were boys from the streets of Kigali, but now they were *Interahamwe*, they were in charge and they were all drunk, with no control of themselves. Now they came to us with machetes and clubs spiked with nails, *masus*, and no one could believe they were going to kill us standing as we were in the forest, away from the road. People began to scream and plead for their lives, mothers trying to shield their children. The Hutus were also screaming, and laughing, too, in a state of excitement as they began to hack with their machetes like we were stalks of bananas. I raised my arm to protect myself from the blade . . ." Chantelle paused again; this time she sipped her drink, closing her eyes for a moment. She said, "This one took hold of my hand and struck as I tried to pull away, my arm extended." She said, "I can see his face," and paused again. "When I fell I was in the crowd of people and others, killed or dying, fell on top of me. It was night and in a frenzy of killing, they didn't make sure we were all dead. For a long time I lay there without moving."

"Did they rape you first?"

"No, but others they did, fucked them like dogs."

"You could have bled to death," Laurent said.

"I was wearing strands of beads I twisted around my arm."

"Still . . ." Laurent said.

"Listen, I know of a woman in Nyarubuye, where a thousand or more were killed, who hid beneath dead bodies more than a week. She would come out at night to find water and food and in the morning return to chase away the rats and bury herself again among the dead. I was very lucky, the friend of mine, the Hutu, found me and brought me back to Kigali to the home of a doctor. He was also Hutu but, like my friend, not an extremist. The doctor closed my wound and let me stay a few days. After that I was able to hide at Mille Collines because I knew the manager, a man who saved hundreds of people's lives. He was hiding even wives of government officials, Hutu men in power whose wives were Tutsi. When it was safe, the Hutu cowards running from your army, I came here again to look for my family." Chantelle's slim shoulders moved in the undershirt, a shrug. "And, I stayed to assist the priest."

"To keep his house with one hand," Laurent said.

She looked toward the rectory. The music had stopped some time ago, but there was no sign of the priest. "You want to believe I go to bed with him, even if you have no way to know if it's true."

"You do or you don't," Laurent said, "it means nothing to me. What I don't see is what he's doing here, why he stays when he performs only some duties of a priest. All the time he's here, he offers Mass when he feels like it? The reasons I've heard people say—he has to save the Communion wafers because the nuns who made them for the old priest are dead. Or he drinks the altar wine with his supper."

He saw Chantelle smile in a tired way.

She said, "Do you believe that?"

"Tell me what to believe."

"He said Mass Christmas, always Easter Sunday. He's a good man. He plays soccer with the children, he reads stories to them, takes their picture . . . Why do you want to find fault?"

"That's his purpose here, to play with children?"

She said, "You ask so many questions," shaking her head in that tired way and looking toward the house again.

"Don't you think," Laurent said, "he's different to other priests you know?"

"In what way?"

"He doesn't hold himself above you, with the answer to everything, all of life's problems."

It seemed to be something she believed, looking at him now like she was making up her mind finally to tell the truth about him. But all she said was, "He came to assist the old priest."

Laurent said, "Yes . . . ?" not letting go.

"Now Fr. Dunn carries on his work."

Laurent said, "He does?" with a tone he could see annoyed her, not wanting to talk about her priest. Still, Laurent pressed her. "You say he came here . . . But wasn't he sent by the religious order, the one the old priest belonged to? I don't think I heard the name of it."

"The Missionary Fathers of St. Martin de Porres," Chantelle said, "the same name as the church."

"And they assigned him to this place?"

She hesitated before saying, "What difference does it make how he came here?"

Laurent believed he had her in a corner. He said, "You look tired," and motioned to the table.

They sat across from each other, Chantelle with her hand cupping the stump of her mutilation. The light was fading now, the air filling with the sound of insects and the sight of dark specks against the sky, bats swooping into the eucalyptus trees.

She said, "You sound like a policeman with your questions. I can tell you only that Fr. Dunn came or was sent here because the old priest, Fr. Toreki, was his uncle, the brother of his mother who died."

Laurent said, "Oh?" It seemed to interest him.

"Every five years," Chantelle said, "Fr. Toreki would go home to America to preach and raise money for his mission. And each time he would stay with Fr. Dunn's family, doing this ever since Terry was a small boy."

Now Laurent was nodding. "So during these visits the old priest was able to brainwash the boy with stories of Ah-fri-ca, how he lived among savages who painted their faces and killed lions with a spear."

Chantelle said, "Do you want to talk or listen?"

Laurent gestured with the glass in his hand saying, "Please," inviting her to go on.

"During these years," Chantelle said, "he and Fr. Toreki became very close and would write letters to each other. He didn't brainwash him, he showed Fr. Dunn the boy how to be the kind of man he was, to care for people and their lives."

Laurent nodded, keeping his mouth shut.

"Fr. Dunn said it was his mother who pressed him to be a priest, saying how proud she would be, as any mother would."

Laurent, nodding again, said, "Yes, I understand that about mothers."

"His," Chantelle said, "went to Mass and Holy Communion every morning of her life, six o'clock, and Fr. Dunn was there also when he was old enough, serving as the altar boy. Fr. Dunn said his mother was very religious, each day praying for him to become a priest."

Laurent watched the housekeeper raise her glass to sip the whiskey, taking time to look at whatever was in her mind. Taking forever.

Laurent said, "And so he did, hmmm? He grew up and became a priest." He waited while the housekeeper remained with her thoughts, her hand idly fingering the stump of her arm.

She said, "Yes, the time came that he went to a seminary in California to study. The place was the St. Dismas Novitiate. I saw it printed on paper he keeps, St. Dismas, the African saint who was crucified with Our Lord. From that place he came here only two or three weeks before the killing began."

Now it was Laurent who paused to put this in his mind and look at it.

"You're certain he was made a priest."

"He told me himself, yes." Now, because Laurent was silent but continued to stare at her, she said, "He doesn't lie to me, if that's what you think. He has no reason to." She said, "What am I to him? I wouldn't hurt him even if I could."

It was in Laurent's mind to wonder again, what was this relationship between the housekeeper and the priest? It seemed something more than sharing the same bed, even if that was true.

He said, "You talk to each other."

"Of course."

"About what he thinks?"

"He tells me things and I listen," Chantelle said.

"And you tell him things?"

"I try to protect him."

"From what?"

She took her time to say, "Thinking too much."

"I thought he used Mr. Walker for that."

"He doesn't drink because he's here or doesn't want to be here, he drinks because it gives him pleasure. He told me the reason he knows he is not alcoholic, he's never been tempted to try banana beer."

"Does he tell you you have beautiful eyes?"

"He tells me of bodies found near Ruhengeri, this time tourists who came to see the gorillas, hacked to pieces, the genocide beginning again."

"They were staying to the Hotel Muhabura," Laurent said, "and went out for a walk—as you say, tourists, visitors. We don't call that genocide."

"But it begins again."

"Or you could say it keeps going," Laurent said, "but as incidents, unrelated atrocities."

"Whatever you want to call it," Chantelle said, "it's going to happen soon in this village."

"How do you know that?"

"He tells me."

"But how does he know?"

"They tell him, in Confession."

4

TERRY'S BROTHER FRAN PRACTICED LAW in Detroit, specializing in personal injury, taking on doctors, big corporations, and their insurance companies. During the winter and the dreary spring months Fran liked to fly down to Florida to play golf and speculate in real estate.

The first morning of this trip he told Mary Pat he was going to look at property adjacent to a new development and drove from Boca Raton to Fort Lauderdale and then thirty miles inland to the Sawgrass Correctional Institution, a medium-security facility for women. Fran was here to visit a young lady named Debbie Dewey, who was finishing up a three-year fall for aggravated assault with a deadly weapon.

Before her incarceration Debbie had been doing investigative work for lawyers, a lot of it for Fran, checking out slip-and-fall victims Fran would represent in legal actions against the places where they had slipped and fallen. Also checking out the records of doctors who, Fran would like to believe, had misdiagnosed and malpracticed on his clients.

Debbie wore a gray-green sack dress, prison issue, she had taken in and shortened. Fran told her she looked cute, he liked her hair clipped short like that. It was light brown today, at other times blond. Debbie ran her fingers through her hair and tossed her head to show Fran that it wouldn't muss, saying she liked it, too, and called it a Sawgrass bob. They sat at a picnic table in the visitors compound surrounded by double fencing topped with razor wire. At the other tables were inmates with parents, husbands, boyfriends, some who had brought little kids to see their mommies.

"How're you doing?"

"Don't ask. Mary Pat and the girls with you?"

"At the condo. Mary Pat comes down to watch the maid vacuum, make sure she gets underneath the furniture good. The girls sit around waiting in their plastic inner tubes. I left, I don't remember if I told her I'm playing golf or looking at property. If I'm playing golf I stop at the club on the way back and change. But if I'm looking at property, why'm I coming home with different clothes on?"

"I wish I had your problems."

"What about your release?"

"Next Friday, if I don't kill a guard."

"You coming back to Detroit?"

"I might as well. You know what I'm thinking of doing? Try stand-up again. But with all new material from here, different situations you get into."

"You're kidding—prison humor? Like what?"

Debbie got up from the picnic table and held the skirt of the dress out to the sides. "I wear this in an extra-large with the white socks and the shitkickers? And model the latest in prison couture. I do a bit on forever standing in lines. Another one, getting hit on in the shower. I'm bare naked and this sexual predator I call Rubella makes the moves. The usual stuff."

"You tell how you tried to kill Randy?"

"I mention him in the opening, the reason I'm here." Sitting down again she said, "What's he up to, anything?"

"Well," Fran said, "we won't be seeing him on the society page anymore."

That perked her up.

"His wife divorced him, threw him out of the house."

It made little Debbie sit up straight, a gleam in her eye. She said, "I knew it. When?"

"It just became final."

"They were married what, a year?"

"A little over. There was a prenuptial agreement, so her fortune won't be seriously broken into. Randy's paid off and gets to keep the restaurant."

"He got a restaurant out of it?"

Little Debbie showing resentment.

"Downtown Detroit, on Larned."

"The son of a bitch. Why didn't you tell me?"

"The divorce was only final a couple of days ago."

"I mean about the restaurant. What's the name of it?"

"Randy's, what else. He bought a bar and put a lot of money into it, his wife's."

"Why does he get to keep it?"

"As part of the settlement. She doesn't like the neighborhood. So it's in his name, but I think there might be a partner involved. At least that's what my source tells me."

"What I don't understand," Debbie said, "why it took his wife over a year to find out he's a fucking snake. She should've known the first time he shed his skin."

"You use that in your act?"

"I just thought of it."

"What's it mean?"

"What snakes do, they molt. I'll see if I can make it work." She said, "I'll bet he got a boat out of it, too, the son of a bitch."

"The ex-wife keeps the boats and the country clubs, Detroit and Palm Beach. Randy can have his membership at the DAC if he wants to pay the bills. I have a lawyer friend in the same firm as the guy representing him. That's how I happen to know about the settlement, the main points. Randy comes away with the restaurant and a few million after the lawyer takes his cut. You would think the ex-wife," Fran said, "a woman with all her dough and clout, would've had Randy investigated before they got married."

"You don't know him," Debbie said, "he's a world-class bullshitter. I believed him, didn't I? And I make a living looking for fraud."

"I didn't mean to upset you."

"I'm not upset, I'm still pissed, that's all." She looked over at a table where a child was crying, brought her gaze back and her expression was calm, a cool look in those blue eyes. "Have you been to the restaurant?"

"Only for a drink. It looks like a men's club. You see tables of business suits, out-of-towners, guys calling on the car companies." Fran paused. "I'm told you might see bimbo-type ladies there in the evening."

"It's a pickup bar?"

"Not the kind you're thinking of. I'm told the ladies are pros, high-class call girls."

"Imagine," Debbie said, "your purpose in life is to give blow jobs to auto execs. I'll have to drop by when I get my release, say hi to Randy. I always knew he was a pimp."

"You realize," Fran said, "I hesitated telling you."

"Don't worry, I won't do anything dumb."

"Now that you know what it's like in here. You're out next week, start with a clean slate . . . Which reminds me, my brother should be home soon, from Africa."

"That's right, the priest."

"If he hasn't gone native on me. He writes a letter, it's about the weather. Or what the place smells like."

"He's due for a vacation?"

"First one in five years. There's still that tax fraud indictment hanging over him. We have to get that cleared up."

"What'd he do, cheat on his income tax?"

"I thought I told you about it."

"You didn't tell me about the restaurant, either."

Randy the snake still on her mind.

"This is state, the Wayne County prosecutor's office. I've been on it since he left. They've just about agreed to drop the indictment, but want to talk to Terry first, when he gets home. It comes down to his word against statements made by two other guys. But since Terry's a priest, and I find out the assistant prosecutor I've been dealing with is a devout Catholic—"

"Fran, I don't know what you're talking about."

"Really? I would've sworn I mentioned it to you. The allegation involves Terry smuggling a truckload of cigarettes from Kentucky to Detroit, the purpose, to avoid paying the state tax, Terry and two other guys, the Pajonny brothers. Terry left right after they were busted and the Pajonnys rolled over on him to plead down, saying it was his idea and he took off with their share. So on the strength of that Terry was indicted, but by then he was in Africa."

"Your brother the priest," Debbie said, "I want to get this straight, is a fugitive felon?"

"He didn't know about the charge. He went over there to help out our uncle Tibor, forty years a missionary, Tibor Toreki. I told you about him, how he used to stay with us?"

Debbie said, "I'm confused."

And now Fran was shaking his head. "I didn't tell it right. Terry wasn't a priest yet when he got involved with the cigarettes. He wasn't ordained till he got over there, and took his vows."

She still looked a little confused, saying, "All right, how does a guy who's about to become a priest get into smuggling cigarettes?"

"He drove the truck, that's all. He didn't know it was the pop crime of the nineties. The state raised the tax to seventy-five cents a pack, but didn't add a stamp, so a lot of people got into it. It was low-risk, no one got hurt—" He could see Debbie, hunched over the table, thinking up another question, and he tried to head her off. "Terry gets home, you'll have to meet him. You remind me of him, your attitude about things."

"The two guys," Debbie said, "the Pajonnys—I love the name—they were friends of his?"

"From school, years ago."

"It was their idea?"

"They hired Terry to drive the truck, period."

"And they tried to put it on him and went down."

"The state," Fran said, "claimed they were losing a hundred and fifty mil a year in tax revenues, so they made an example of the Pajonnys, hit 'em with five to ten. Johnny's already out."

Debbie said, "Johnny Pajonny. It gets better. Was he in any trouble before?"

"On occasion, but he'd never done state time."

"What about Terry?"

"Never in any trouble before this—even though he was always kind of a tough kid. When we were little and I was what you might call pudgy?"

"What're you now, hefty?"

"Be nice. Who else comes to visit?"

"The other kids picked on you."

"The morons, they'd call me Fat Francis, make fun of my name. 'Oh, Fran-cis, where're your dolls?' Or they'd call me Frannie, which I hated. But if Terry was around, uh-unh, they left me alone."

"Your big brother."

"Actually he's two years younger, but was a real hardnose, played football three years in high school, liked to box—he'd take on bigger guys, it didn't matter. Even if he was getting beat up he always hung in." Fran's expression softened, seeing Terry the priest now in his white cassock. He said, "I've been thinking, five years in an African village—he comes home, I might not even know him."

"Maybe he's a saint," Debbie said.

Fran smiled at the idea. "I wouldn't go that far. But who knows?"

Ten women, seven of them black, occupied the wooden benches that faced the TV set in C dorm, waiting for their favorite sitcom to come on. Debbie came down from the second-floor tier above their heads and stepped in front of the TV set.

"What she doing?"

"Gonna try her act on us."

"I'm still working on it," Debbie said. "How I got conned out of fifty thousand and ended up in the joint."

"Is it funny?"

"That's what I want you to tell me."

"Fifty thousand? Where you rob that kind of money from?"

"I worked for it."

"Hookin'?"

"Shame on you. Debbie's a lawyer, fucks people in court 'stead of the bed."

"I'm not a lawyer. I took pre-law, but that was it."

"Then why you go to school?"

"I thought I wanted to practice law." Debbie paused, changed her mind about trying out the bit and said, "Let me ask you something. What's the best way to make a lot of money without working for it?"

"Hit on the five-number lottery."

"Find a man has some."

"Yeah, and have to put up with his shit."

Debbie said, "What about armed robbery?"

"You want to get high, you rob."

"Have any of you ladies ever robbed a bank?"

They looked around at each other saying, "Yeah, I know people have." Saying, "Rosella in B has. You know who I mean?" Saying, "Yeah, Rosella." Saying, "Rosella owed five hundred to a shy. She went in the bank with her boyfriend's gun and said, 'Gimme five hundred dollars, girl,' to the teller? Took it and paid the shy."

Another one saying to Debbie, "What you think is the best way to make it?"

"I want to do stand-up," Debbie said, "but I also want to con the son of a bitch who conned me."

The mother of this group, twenty-four years inside for killing her husband with a cast-iron frying pan, said, "Save the comic shit, baby, and do the con. You haven't said nothing funny since you been standing there."

————

Driving back to Mary Pat and his two little girls, Fran turned on his current favorite daydream:

Debbie comes out and he has a furnished apartment waiting for her in Somerset, where she used to live, not four miles from his home in Bloomfield Hills. He helps her get settled, maybe paint a room, re-arrange the furniture, get in some groceries, booze. They have a drink, kick back. "Boy, it's good to sit down, huh?" Debbie gets high. Naturally she's a little horny, not having been with a man in almost three years. She gives him the look . . . one Fran has been waiting for ever since he and Debbie met and she started doing investigations for him: the look that says it would be okay to become intimate, not seri-ously intimate but for fun. Fall into it and say, after, "Wow, how did that happen?"

He had told Terry one time, years ago, he had never picked up a girl in a bar, even when he was single. Terry said, "You never tried or you never made it?" Fran told him he'd never tried. Why didn't he have the same confidence in a bar he had in a courtroom? Terry said that time, "You're too buttoned up. Lose some weight and quit get-ting your hair cut for a while."

Terry's answer to any problem was based on the serenity prayer. If you can handle it, do it. If you can't, fuck it.

5

AT NIGHT CHANTELLE KEPT HER pistol close by, a Russian Tokarev semiautomatic she bought in the market with money Terry had given her. There were hand grenades for sale, too, but they frightened her.

This evening she brought the pistol outside with her and laid it on the table where he was twisting a joint he called a yobie. She had told him that here marijuana was sometimes called *emiyobya bwenje*, "the stuff that makes your head hot." From that he had made up the word *yobie*. They had smoked one before supper—goat stew left over from last night, Terry complaining always about the fine bones—and now they would smoke another one with their brandy and coffee, the mugs, the decanter, and a citronella candle on the table.

Always before when they smoked he would tell her funny things he heard in Confession, or about his brother the lawyer, what he did to get money for people who were injured. Or he'd tell jokes she never understood but would laugh because he always laughed at his jokes. This evening, though, he wasn't saying funny things.

He was serious this evening in a strange way.

He said he had never seen so fucking many bugs in his life. He used that word when he was drinking too much. The fucking bugs, the fucking rain. He said sometimes he would turn on a light in the house and it would look like the fucking walls were moving, wallpaper changing its pattern. She said, "There is no wallpaper in the house." He said he knew there wasn't any wallpaper, he was talking about the bugs. There were so many they looked like a wallpaper design. Then with the light on they'd start moving.

She was patient with him. This evening there were lulls, Chantelle waiting through minutes of silence.

Now he surprised her, coming out of nowhere with "Some were mutilated before they were killed, weren't they? Purposely mutilated."

Lately he had begun to talk about the genocide again.

She said, "Yes, they would do it on purpose."

He said, "They chopped off the feet at the ankles."

"And took the shoes," Chantelle said, "if the person was wearing shoes." She believed he was talking about the time they came in the church, an experience of the genocide he had not spoken of in a long time.

He said, "I don't recall them hacking the feet off with one whack."

It sounded to her so cold. "Sometime they did."

He said, "This was your observation?"

She didn't like it when he spoke in this formal manner. It didn't sound like him and was another sign, along with that word, he had been drinking too much. She said, "Some they did with one blow. But I think the blades became dull, or were not honed to begin with. The one who injured me—I raised my arm to protect myself as he struck.

He then took hold of my hand as I tried to pull away and he struck again, this time severing the arm. I saw him holding it by the hand, looking at it. I remember he seemed surprised. Then his face changed to a look—I want to say horror, or disgust. But was he sickened only by what he saw or what he did to me?"

"What if you run into him again?"

"I hope I never see him."

"You could have him arrested and tried."

"Yes? Would I get my arm back?"

Terry smoked in the light of the candle. After a moment he said, "The ones they murdered in the church stood waiting, crowded together, holding each other. The Hutus would drag them into the aisle and some of them called to me. I never told you that, how they called to me, 'Fatha, please . . .' "

She didn't want him to talk about himself, what he was doing or not doing that time. "You know," she said, "all over Rwanda they were cutting off the feet of Tutsis, so they not taller than the Hutu killers anymore."

He brought it back to the church saying, "They stood there and let it happen."

She wished he'd be quiet. "Listen to me. If they had no weapons they knew it was their fate to die. I heard of people in Kigali, they paid the Hutu killers to shoot them rather than be hacked to death with the machetes. You understand? They knew they would be dead."

Her words meant nothing to him. He held the yobie to his mouth but didn't draw on it, saying, "I didn't do anything to help them. Not one fucking thing. I watched. The whole time they were being killed, that's what I did. I watched."

He said it without feeling and it frightened her.

"But you were offering the Mass. You told me, you were holding the Host in your hands when they came in. There was nothing you could do. You try to stop them they would have killed you. They don't care you're a priest."

Again he raised the yobie to draw on it and paused.

"Let me ask you something."

He paused again and she said, "Yes, what?"

"You think I do any good here?"

Sounding like he was feeling sorry for himself.

She said, "You want the truth? You don't do as much as you could." She said, "Do more. Talk to people, preach the word of God. Do what a priest is suppose to do. Say Mass every Sunday, what people want you to do."

"You really believe," he said, staring at her in the candlelight, "I can take bread and change it into the Body of Christ?"

What was he doing asking her that? She said, "Of course you can. It's what priests do, in the Mass. You change the bread, and also the wine." What was wrong with him? "I believe that, as all those who come to Mass believe it."

"Sally, we believe what we want to believe."

Calling her that, Sally, from *asali*, the Swahili word for honey, which he did sometimes.

He said, "You want to know what I believe?"

"Yes, I would like to know."

"I did come here with a few good intentions. One thing in particular I wanted to do was paint Fr. Toreki's house. Every picture I ever saw of it, going back years, the house needed painting. I knew how, I used to help my dad sometimes when he had a big job, the outside of a two-story house."

Why was he telling her this? She believed she was listening to his mind wander from having too much to drink.

"My dad was a housepainter all his life. Forty years at least he stood with a wall in front of his face painting it, smelling it, going to his truck with the ladders on top to smoke a cigarette and drink vodka from the bottle. He said to me—it was when I dropped out of college and was helping him—he said, 'Go back to school and get a good job.' He said, 'You're too smart to spend your life pissing in paint cans.' The only time he took off was to go deer hunting in the fall. Never saw a doctor, he was sixty-three years old when he died, my brother Fran said watching the Lions on TV. Not real ones, the Detroit Lions, a professional football team. Fran said in a letter our dad's last conscious experience was seeing the Lions march all the way down the field, fumble on the two-yard line and lose the ball."

She watched his expression looking at her. He seemed to smile. Or she could be wrong.

"You have to know my brother," Terry said. "He wasn't being disrespectful."

Was he speaking to her in that quiet voice or to himself? She watched him draw on the yobie. It had gone out.

"You should go to bed."

"In a while."

"Well, I'm going." She got up from the table with her Russian pistol and stood looking at him. "Why do you talk like this to me?"

"Like what?"

Walking away she said, "Never mind."

And heard him say, "Why are you mad at me?"

Lying still to listen, she heard him taking a shower and then could hear him brushing his teeth, in the bath between the two bedrooms. Always he brushed his teeth and smelled of toothpaste when he came to her bed. Once a week he brought two Larium pills, so they wouldn't catch malaria, and a glass of water they shared. The pills were hallucinogenic and in the morning they would try to describe their dreams.

Tonight he slipped in next to her beneath the netting and remained lying on his back, not moving, leaving to her whatever would come next.

She said, "You tell me you come here to paint a house. That's the reason?"

"It's something I wanted to do."

"Then why don't you paint it?"

He didn't answer, but said after a few moments, "I want to have the bodies buried, the ones lying in the church, the bones."

She said, "Yes?"

But now he was silent.

She said, "Can't you talk to me?"

"I'm trying to."

She said, "Give me a break." One of his expressions she liked.

For several minutes she listened to the sounds in the night, outside, before turning onto her side and was closer to him now, close enough to see his face, close enough to rest the stump of her arm on his chest. Now if he takes it in his hand . . .

He did, he took the hard, scarred end of what remained of her arm and began to caress it lightly with his fingers. She raised her head and he slipped his arm around her.

She said, "I know why you don't talk to me."

She waited and he said, "Why?"

"Because you going to leave and not come back."

This time when she waited and he said nothing she raised her head and put her mouth on his.

She awoke in the morning looking at sunlight through the netting and closed her eyes again to listen for sounds in the house. She knew he was gone but continued to listen. Sometimes he would return to his own bedroom during the night. Sometimes he rose before she did and would put the coffee on the stove to boil. She listened to hear him cough and clear his throat. She believed if she didn't see him for a long time and heard him clear his throat in a crowd of people she would know it was Terry. There were times she believed he loved her: not only when they were in bed and he showed his hunger for her, but other times, seeing the way he looked at her and she would wait for him to say it. When she said it to him she would smile, so the words wouldn't frighten him. After they went to bed the first time he was so quiet she said to him, "Listen, there were always priests who want me, Rwandese priests, French priests, it's nothing new. Do you think people care if we sleep together?"

Opening her eyes she turned her head on the pillow.

He was gone.

Now she turned to her side of the bed to get up, looked at the night table and saw her pistol was also gone.

6

IT TOOK HIM THREE HOURS to drive the hundred miles from Arisimbi to the Banque Commerciale and the Sabena ticket office in Kigali, and then three hours back, the road through Rwanda like nothing from past experience.

Get to the top of a long grade and look around, all you saw were hills in every direction, misty hills, bright green hills, hills that were terraced and cultivated, crops growing among groves of banana trees, the entire country, Terry believed, one big vegetable garden. The red streaks on distant hills were dirt roads, the squares of red dotting the slopes, houses, compounds, a church. He cruised the two-lane blacktop with all the windows in Toreki's Volvo station wagon cranked open. He drove with a sense of making his move, his life about to turn a corner.

The downside was getting stuck behind trucks on the blind curves and grades, trucks piled high with bananas and bags of charcoal, trucks carrying work crews, a big yellow semi with PRIMUS BEER lettered across the rear end that Terry stared at for miles. The trucks, and the people along the side of the road, people standing in groups like they were waiting for a bus and people going somewhere, women in bright colors carrying plastic buckets on their heads, clay pots as big around as medicine balls, boys pushing carts loaded with plastic chairs grooved together, goats grazing close to the road, Ankole cows with their graceful horns and tough meat taking their time to cross. But no dogs. Where were the dogs? A roadside poster warned against AIDS. A sign on a Coca-Cola stand said ICI SALLON DE COIFFURE. People strayed onto the blacktop and he would lean on his horn, something he never did at home.

Finally cresting a grade he descended toward Arisimbi, the village laid out below him left to right, the marketplace of concrete stalls on the offside of the main road, away from the sector office and the squares of red brick among plots of vegetation, the bar, the beer lady's house, the compound where Laurent's squad lived, the well, the charcoal seller's house, the compound where Thomas the corn man lived, all of it a patchwork of red and green leading up to the white church and the rectory in the trees.

Terry parked the Volvo wagon in front of the sector office and went in.

Laurent Kamweya in his starched camies looked up from the only desk in the room and then rose saying, "Fatha, how can I be of service?"

Terry liked Laurent and believed he meant it. "You know where I can find Bernard?"

It seemed to stop him for a moment. Laurent turned enough to indicate the window, the heavy wooden shutters open, the street outside that trailed through the village. "You see the white flower by the door of the beer lady's house," Laurent said. "She has banana beer today, so that's where he is, with his friends. Tell me what you want with him."

"Have a talk," Terry said. "See if I can get him to give himself up."

"Persuade Bernard Nyikizi to confess to murder?"

"To save his immortal soul."

"You serious to do this?"

"I'll give it a try. Are you busy?" Terry said. "There's something else I want to ask you."

Laurent said, "Please," gesturing over his desk, the surface clean except for a clipboard holding a few papers. The brick walls of the office were as clean as the desk. A woven mat covered the floor. The place always looked the same, temporary, never much going on. Laurent was watching now as Terry slipped his hand inside his white cassock and came out with currency, ten five-thousand-franc notes, the new one illustrated with tribal dancers, and laid the money on the clean desk.

"Fifty thousand francs," Terry said. "I'd like you to do me a favor, if you would. Use half of this to pay for graves dug in the churchyard, forty-seven graves."

"You have permission of the *bourgmestre*?"

"Fuck the *bourgmestre*, it's private property, the state has nothing to say about it."

Laurent hesitated. "Why do you ask me? You could see to it."

"I'm leaving, going home."

"For good?"

"For good or bad. This afternoon."

"You have someone to take your place?"

"That's not my problem. Ask the bishop."

"Will you continue to be a priest?"

Terry hesitated. "Why do you ask that?"

"You seem different to other priests I've known. I say this as a compliment to you." Laurent paused, waiting for Terry to tell if he would still be a priest. When he didn't answer, Laurent said, "Twenty-five thousand to dig graves is very generous."

"What does it come to," Terry said, "a dollar and a half each?" He picked up five of the notes and dropped them closer to Laurent standing behind the desk. "This is for another favor. I need a ride to the airport."

"Take the bus," Laurent said, "is much cheaper."

"But what I'd like you to do," Terry said, "is use the Volvo. Bring it back and give it to Chantelle, or sell it in Kigali and give her the money."

"I have to ask again," Laurent said, "why you want me to do it, not someone else."

" 'Cause you're the man here," Terry said. "You may have your doubts about me, but I don't have any about you. If I'm wrong and you keep the car or the money for yourself, well, Chantelle's the one who's out. So it's up to you, partner."

Let him chew on that.

Terry turned to the door, then looked back. "I won't be long." He paused again, remembering something, and said, "Where're all the dogs? I've been meaning to ask that for a long time."

"People don't like to have dogs anymore," Laurent said. "The dogs ate too many of the dead."

The only difference between the beer lady's house and what was called the bar—both mud brick with metal roofs—the beer lady made her own banana brew, *urwagwa*, and sold it in used Primus litre bottles with a straw for five to fifteen cents depending on the supply. The bar offered commercial brands, too, Primus, made with sorghum, and Mutzig, which Terry drank once in a while. He walked into the beer lady's house breathing through his mouth against the stench of overripe bananas and body odor, into a bare-brick room that could be a prison cell.

There was Bernard in his shirt, one of his buddies next to him, both against the wall behind a plywood table, both sucking on reed straws stuck into brown litre bottles, the Primus label worn off from reuse. The third one sat to the left of Bernard in a straight chair with his bottle and straw, the chair tilted against the wall, his bare feet hanging free. The fourth one was just now coming out of a back hall. Terry waited until he was in the room—the same four from the market the other day—all of them watching him now, Bernard murmuring to them in Kinyarwanda. There was no sign of the beer lady.

Terry said to Bernard, "Any more visions?"

"I told you in the Confession," Bernard said, "what thing is going to happen." He spoke with the reed straw in his mouth, holding the bottle against his chest. "I don't tell my visions in this place."

"It doesn't matter," Terry said. "You told everyone at the market you saw me and I saw you. Talking about the time you came in the church with your machete, your panga. Your words, 'I saw him and he saw me.' Isn't that right? I saw you hack four people to death, what you told me, and you saw me do nothing to stop you. Now you say you're gonna do it again. Cut anybody you don't like down to size, including me. Right? Isn't that what you said?"

"I speak only to my friends in this place," Bernard said, still with the straw in his mouth. "We don't want you. What do you come here for?"

"To ask you to give yourself up. Tell Laurent Kamweya what you did in the church."

Bernard, smiling now, said, "You must be a crazy person." He spoke to his friends in Kinyarwanda and now they were smiling.

Terry said, "They were with you that day?"

"Oh yes, these and others. It was our duty," Bernard said. "We say, '*Tugire gukora akazi*.' Let us go do the work, and we did, uh? Go now, we don't want you here."

"Soon as I give you your penance," Terry said.

He pulled Chantelle's pistol out of his cassock and shot Bernard, shattering the bottle he held against his chest. He shot the one next to Bernard trying to get up, caught between the wall and the plywood table. He shot the one in the chair tilted against the wall. And shot the one by the back hall as this one brought a machete out of his belt and shot him again as the blade showed a glint of light from the open door.

The shots left a hard ringing sound within the closeness of the brick walls. Terry held the pistol at arm's length on a level with his eyes—the Russian Tokarev resembling an old-model Colt .45, big and heavy—and made the sign of the cross with it over the dead. He said, "Rest in peace, motherfuckers," turned, and walked out of the beer lady's house to wait at the side of the road.

Pretty soon the Volvo appeared, coming around from the front of the sector office.

They stood in the rectory kitchen, Chantelle watching Laurent taking things from the deep pockets of his combat fatigues, a mist showing in the window behind him, the light fading.

"The keys to the Volvo and the house and, I believe, the church." Laurent laid them on the kitchen table. "Your pistol. I can get you another one that holds twice the number of bullets. There are only two in here now." He laid the Tokarev on the table. "Four men with five shots tells me he concentrated, this priest of yours. He knew he could not waste the shots."

"How do you report it?"

"Unknown assailant."

"No one will question it?"

"The witnesses are dead. As always." Laurent's hand went into the big pocket of his tunic. "Sabena Air tickets, he said to give you. I told him even the Belgian ambassador will do anything to avoid flying Sabena. I drove the priest to Goma and introduced him to a man who runs arms into Congo-Zaire, a friend of everyone. He'll take the priest to Mombasa. From there he can fly to Nairobi and take British Air to his home."

Chantelle said, "He could have exchanged the tickets."

"He wants you to have them, to cash in or go to Brussels for a holiday. Why not?"

"He was always generous," Chantelle said, "giving me money to spend."

"A priest," Laurent said, "who took vows to be a holy man. Or maybe he forgot to take them. I always said he was different to any priest I ever knew."

Chantelle seemed about to speak, perhaps to give her opinion, defend her priest. No—she pulled the cord to turn on the electric light in the ceiling, brought an unopened bottle of Johnnie Walker black, not the red, from the cabinet above the refrigerator she reached into now for a tray of ice. When she spoke again the priest was gone. She said to Laurent, "Have you had your supper?"

7

"HEY. EVERYBODY HAVING A GOOD time tonight? . . . Yeah? Well, come on, let's hear it, okay? We're up here working our asses off. No dogs or ponies, man, just us."

The comic acting as MC, the bill of his baseball cap funneled around his face, got a pretty good response: half the tables filled this evening, the back part of the big room dark; not bad for an open-mike night.

"Right now it's my pleasure to welcome back to Mark Ridley's Comedy Castle a chick who's smokin', so fucking hot that I ask myself, 'Rich, why would a killer chick like Debbie ever stoop to doing stand-up?' And the answer that flashed immediately in my tired brain, 'Because she's funny, dude. Because she's a very funny chick, fast on her way to becoming a headliner.' You with me? . . . Yeah? Then give it up for . . . Detroit's own Debbie Dewey!"

She appeared out of the center-stage door in a gray-green prison dress, extra-large, ankle-high work shoes and white socks, the outfit keeping the applause up. The right thing to do now was point to the comic-as-MC in his baseball cap leaving the stage and shout in the noise, "Richie Baron! Yeah! Let him hear it!" But she didn't. When the room was quiet enough she said:

"Hi. Yes, I'm Debbie Dewey," and turned to show herself in profile. "Or, eight nine five, three two nine." Then, facing the room again, "That was my Department of Corrections number while I was down most of three years for aggravated assault with a deadly weapon. True story. I was visiting my mom in Florida and happened to run into my ex-husband . . . with a Buick Riviera."

She paused, getting a pretty good response, and said, "It was a rental, but it did the job."

More laughs this time, the audience warming up to her conversational delivery, Debbie holding back, not giving it too much.

"I was stopped for a light on Collins Avenue, Miami Beach, and there was Randy, Mr. Cool in his yachting cap and shades, he's crossing the street right in front of me as the light turned green."

A few laughs now in anticipation.

"I said to the arresting officer, 'But I had the right of way.'" More laughter and she shook her head at the audience. "Randy's another story. He seemed like such a sweet, fun guy, a real free spirit. How many people do you know have a pet bat flying around the house?" Debbie hunched her shoulders and ducked her head, waving her hand in the air. Now she stood with her eyes raised, a cautious expression, until she shook her head again.

"By the time the bat disappeared I'd come to suspect Randy was a snake. There were certain clues . . . like his old skin lying on the bathroom floor. So when I noticed the bat was no longer around, I thought, My God, he ate it."

Some laughs, but not the response she'd hoped for.

"But his molting wasn't the worst." She waited for the few laughs that came from people who knew what molting meant. "Finding out he had another wife at the same time we were married didn't sit too well. Or the fact he used up my credit cards and cleaned me out before he skipped. So when I happened to see him crossing the street . . . I thought, Where can I get a semi, quick? Like an eighteen-wheeler loaded with scrap metal. You know, do it right. Or do it again—I thought about this later—as soon as Randy's out of his body cast. But by then I'd been brought to trial, convicted, and was one of six hundred ladies making up the population of a women's correctional institution, double-fenced with razor wire."

Debbie held the sack dress away from her legs as though she might curtsy.

"This is the latest in prison couture. Can you imagine six hundred women all wearing the same dress? You're also given a blue-denim ensemble—shirt, jacket, and slacks with a white stripe down the sides. You can wear the jacket with the dress if you like to mix and match. You're given underwear and two bras that come in one-size-fits-all. . . . Honest. You knot the straps trying to get the bra to fit, and you keep knotting till you get your release."

Debbie had reached into the dress to fool with the straps and could feel the audience with her. Especially the women.

"I thought of stuffing the cups, but you're only given four pairs of socks. The dress, by the way, comes in small, medium, large, and extra-large." She held the skirt away from her legs again. "This is the small. I made a suggestion to the superintendent one time, a nice guy, I said, 'Why don't you offer more smaller sizes, even a petite, and send all the ladies who wear extra-large to a men's facility?' As you might imagine, large women have a way of making the prison experience more to their liking. The kind of thing that can happen . . ."

Debbie raised her face, eyes closed, and moved her hands over her arms and shoulders, her breasts.

"Imagine luxuriating in the shower, rubbing yourself all over with the industrial-strength soap they give you . . . the water soothing, rinsing the blood from your abrasions, and you hear a voice murmur, 'Mmmmmm, you pretty all over.' You think fast, knowing what you'll see when you open your eyes."

Debbie turned her head to one side and looked up, way up, as if gazing at someone at least seven feet tall.

" 'Hey, Rubella, how you doing, girl?' You want to keep reminding Rubella she's a girl. 'Girl, you feel like a cocktail? I've got some hairspray if you have the Seven-Up.' Or, 'You want me to fix your hair? Get me a dozen pairs of shoelaces and I'll make you some cool extensions.' "

Debbie had been looking up with a hopeful smile. Now she turned to the room with a solemn expression.

"And if you can't think of a way to distract a three-hundred-pound sexual predator, you're fucked. Literally. Whatever way Rubella wants to perform the act."

It was working and she felt more sure of herself, the audience laughing on cue, waiting for the next line.

"Actually, though, being molested or raped by some tough broad isn't as common as you might think. Girl prison movies like *Hot Chicks in the Slammer*, with inmates running around in these cute Victoria's Secret prison outfits? It isn't anything like that. No, in women's facilities chicks form family groups. The older ones, usually in for murder, are mothers . . . Really. There may be a father played by a dyke senior citizen. There are sisters and what pass for brothers. And there are, of course, chicks with chicks. Hey, even in the joint love is in the air. What I did, whenever one of the chicks found me attractive, I'd go, 'Oh, hon, I hate to tell you this but I'm HIV positive.'

And it worked until this one grins at me and goes, 'I am, too, sweetie pie.' No, my most serious problem inside . . . What do you think it was?"

A male voice called out, "The food."

"The food's another story," Debbie said, "but not my number one complaint."

Another male voice said, "Standing in line."

And Debbie smiled, one hand shading her eyes as she looked out at the audience. "You've been there, haven't you? You know about standing in line. And what happens to anyone who tries to cut in? You can buy your way in, give someone in the canteen line a couple of cigarettes and she comes out and you take her place—that's okay. But if anyone tries to cut in . . . ? Listen, since I'm home I do all my grocery shopping at two A.M., so I won't have to stand in line. If I happen to shop during the day, I never buy more items than the express checkout will take, like ten items or less. I watch the woman in front of me unloading her cart and I count the items. If she has more than ten? Even one more? I turn the bitch in. I do, I blow the whistle on her, demand they put her in a no-limit checkout line. I know my rights. Listen, even if the bitch picks up some Tic-Tacs or a pack of Juicy Fruit, and it puts her over ten items? She's out of there—if I have to shove her out myself."

Debbie had struck a defiant pose. She began to relax and then stiffened again.

"And if some guy in a hurry tries to step in front of me? . . . You know the kind. 'Mind if I go ahead of you? I just have this one item.' A case of Rolling Rock under his arm. Do I mind? All he has to do is make the move I've got a razor blade off the rack ready to cut him . . . and I'm back with the ladies on another aggravated assault conviction. Let me just say, you haven't waited in line till you've waited in line in prison. But even that wasn't the worst thing. To me, anyway."

Debbie paused to look over the room and the audience waited.

"I should tell you, a number of my dorm mates were in for first- or second-degree murder. Brenda, LaDonna, Laquanda, Tanisha, Rubella you've met, Shanniqua, Tanniqua and Pam, two Kimberleys who went bad and a Bobbi Joe Lee, who played a couple of seasons with the Miami Dolphins till they found out she was a chick. There are ladies you don't want to mess with unless you're behind the wheel of a Buick Riviera, with the doors locked. So in the evening when it's time to turn on the TV? Guess who decides what we watch. Me? Or bigger-than-life Rubella. Me? Or the suburban housewife who shot her husband seven times and told the cops she thought he was a home invader . . . coming in the back door with a sack of groceries, four in the afternoon?" Debbie paused. "To me, the worst thing about prison was a sitcom the dorm ladies watched every evening on local cable TV. Guess what it was."

8

DEBBIE CAME OUT TO THE lobby bar wearing jeans and a light raincoat, her prison dress and shoes in a canvas bag. She saw Fran waiting and was sure he'd say something about the set—nice going, anything. No, her first gig in more than three years and Fran goes, "Here, I want you to meet my brother."

The one turning from the bar with a drink in his hand, Fr. Terry Dunn, black Irish in a black wool parka, the hood hanging about his shoulders. Now she saw him as a friar, the beard, the gaunt face, giving him kind of a Saint Francis of Assisi look. He came right out with what she wanted to hear:

"You were terrific"—with a nice smile—"really funny, and you made it look easy, the conversational style."

"That either works," Fran said, "or it doesn't." Fran serious about it. "You have to have the personality and be naturally funny. You know what I mean? Not just recite punch lines." He said, "Debbie, this is my brother Terry."

He held her gaze as they shook hands, still with the nice smile. She glanced at Fran and back to the priest.

"I don't have to call you Father?"

He said, "I wouldn't."

Now she didn't know what to say. How was Africa? But then wondered if they were there for the whole set. "I didn't see you before I went on."

"You'd just come out," Fran said, "giving your DOC number as we sat down, in back."

Terry was nodding. "You were about to run into your ex with the Buick."

"The Buick Riviera," Debbie said.

He smiled again. "I wondered if you tried other makes. A Dodge Daytona?"

"That's not bad."

"Cadillac El-do-ray-do?"

"Eldorado was on the list, but what'm I doing driving a Cadillac? So I went with the Riviera."

"Yeah, that worked."

Fran, antsy in his tweed sport coat, a sweater under it, said, "We'll go someplace we can talk and get something to eat." Debbie lit a cigarette, Terry holding her bag, while Fran told them he'd forget to eat with Mary Pat and the little girls in Florida. "This guy"—meaning Terry—"all he eats is peanut butter since he got home. Eats it with a spoon." That was something she could ask: why there wasn't any peanut butter in Africa. Fran led them out of the Comedy Castle, on Fourth in Royal Oak, and around the corner to Main, Fran telling his brother how he'd suggested she act nervous when she comes out, scared, so if the act doesn't exactly rock, the audience would still sympathize with her, like her spunk.

The priest said, "Debbie doesn't need spunk. She's cool." Surprising the hell out of her.

She hunched her shoulders saying, "Actually I'm freezing," almost adding, "my ass off," but didn't. The priest, huddled in his parka, said he was too. So then Fran had to tell them it wasn't cold, it was spring, forty-seven degrees out. Terry said, "Oh, then I guess I'm not cold," and she felt in that moment closer to him and knew that if she'd said, "my ass off," he still would've agreed, maybe given her the smile.

They got a table at Lepanto. Fran, still on, asked the waitress if they had banana beer, the only kind his brother here from Africa would drink—Debbie wishing he'd please get off the fucking stage. The waitress said with no expression, or showing any interest, "We don't carry it," and Debbie could've kissed her. Fran was out of it while she ordered an Absolut on the rocks, but then got back in when Terry said all he wanted was a Scotch, Johnnie Walker red if they had it. Fran told him he should eat something besides peanut butter. How about an appetizer and a salad? Terry said he wasn't hungry. Fran was studying the menu now while Terry sat there in his parka.

Debbie thought he looked beat, maybe some African disease like malaria hanging on. She loved his eyes, his quiet expression. She said to him, "I've been trying to picture where Rwanda is exactly."

"Right in the center of Africa," Fran said, his nose still in the menu, "practically on the equator. You're a missionary over there you come home every five years to cool off and get your health back." He looked up now to say, "If you're not gonna eat I'm not either." But now the waitress was back with their drinks and he ordered a Caesar salad and some rolls.

Looking at Terry she said to Fran, "Did he always want to be a priest?"

Terry smiled as Fran said, "Even as a kid he felt he had a vocation. Like you might've thought of becoming a nun when you were at Marian."

"The Academy of the Sacred Heart, please. I was a rich kid." She was dying to ask Terry about smuggling cigarettes, but would lose her nerve when he looked at her. She asked what order he belonged to. He told her the Missionary Fathers of St. Martin de Porres.

"There's a school in Detroit with that name," Fran said, "all black kids, but there's no connection."

"Other than Martin de Porres was black," Terry said, "on his mother's side. His dad was a Spanish nobleman. They weren't married and for a long time the father wouldn't have anything to do with Martin, since he was a mulatto. Or you could say he was African–South American. This was in Lima, Peru, around sixteen hundred. He was canonized because of his devotion to the sick and the poor." There were no comments, a silence, and Terry said, "Martin de Porres is the patron saint of hairdressers."

Fran said, "Yeah, well that was a long time ago."

Debbie passed. She might ask why some other time. So she asked if he'd run into any comedy over there. "Any African stand-up?"

Terry seemed to think about it as Fran said, "Deb, it's hard to think of anything funny when hundreds of thousands of people are being killed. Terry was right there during the entire period of the genocide."

Debbie said, "I can't even imagine that." She couldn't remember hearing much about it, either, the genocide.

"On the altar saying his first Mass," Fran said, "when they broke into the church. A scene that'll stay with him the rest of his life."

Terry's expression didn't change. She thought of it now as kind of a saintly look, the dark hair and beard part of the image, the hood of the parka hanging like a monk's cowl. She hoped he might add something, so she'd know what Fran was talking about.

But now Terry was telling her again, "You were really funny. You must've felt good about it."

"Most of it," Debbie said.

"Where'd you get the pet bat?"

"Out of the air. I wanted to describe Randy as evil in a funny way, if you know what I mean, this good-looking but sinister guy with a bat flying around the house. It didn't get much of a laugh."

"It worked for me," Terry said, "but then I'm used to bats. They'd come out every night and eat a few tons of bugs. I liked the skin on the bathroom floor, too, Randy the snake molting."

"That's right," Fran said, "you were gonna see if you could make that work."

"It either didn't," Debbie said, "or only a few people got it. Or if you're gonna do weird humor you have to establish it right away, not slip it in somewhere."

"The only thing I didn't get," Terry said, "was the worst thing in the joint being the TV show. But then I never saw it. What's the name of the show? *Urkel?*"

"He's the character," Debbie said. "The show's called *Family Matters*. Urkel's a nerdy black kid with the most annoying voice I've ever heard, and the ladies in the dorm'd cry laughing at him. But you're right, it doesn't work. I'm getting rid of Urkel."

"Maybe do more with Randy."

"I could; but I get mad thinking about him and then it's not funny. I didn't hurt him enough."

"You mean there is a Randy and you hit him with a car?"

"A Ford Escort. But you say you happened to run into your ex-husband, beat, with a Ford Escort, it doesn't make it. And I didn't just happen to run into him."

"She ambushed him," Fran said, eating his salad now, "laid in wait."

"You have to understand," Debbie said, "the guy wiped me out, totaled my Beamer, got rid of my dog, stole cash I'd hidden away . . . He's the only guy I know comes out of the bathroom he doesn't have a magazine or the newspaper under his arm. He'd be in there forever. Finally it dawned on me, he's snooping around, looking in the medicine cabinet, the drawers . . . I'd hide extra cash in there, 'cause if I had it in my bag I'd spend it. I'd put it in a roll of toilet paper in the bathroom closet, in that hollow center, or in a box of tampons. The sneak found twelve hundred bucks and then lied about it. 'No, it wasn't me.' Or I'd forgot where I hid it. Another time I come home, my dog's gone. 'Where's Camille?' Randy goes, 'Oh, she must've run away.' This is a Lhasa Apso that had the dog world by the ass, had anything she wanted, toys, gourmet pet chow—and she ran away? I know what he did, he took Camille for a ride and threw her out of the fucking car, a helpless little dog." Debbie took a sip of vodka and looked up to see Terry's quiet gaze on her. She said, "I get upset, I don't normally use that kind of language."

"You don't," Fran said, "since when?"

She watched Terry grin, like he thought his brother was being funny, then surprised her with, "How much did he take you for altogether?"

"He hit her at the perfect time," Fran said. "I'd just paid Deb her commission on a big case we settled."

"The total," Debbie said, "counting what he borrowed, comes to sixty-seven thousand. Plus the car and the cash, all in less than three months."

"And Camille," Terry said, "she's worth something."

Looking at her with his innocent eyes. Was he putting her on? Now he said, "The guy must've charmed you out of your socks," not sounding much like a priest.

"What he does," Debbie said, "Randy looks you right in the eye and lies, and you want to believe him. We met at a wedding reception at Oakland Hills I find out later he wasn't invited to. Read about it in the paper. We're dancing, drinking champagne, he asks me if I like to sail. I told him I'd only been out a few times, on Lake St. Clair. We're dancing, Randy whispers in my ear, 'I'm getting ready to sail around the world and I want you to come with me.' You have to understand, this guy is movie star good-looking, early forties, he's tan, buff, gold ring in his ear; he has hair like Michael Landon, a home in Palm Beach he tells me he's putting on the market, asking price eight mil. I was ready to go to Hudson's and buy a little sailor suit. He draws a map on a napkin how we'd sail from Palm Beach to the Gulf of Mexico, through the Panama Canal to Tahiti, Tonga, New Caledonia—"

"Only," Fran said, mopping up salad dressing with a roll, "the guy didn't have a boat."

"A yachting cap," Debbie said, "and a picture of a boat he tells me is in drydock in Florida, getting it ready for the trip. This was his excuse to start borrowing money. First a couple of thousand, then five, then ten—for navigational equipment, radar, all boat stuff, because his money was tied up in investments he didn't want to move just yet."

Terry said, "What's he do for a living?"

"Preys on stupid women," Debbie said. "I still can't believe I fell for it. He tells me he's retired from Merrill Lynch, one of their top traders, and I believed him. Did I check? No, not till it was too late. But you know what did me in, besides the hair and the tan? Greed. He said if I had a savings account that wasn't doing much and would like to put it to work . . . He shows me his phony portfolio, stock worth millions, and like a dummy I said, 'Well, I've got fifty grand not doing too much.' I signed it over and that's the last I saw of my money."

"But you saw Randy again," Terry said, "on Collins Avenue?"

"You've got a good memory," Debbie said. "Yeah, a couple of months later. In the set, the opening, I say I was in Florida visiting my mom, and that part's true. She's in a nursing home in West Palm with Alzheimer's. She thinks she's Ann Miller. She said it was hard to dance in her bedroom slippers, so I gave her an old pair of tap shoes I had."

"She any good?"

"Not bad for not having taken lessons."

"It was on Royal Poinciana Way you ran him down," Fran said, finished with his salad, wiping the plate clean with half of a roll he stuffed in his mouth.

"If you want to get technical about it," Debbie said, "but Collins Avenue works better in the set."

Fran was pushing up from the table. He said to his brother, "You know I'm going to Florida in the morning, early. We better leave soon as I get back."

Debbie watched him heading toward the men's. "He was in Florida last week."

"The girls are out of school," Terry said, "so Mary Pat stays down with the little cuties and Fran's joining them for a long weekend. But I think he wants to go home 'cause he's still hungry. Mary Pat loaded the freezer with her casseroles, and they're not bad. Mary Pat's a professional homemaker."

"I've never met her," Debbie said. "I've never been invited to the house."

"Fran's afraid Mary Pat would see you as a threat."

"He told you that?"

"I'm guessing, knowing Francis. I think he would like to believe you're a threat."

"He's never made a move that way."

"Doesn't want to risk being turned down."

"You're saying he has a crush on me?"

"I can't imagine why he wouldn't."

Looking right at her, like he was saying he'd feel that way if he were Fran. It startled her. She said, "Oh, really?" and it sounded dumb.

His gaze still on her, he said, "I was wondering, when you hit Randy, were you still married to him?"

"We never were. In the bit I call him my husband and I've got the divorced women in the audience with me. I say I hit my ex-boyfriend it doesn't have the same, you know, emotional effect."

"But you lived with him?"

"He lived with me, in Somerset. Where I am now, back again. Fran got me the apartment." She said, "Does that sound like I'm being kept?"

"If it was anyone but Francis," Terry said. "Did you really put Randy in a body cast?"

He kept going back to Randy.

"No, but I banged him up pretty good."

"Have you seen him since?"

"You mean, did he visit me in prison?"

"That's right, you've been out of circulation. What I was thinking," Terry said, "the next time you see him, get him to hit you and sue him for sixty-seven thousand. I thought working with Fran, the personal-injury expert, you might know how to arrange that kind of accident."

The priest sneaking up on her with a straight face. Playing with her.

"Fran and I," Debbie said, "have never staged a car wreck, ever. Or hired people who do it." She paused for a beat. "And I've never smuggled cigarettes."

It brought his smile. It told her they could kid around, not take each other too seriously. She said, "We're not in a confessional, Father, so I'm not telling you any of my sins, business-related or otherwise."

"You still go?"

"Not in years."

"Well, if you ever feel the need—I never give more than ten Our Fathers and ten Hail Marys."

She said, "Really?" She said, "Do you hear the same kind of sins in Rwanda you do here?"

"A typical one over there, 'Bless me, Fatha, for I have sin. I stole a goat by Nyundo and my wife cook it en brochette.' Here, you don't get as many goat thieves."

"Did you ever try it?"

"Goat? We had it all the time."

"What about adultery?"

"I was never tempted."

Having fun behind his innocent expression.

"I meant, did you hear it much in Confession?"

"Now and then. But I think there was a lot more fooling around than I was told about."

"What's the penance for fooling around?"

"The usual, ten and ten."

"What about murder?"

"I only had one person confess to it."

"What did you give him?"

"That one, I laid it on."

She paused to see if he'd tell her what that meant. When he didn't, she said, "Have you ever called a man 'my son'?"

"That's only in movies."

"That's what I thought." She said, "Well, now that you're home"—and saw Fran coming back from the men's—"what'll you do, take it easy for a while?"

"I have to see about raising some money."

"For your mission?"

Fran reached the table saying, "You ready?" and Terry didn't get a chance to answer.

He said, "I am if you are, my son."

Fran said, "What's this 'my son' shit?"

In the parking lot Terry took her hand and told her again how much he liked the set and enjoyed talking to her; all that. Then, as Fran stepped toward his Lexus and pressed the key remote to unlock the door, Terry said to her, "I'd like to see you again."

Sounding like a guy after a phone number.

It gave her a funny feeling, a priest saying it. She turned to Fran and said, "Why don't I drive your brother?" Saying it before she had time to think about it and change her mind.

"He's staying at my house," Fran said, sounding surprised because he'd told her that.

"I know where you live," Debbie said. "I want to hear more about Africa."

9

IN THE CAR HE TOLD Debbie he almost wasn't invited to stay at Fran's, Mary Pat worried he might leave an African disease around the house like cholera or a tapeworm on the toilet seat. But now, since Mary Pat and the girls were in Florida and Fran was flying down, it was okay.

"Did you have any African diseases?"

"We boiled the water and always slept under mosquito netting," Terry said, catching a glimpse of Chantelle's slim body. "So I'm pretty sure I'm clean. I did worry about worms, but never spotted any."

When they got in and Debbie started the car—a Honda Fran had leased for her—the radio came on, Sheryl Crow and the sun coming up over Santa Monica Boulevard. Lowering the volume she asked if he listened to music in Africa. Terry told her Congo-Zaire rock until Fran sent some CDs. Joe Cocker, Steely Dan, Ziggy Marley and the

Melody Makers. She asked if the natives liked reggae and he said he never thought of Rwandans as natives, since they wore clothes. He told her his housekeeper, Chantelle, wore cool skirts she wrapped around her hips, a lot of colors in the design, and told how Chantelle had lost part of her left arm during the genocide. Debbie asked how she cleaned the house and cooked with one hand. Terry said she managed. Debbie asked if he'd brought any mementos home with him and he said only one, a machete.

He knew it wasn't Africa she wanted to talk about but maybe would get to it by way of Africa—driving up Woodward Avenue now toward Bloomfield Hills, a five-mile strip where, Terry said, serious Motor City cruising used to happen, only it was called Woodwarding. Debbie said it was before her time. Terry said they'd always lived on the east side, so he hadn't got over this way too often. He said he and Fran both went to Bishop Gallagher and, before that, Our Lady Queen of Peace. Both keeping the chitchat going until Debbie said:

"Where they had the Mass for your mother."

"You went to the funeral?"

"And to your house after, where you grew up. I met your sister—"

"Did she talk?"

"She never stopped. She called you harum-scarum, whatever that means, but you loved to have her read to you. One of your favorites was *The Lives of the Saints*, especially stories about martyrs."

"Saint Agatha," Terry said, "had her breasts cut off and then was thrown on a pile of hot coals."

"Bummer," Debbie said.

And he knew what she was thinking.

"Do a martyr bit. The Christian chick trying to talk her way out of being thrown to the lions."

Debbie picked it up. " 'Hey, some of my best friends are pagans. Love their idols.' Did you see *The Life of Brian*?"

"Monty Python, yeah—'Blessed are the cheesemakers.' What was it they sang at the end, when they were crucified?"

"Yeah, it was perfect, but I can't remember."

They passed lights shining down on rows and rows of sparkling used cars.

"I understand you were an altar boy."

"Six o'clock Mass every morning."

"Your sister thinks that's why you became a priest."

"Except that by the eighth grade I was staring at Kathy Bednark's rear end."

It seemed to stop Debbie for a moment.

"But later on you did enter a seminary."

"In California," Terry said.

"But you weren't ordained till you got to Africa?"

"The way it worked out."

"You took your vows there?"

Getting to poverty, chastity, and obedience now.

"They're part of becoming a priest," Terry said, wondering where she was going with it.

"I would imagine," Debbie said, "living in an African village, you'd have no trouble keeping your vows."

He had to ask, "Why do you say that?"

"Well, living in a third-world country on a poverty level? On your own, no one you had to answer to . . ."

That took care of two of the vows. Terry said, "Yeah?" and waited to see how she'd handle chastity.

When she ducked it, saying, "And now you'll try to raise money for the mission?" he was surprised.

"It's why I'm here. The priest whose place I took, Fr. Toreki—?"

"Your uncle. Fran told me about him."

"He'd come home and visit parishes around Detroit, and make a pitch at the Sunday Masses. I don't think I can do that. I'm not any good as a preacher. Any time I gave a sermon there'd be a guy there doing a translation, and it always sounded better in Kinyarwanda. I have a lot of pictures of kids, most of them orphans, that'll hit you right in the heart, but I don't know what to do with them. I remember in grade school there'd be a jar in the classroom and a sign that said FOR THE PAGAN BABIES, and we'd put change in it left from our lunch money."

"What would that bring, ten bucks a week?"

"If that."

"About what you made smuggling cigarettes?"

She did it. Got to what she wanted to talk about by way of Africa. Sneaked up on him.

"I can tell you," Terry said, "the money we made on cigarettes wasn't cigarette money. We'd drive a U-Haul to Kentucky, six, seven hours, and come back with ten thousand cartons at a time. Make three bucks a carton, thirty grand a trip, a day's work. Fran told you about it, uh?"

"He said you were an innocent victim."

"That's right, and he explained it to the prosecutor. All I did was drive."

"Not knowing you were committing tax fraud."

"That's all it was. You ever cheat on your income tax, list phony expenses? That's fraud, too."

"As a matter of fact," Debbie said, "I've never cheated on my income tax."

"And I've never run over anyone with a Buick."

"Riviera."

Terry smiled. "You see us as a couple of cons, don't you, talking in the yard? Only I've never done time."

They stopped for the light at 13 Mile Road and he saw her turn to look at him, maybe for the first time.

She said, "You don't count Africa?"

"I went there of my own free will."

"With an indictment hanging over you. And, according to Fran, a guilty conscience, worried your mother'd find out what her little altar boy was doing."

"He told you that?"

"He said you took off and the Pajonny brothers went down, and that's all I know."

"It was the other way around. They were picked up before I left."

"You make those plans pretty fast?"

"I'd been thinking about going over there for some time, help out my uncle Tibor. He was a saint."

"Whatever you say, Father."

He could feel her confidence, little Debbie sitting there in the dark looking straight ahead at the traffic lights, knowing exactly where she was going, Terry paying close attention.

So when she said, "I met a friend of yours at the funeral."

He knew right away who she meant and said, "Does he have bad teeth and stands real close when he's talking?"

"His breath could use some help, too," Debbie said. "How'd you know?"

"You've been working up to this," Terry said, "and now you're there. You met Johnny Pajonny."

She looked over at him, this time with a smile.

"He's a beauty."

"You want to use him in your routine."

"I'm thinking about it."

The light changed and they were moving again, Debbie keeping to the right-hand lane, taking her time. She said, "He thought you'd be at the funeral."

"Was Dickie there?"

"He's still in. Johnny says he fucks up and spends most of his time in the Hole."

"What else did he say?"

"He mentioned you owe them each ten thousand."

"Just happened to mention it?"

"It seemed to be on his mind."

"He thinks I stiffed him?"

"He seemed a little bummed, yeah. Mostly he wanted to know if you still had the money."

"That was five years ago. Why was he asking you?"

"He seemed to think I was your girlfriend."

"Come on—doesn't he know I'm a priest?"

"Your old girlfriend."

As she said it, watching the road, Debbie turned into a lane that ran along a strip of storefronts and angle-parked close to a party store.

She said, "I have to get some cigarettes," and opened her door.

"Wait a minute. What old girlfriend?"

"The one you were living with in L.A.," Debbie said, "when your mom thought you were in the seminary. I'll be right back."

10

HE COULD SEE HER INSIDE the store talking to the young Arab-looking guy behind the counter, the guy laughing at something she said, Debbie winning a fan while she bought a pack of cigarettes. The guy would tell his friends about this cool blond chick who came in and was funny, man. The guy not knowing how cool she really was—the way she could zing you when you weren't looking; set you up first, see if you'd admit things she already knew, things Fran would've told her, Fran and now Johnny Pajonny, who loved to talk and act like an insider, thinking Debbie was the girl in L.A. and Debbie no doubt letting him think it.

He should never've told Johnny in the U-Haul coming back from Kentucky about the girl in L.A.

Debbie had moved away from the counter, down an aisle toward the back of the store, out of view. Now she was at the counter again, the Arab-looking guy ringing up the sale with a big grin, Debbie standing in her raincoat talking, opening a pack of cigarettes, the guy stopping to give her a light, then handing her the Bic, or whatever it was. Terry couldn't see what she'd bought, but it looked like more than cigarettes the guy was putting in the paper bag.

The whole time in the car had been an interrogation: Debbie showing a keen interest in his life, more than just curiosity. But now where would she go with it? He'd have to bring her along to find out.

So when she came out and got in the car Terry said, "I can understand why Johnny asked about the money."

"I can, too," Debbie said, "thirty thousand in cash."

She started the car, but then sat back with her cigarette, the grocery bag on the seat next to her.

"He thinks I took off with it, uh?"

"Didn't you?"

"Let me tell you," Terry said, "how it worked on a run to Kentucky. We'd come back with a load, drop it off, and return the U-Haul. The next day we'd go to an office downtown in the Penobscot Building and the woman there, Mrs. Moraco, would pay us. Count out hundred-dollar bills without saying a word, mostly old bills, and we'd put the money in athletic bags we'd brought along."

"You know who the buyer was?"

"I didn't ask. Anyway, the first couple of times we made the run, no problem," Terry said. "The time we're talking about, only Johnny and I made the trip. Dickie wasn't feeling good and stayed home. But when I say home I mean Johnny's house in Hamtramck. Dickie lived with Johnny, his wife Regina and their three kids—two little boys swore all the time, did whatever they wanted, and a fifteen-year-old girl, Mercy, who was studying hard to become a hooker."

Debbie said, "Mercy?"

"Regina's born again."

"Don't tell me," Debbie said, "this is about Mercy and Uncle Dickie."

"Yeah, but which one needed protection? Dickie said Mercy was always showing off her young body—and it was all there, believe me. I stopped by to pick Johnny up one time, Mercy comes out to the car in a little sunsuit. The way she leaned on the windowsill showing herself, I thought she was gonna ask if I wanted to have a good time. What Regina wanted was Dickie out of the house, but Johnny wouldn't hear of it. He said if Dickie wasn't around he wouldn't have anybody to talk to. They watched sports on TV together and argued."

"At the wake," Debbie said, smoking her cigarette, "he asked me to go have a drink with him."

"What'd you tell him?"

"I met him at the Cadieux Café, looking for Johnny Pajonny material. The name alone. So then what happened?"

She'd zing him and Terry would have to remind himself this nice-looking girl was not only an entertainer, she'd done time. And smoked a lot. He pressed the button to lower his window halfway.

"Regina comes home from working a checkout counter at Farmer Jack's and finds Mercy and Dickie in the bathroom together." Terry paused. "You had a drink with Johnny at the Cadieux? That's a popular spot."

"He wanted to go to a motel."

"Yeah . . . ?"

"I told him I was a nun."

It hung there, Terry not sure if she was kidding, had actually said that.

"I handled it, Terry. Okay? So Regina finds Mercy and Dickie in the shower."

"They were in the bathroom with the door closed."

"The shower running?"

"I don't know if they were doing anything or not. I wasn't around to hear. But what happened, Regina called the cops. They arrive and find Dickie trying to stash about a hundred cartons of cigarettes under his bed, ones Dickie sold on the side. Johnny and I are on the way home, his cell phone rings and it's Regina. She says the cops are there on account of Dickie molesting Mercy, his own niece, but doesn't mention the cops finding the cigarettes; that's not her problem. We get to Detroit, Johnny wants to go right home. He's as upset as Regina 'cause now he's afraid Dickie'll have to move out. I told him I wasn't going near the house with cops there. I dropped him off at a bar on his street, Lili's, it's just off Joseph Campau, and went on to the warehouse, dropped the load, and returned the truck. Later on I called the house. Regina tells me Johnny and Dickie are in the Wayne County jail and people from Alcohol, Tobacco and Firearms are going through the house as we speak. See, at that time no one knew if it would be taken state or federal. So the next day I collected from Mrs. Moraco—"

Debbie stopped him. "Did you tell her?"

"I told her she better close the office for a while, and left town."

"You had a passport?"

"I told you, I'd already made plans to leave, go to Africa. But that doesn't mean I planned to skip."

She shrugged, maybe not caring one way or the other. "So the Pajonnys were brought in and they gave it up."

"They gave *me* up. The prosecutor worked on them a few days and offered a plea deal. They said I hired them; I was the one always delivered the load and collected the money. They knew better than to give 'em Mrs. Moraco. But then once I was involved Fran got on it and talked to the prosecutor. Fran said there must be some mistake, as I was an ordained Catholic priest at a mission in Rwanda. By now a few weeks had passed. I'm over there and the genocide's going on, hundreds of thousands of people being killed and I'm in the middle of it. Did the state really want to indict me? Fran says I'm in the clear, but still have to talk to an assistant prosecutor, Gerald Padilla, downtown at the Frank Murphy, what they call Recorders Court; it's all criminal. I have to get a black suit and a collar and shine my shoes."

"Why don't you have a suit?"

"When I left, I gave it to a man less fortunate than myself. There's always a need for clothing over there."

She said, "Terry?"

"What?"

"Bullshit."

He watched the glow of her cigarette as she drew on it and blew the smoke out in a slow stream, directly into his face. Terry closed his eyes. He didn't wave his hand at the smoke, he closed his eyes and opened them again, knowing what was coming.

She said, "You're not a priest, are you?"

He heard himself say, "No, I'm not," sitting there in the dark.

"Were you ever a priest?"

"No."

"Or in a seminary in California or anywhere else?"

He felt the interrogation winding down.

"No."

She said, "Don't you feel better now?"

They were on their way again following taillights, Terry with a sense of relief, because he'd wanted to tell her even while they were in the restaurant talking and knew he would sooner or later. But not with Fran around. Fran needed to believe he was a priest. Debbie didn't want to believe it—he could tell—so he was himself with her most of the time, even talking about Confession when Fran was away from the table. That part was easy because it was true, and he almost told her then, tired of acting a part. After that he was open, giving her a chance to have a funny feeling about him, suspicious, and if she had the nerve she'd ask the question. And she did.

In the dark he offered a little more.

"You're the only person who knows."

"You haven't told Fran?"

"Not while he's talking to the prosecutor."

"No one during all that time in Africa?"

"No one."

"Not even your one-armed housekeeper?"

Look at that—she'd picked up on Chantelle.

"Not even her."

"She lived with you?"

"Almost the whole time I was there."

"Is she pretty?"

"Miss Rwanda, if they ever have a pageant."

"Did you sleep with her?"

Debbie asked it looking straight ahead.

"If you're wondering about AIDS it was never a threat."

"Why would I worry about AIDS?"

"I said 'If you were wondering.' "

Debbie dropped her cigarette out the window.

"She believed you were a priest?"

"It didn't matter to her."

"Why've you told me and no one else?"

"I wanted to."

"Yeah, but why me?"

"Because we think alike," Terry said.

She glanced at him saying, "I felt that right away."

"And when I explain how it happened," Terry said, "you'll think it's funny and see it as a skit."

They came to an intersection, the light green, and Debbie turned right onto Big Beaver. Now they were passing low rolling hills on the left, a heavy cover of trees lining the other side of the road and Terry said, "Shouldn't we have turned the other way?"

"I thought we'd go to my place," Debbie said. "Okay?"

Terry picked up the party store bag and felt packs of cigarettes inside and a bottle with a familiar shape, four sides to it rather than perfectly round, like most fifths of whiskey.

"Red or black?"

"Red."

"You knew what I'd say before you went in the store."

"Yeah, but I had to set it up."

"You have some kind of scheme working and you want my blessing. Is that it?"

She said, "Terry, you're too good to be true."

11

DEBBIE USED THE PHONE IN the kitchen to call Fran. She could see Terry in the living room by the glass door to the balcony, looking out at the grounds in the dark. She saw him turn to say, "All that space and no crops growing. You could have an acre of corn out there."

"It's a three-par golf course," Debbie said, "nine holes," as Fran came on the line. She spoke to him less than a minute, unhurried, but anxious to have the call out of the way. Terry came in the kitchen as she hung up.

"What'd he say?"

"He said, 'Oh . . . ?' I told him I'd drop you off after we have a drink, or you could stay if you want. Fran said, 'You sure you have room?' "

"Who doesn't he trust, you or me?"

"Well, since he thinks you're celibate, and he knows I haven't scored or been scored on in quite some time . . . I imagine he sees me seducing you. Or trying to."

"Wishing he was here instead of me."

She said, "I won't comment on that. Fran and I are strictly business. You want to know how we got together?"

"He told me he used to see you around Circuit Court, you'd be testifying for other lawyers."

"Yeah, and I always thought he was a decent guy. What happened, I saw a skycap out at Metro drop a suitcase on a woman's foot and I brought her to Fran. He sued Northwest at a time when everyone in Detroit hated the airline. They settled and we've been friends ever since."

"What do you do," Terry said, "show people how to limp?"

"How to limp convincingly," Debbie said, making drinks now, a tray of ice on the counter with the Johnnie Walker and a fifth of Absolut. "But we're still on you. Tell me why, when you were in California, your mom thought you were in a seminary."

"Because all my life she was after me to become a priest. What I couldn't understand, why me and not Fran?"

"You have that sort of haunted look," Debbie said, "like Saint Francis. Haunted or maybe shifty. She probably worked on Fran but you didn't notice."

They were both sipping their drinks now.

"Listen, if you had my mother praying for you, I'm not kidding, you could be a Carmelite nun, like my sister. She was on me even after I quit school, U of D, and went to work for my dad painting houses. I quit that and started selling insurance."

"That sounds like Fran's idea."

"It was, and I hated it."

"You hadn't found your true calling yet, smuggling."

"I ran out of friends who might buy a policy and moved to Los

Angeles. My mother put holy cards in her letters, prayers to Saint Anthony to help me find myself. Saint Jude, the patron saint of hopeless
cases. What I did, I told her, 'You win, I'm going in the seminary,'
and had stationery printed up that said across the top, 'The Missionaries of St. Dismas Novitiate.' "

Debbie said, "Wasn't he one of the guys crucified with Christ?"

"Known as the good thief."

"What were you, kind of a smart-ass?"

"I thought I was a genius. I used it whenever I wrote to Mom. I'd
sign the letters, 'Yours in Christ, Terry.' "

"This is while you were living with the girl?"

"Part of the time. Jill Silver, she was from around here originally,
that's how we came to be introduced. I think she was in a high school
production of *Fiddler on the Roof* and decided she wanted to be a
movie star."

"She make it?"

Terry finished his drink. "Not till she had breast implants," as he
poured himself another. "Though it could've been a coincidence. I
told her small ones were more stylish. Jill comes home from an audi-
tion at the studio and goes, 'Well, smartie, guess what? My new rack
got me the part.' So maybe it did. Within a month she's living with
the director."

"Tits," Debbie said, "can make a difference. I'm thinking of getting just a lift."

"For what?"

"My self-esteem, what else?"

"The movie Jill was in, she played a flight attendant who's hooked
on 'ludes. Pops one in the lavatory and spills coffee all over the pas-
sengers. The other flight attendant was the star, but I can't think of
her name."

"What were you doing at the time?"

"Insurance, the only thing where I had any experience. But as a claims adjuster. Out there it was mostly fires and mud slides."

"No personal injury?"

"Some."

"Could you tell when they were faking it?"

"Only if they got nervous and offered me a piece of the action."

"Would you take it?"

"If I felt sorry for the guy."

"Compassion," Debbie said, "influencing your report. Even though you were helping the guy commit fraud."

"You have to look at it more as a tip than a bribe," Terry said. "The lawsuit pays off, the guy gives you a tip. It's like when you win big playing blackjack. You tip the dealer, even though he hasn't done anything to help you."

"You see it as a gray area," Debbie said.

"Exactly. I called Fran one time with a gray-area situation, see what he thought about it. He wouldn't even discuss it. You know what I mean? Fran doesn't like to go on record."

"He's a gray area himself," Debbie said. "If the injury isn't one hundred percent legit, don't tell him. And you know he won't ask. So he knew you weren't in a seminary."

"Just my mother."

"But Fran believes you're a priest."

"Because of Uncle Tibor. He told my mom I got ordained."

"He lied for you?"

"That part gets tricky."

"Wait. First you came back from L.A."

"The low point of my life," Terry said. "I was working for my dad again. I was drinking—I mean more than I usually did. I didn't have any money to speak of. No direction. I was in Lili's one night to hear a band, I think it was the Zombie Surfers, and the Pajonny brothers walked in."

"Your old buddies."

"I wouldn't say we were buddies. We played football together in high school. Had some fights—they used to pick on Fran because he had a girl's name."

"I was thinking in the restaurant," Debbie said, "you should have that name. Didn't I say you remind me of Saint Francis?"

"You mean, what you think he looked like? If I'd been named Francis I'd be dead or punch-drunk by now, all the fights I'd get into. You know what's the worst thing about a fistfight? How long it takes your hands to heal."

"Okay," Debbie said, "and now you're in the cigarette business. You make a few runs and take off for Rwanda with the thirty thousand. Or maybe more."

"You want to know if I've got any money?"

"That's what Johnny's wondering," Debbie said. "I wouldn't want to owe him ten grand and not have it."

"I'll talk to Johnny. Don't worry about it."

She wondered if it would be that simple, but decided to move on. "Let's get back to Uncle Tibor. He told your mom you were a priest—"

"You know why I went there? Outside of who's gonna look for me in Rwanda? I liked Tibor. I knew him all my life, from when he used to stay with us, and I wanted to do something for him. Paint his house, cut the grass, whatever'd make him happy. I get over there he says, 'I don't need a painter, I need you on the altar saying Mass, or you're no good to me.'"

Debbie said, "Your mom'd told him you'd gone to a seminary."

"That's right, and I didn't tell him I hadn't. But I knew the liturgy anyway, from being an altar boy."

"You were just a little short on theology."

"When would I use it? Most of the people only spoke

Kinyarwanda and some French. Tibor's idea was to get me ordained right away. He was eighty years old, had a bad heart, a couple of bypasses already, he felt he wasn't gonna be around too much longer. He said he'd work it out with a bishop friend of his to get me ordained. I thought, well, the bishop can say the words over me, but that won't in conscience make me a priest, will it? If I don't want to be one? You understand what I mean? I go through the motions—who knows I'm not a priest?"

"Another gray area."

"But before it's arranged, Tibor has a heart attack and I take him to the hospital in Kigali, the capital. I said to him, 'Uncle Tibor, just in case, why don't you write to Marguerite'—that's my mother—'while you still can, and tell her I'm finally a priest? The news coming from you would make her even happier. Write the letter and I'll mail it after I'm ordained.' "

"He wrote the letter," Debbie said.

"Yes, he did."

"And died?"

"Not right away."

"But you mailed the letter right away."

"So I wouldn't lose it."

"You went all the way to Rwanda and stayed five years," Debbie said, "to get your mother off your back."

"She's not why I stayed."

Debbie opened a cupboard and brought out a box of crackers. "You know what it looks like? You were waiting for her to die so you could come home."

"I hadn't thought of that."

Debbie brought a wedge of Brie out of the refrigerator.

"You came, but not in time for the funeral."

"There was something I had to do before I left."

Debbie placed a knife next to the cheese. She said, "Five years in an African village—"

"Fran had to work on the prosecutor."

"I know, but Rwanda. Couldn't you have gone someplace else? How about the South of France?"

"I was there," Terry said. "Fran liked my taking Uncle Tibor's place, the family tie-in. The prosecutor liked it, too."

"You told me you heard Confessions," Debbie said, handing him a cheese and cracker. "Is that true?"

"Once a week," Terry said with his mouth full.

"Come on—really?"

"They tell you their sins, you tell them to love God and don't do it again. And give 'em their penance."

"The guy who stole a goat was real?"

"From around Nyundo."

"The one who committed murder?"

"I took care of him, too. Gave him his penance."

"Don't tell me you said Mass."

She watched him fix another cheese and cracker and put the whole thing in his mouth.

He said, "The first time," and stopped to finish chewing and swallow. "I was visiting Tibor, still in the hospital. There was already talk about a genocide being organized. Now we hear on the radio that it's started—Hutu militia, the bad guys, armed with AK-47s, machetes, spiked clubs, are killing every Tutsi they can find. Tibor tells me to go home and get everybody in the church, quick, and they'll be safe."

Sanctuary. Debbie knew about that from *The Hunchback of Notre Dame*.

"We're in the church, everybody's scared to death and want me to say Mass. I thought, well, we could say some prayers. No, they want a regular Mass and Communion, 'Because we know we going to die.'

That's what they told me. They've already accepted it and there was nothing I said made any difference. I put on the vestments—I look like a priest and I know how to say Mass, so I did. I got through the first part, right up to the Consecration, and that was when they came in, all of a sudden shooting, hacking with their machetes . . . I stood there and watched them kill everyone in the church, even the little kids, infants they held by the feet and swung against the wall, the mothers screaming—"

Debbie said, "They didn't fight back?"

"With what? They knew they were gonna die and were letting it happen."

She stood with him at the counter not saying a word now. She watched him take a drink, then another, finishing what was in the glass. She picked up her cigarettes and offered him one. He shook his head. She poured Scotch into his glass, added an ice cube. He let the drink sit on the counter. She lit a cigarette. Now he took one from the pack and she flicked the lighter again, the one the guy in the party store had given her. Terry drew on the cigarette and laid it on the edge of the ashtray.

He said, "I didn't do anything. I watched."

"What could you do?"

He didn't answer.

"You keep seeing it happen."

"I think about it, yeah."

"Is that why you stayed? You didn't do anything and it bothered you? You felt guilty?"

It made him hesitate, maybe surprised, hearing something he hadn't considered.

"Why you spent five years there?"

"I told you why."

"You felt if you left—"

"What?"

"You'd be running away?"

He shook his head. "It didn't—I can't say it made me want to, you know, get revenge. I couldn't believe I'd seen all those people killed, most of them hacked to death by people they knew, their neighbors, friends, some even related by marriage. The Hutus were told to kill all the Tutsis and they said okay and tried as hard as they could to do it. How do you understand that and take sides if you're not with one or the other? Even when I saw a chance to do something it wasn't planned or something I'd even thought about."

"What did you do?"

He picked up his drink, sipped it, and put it down.

"The day I left I killed four young guys, Hutus. They were in the church that time five years ago. I killed them because one of them bragged about it and said they were gonna do it again. They were sitting at a table in the beer lady's house drinking banana beer and I shot them with my housekeeper's pistol."

There was a silence.

Debbie drew on her cigarette, patient.

"You're not kidding, are you?"

"No, I killed them."

"Did it help?"

"I don't know what you mean."

"Like now you've done something? Struck back?"

He said after a moment, "It didn't seem to have anything to do with what happened in the church."

"You weren't arrested?"

"The military are Tutsi. One of them helped me get away."

He was solemn about it, his expression, his tone. Still, he seemed at ease with what he had done. Debbie moved closer and touched his face, feeling his beard and cheekbone. She said, "Tell it that way, the scene in the church. That's your sermon." She gave his cheek a pat, brought her hand down and picked up her drink.

Terry said, "Yeah, well, that's the idea. Visit parishes and get permission to make a special appeal at Sunday Mass. Fran got me a directory of the Archdiocese and I wrote down the parishes I want to visit and the names of the pastors. I'll start on the east side, the ones I'm familiar with."

"You'll work your tail off," Debbie said, "and it's nickel-and-dime."

"I've got pictures of little kids, orphans."

"Are they heart-wrenching?"

"They're alone in the world and they're hungry. I have shots of them digging through garbage dumps—"

"The only way to do it," Debbie said, "and score big, you buy a mailing list of Catholics. Start with one area, a few thousand. Send a brochure that features your story, your pitch, pictures of the starving kids, flies crawling around on their little faces, in their mouth—"

"I'm not sure I have any with flies."

"That's all right, as long as they're heart-wrenching. And, you include a postage-paid return envelope."

Terry said, "The cost of that alone—"

He stopped, Debbie shaking her head.

"There's a little note on the envelope that says, 'Your stamp will help, too.'"

"What's all that cost?"

"A lot. Way too much. And it's work." She said, "Wait," and stubbed out her cigarette. "You get a Web site on the Internet and do it, paganbabies dot com."

"There aren't that many pagans anymore. They've all been converted to something. A lot of Seventh Day Adventists."

"Orphans dot com. Missions or missionaries dot com." Debbie

stopped. "It's still a lot of work. You know it? I mean like stoop labor, no fun in it. We could get into it and find out the Web sites are already taken." She said, "I don't even like computers, they're too . . . I don't know, mechanical." She went into the refrigerator for another tray of ice, turned with it to the counter, to Terry, the face she thought of as saintly, and said, "What's the matter with me? You're not raising money for orphans."

He said, "That's what you thought?"

"You're using them."

He said, "I don't like the idea especially, but do you think they care?"

Debbie levered open the ice tray. "Well, if all you're looking for is a score, to get you back on your feet—"

He said, "I thought you understood that, once you had me unfrocked."

She dropped ice cubes in their glasses saying, "You know, that gives me an idea," taking her time, as though the thought was just now creeping into her mind. "I'll bet if you helped me out—"

"Yeah . . . ?"

"You could make more than you ever would with your sermon, as good as it is."

"Help you get Randy?"

She said, "Would you?" and watched him grin and shake his head in appreciation, bless his heart, at times appearing to be a simple soul.

"Get him to hit you this time? I think I might've suggested that."

"You did, but I don't want to be seriously injured. Like settle but never walk again. Accidents, you never know what might happen."

He said, "Yeah, but it's your specialty. You must have all kinds of ways to fake it, you little devil."

Debbie let that one go. She put a fresh hit on their drinks and turned to Terry with his.

"You said, 'They were sitting at a table in the beer lady's house drinking banana beer and I shot them with my housekeeper's pistol.' Your exact words. I may never forget them."

She watched him sip his drink.

"Were you scared?"

She watched him shake his head.

"In my mind it was done before I stepped inside."

"Didn't they . . . come at you?"

"I didn't give them a chance to."

"You walked in and shot them?"

"We exchanged a few words first. I asked 'em to give themselves up. I knew they wouldn't. So you could say I knew going in I was gonna kill them."

12

TERRY, IN HIS PARKA, WAITED as Debbie drove off past hedges and old shade trees. No palms or eucalyptus, no banana trees in sight, or hills rising out of a morning mist, only manicured lawns like fairways and homes Terry saw as mansions. Debbie gave her horn a toot and he waved with a lazy motion of his arm, raised it and let it fall. He turned to see Fran standing in the entrance, one of the double doors open, and followed the brick walk up to the house; a wide expanse of limestone blocks painted beige, the windows and twin columns of the portico trimmed in white. "Regency," Fran had told him, "copies from a picture Mary Pat clipped out of *Architectural Digest*."

"Another five minutes," Fran said, "I'd be out of here. You wouldn't be able to get in the house."

He had on white poplin warm-ups that gave him a puffy look, Terry seeing a snowman in elaborate tennis shoes.

"I thought you were going to Florida."

"I am, I got a limo service takes me to the airport."

He didn't seem happy about going. Or something else was bothering him.

"That's what you wear on the plane?"

"For comfort," Fran said, "it's a three-hour flight. You have your breakfast?"

"I wouldn't mind a cup of coffee. All Debbie has in the house is instant."

"She's a kid," Fran said. "Her idea of coffee is cappuccino, in a restaurant."

"How old would you say she is?"

"I know exactly how old, she's thirty-three, still a kid."

"What're you trying to tell me," Terry said, following Fran inside, "even if I wasn't a priest she's still too young for me?"

Fran brought him from the foyer past a curving staircase, through the formal dining room and butler's pantry to the kitchen before he spoke, Fran facing him now from across a big butcher-block table. "Somebody sees you leaving her apartment, seven in the morning, what're they supposed to think?"

"We grilled hot dogs last night, kosher," Terry said, "with the skin. After that we sat around talking. It got late, I could see she was tired—"

"I told her on the phone, call me, I'd pick you up."

He thought Fran would ask where he'd slept—it was a one-bedroom apartment—but didn't seem to want to touch that. So Terry said, "You worried I might've gotten laid?"

No smile, Fran's tone almost grim saying, "I'm talking about appearances."

No, he wasn't, but Terry went along. "I appear, seven in the morning or whenever, who knows who I am? Do I look like a priest in this?"

"You told me you bought a suit."

"I did." Fran had given him his Brooks Brothers credit card and he'd driven to the mall in Mary Pat's Cadillac—Fran having a fit when he found out and had to inspect the car for dings. "I pick up the suit today, after five."

Fran said, "Aw shit," sounding worn out. "Your meeting with the prosecutor's at one o'clock."

"I'll be there."

"One o'clock sharp at the Frank Murphy. I know I told you."

"You did, I just don't have a suit. I have the Roman collar, one of Uncle Tibor's, and one of his Mandarin shirts—has a little notch up here to show the collar. I tried on his suit. It was so shiny you could use it as a mirror to comb your hair."

Terry grinned, hoping Fran would, but he didn't.

"Fran, I could wear a dress, I'm still a priest."

"You scare me sometimes, you know it? Mr. Casual."

"Fr. Casual. I'll speak to him in Latin."

"You're not funny." Fran seemed about to say something else, but then looked at his watch and hurried out of the kitchen.

Terry had already spotted the coffeemaker. He found a can of Folgers in the first cupboard he opened and was running water from the tap, waiting for it to get cold, when Fran appeared again.

"My car's here."

"How'd you know?"

"It's supposed to be here at seven-fifteen and that's what time it is. Listen, Terr. Don't fuck up, okay?"

"I won't."

"The wrong attitude alone could keep the indictment active." Fran paused. "Buddy, I went way out on a limb for you. I said the Pajonnys hired you to drive a truck, ten bucks an hour. You were going to Africa and needed some extra expense money. I offered to give you whatever you needed, but you wanted to work for it—it's the kind of guy you are, hardworking. Yes, you knew you were transporting cigarettes but had no idea it involved tax fraud or you wouldn't have taken the job. You don't know who bought the cigarettes or what they did with them. That's your story and you stick to it. You nervous?"

"Why? I've got nothing to hide."

"That's good," Fran said, "that's the attitude to have. Any questions?"

"I can't think of any."

"You gonna walk me out?"

Terry said, "Sure," and turned the water off.

Fran hadn't moved. "I forgot to tell you, Johnny called. His number's by the phone in the library. Call him—you don't want to piss him off. But you also want to hold your ground. By that I mean you don't owe him anything, not a dime. You can't admit to anybody you received a payment. Johnny tries to get tough, back off, you're not kids in the schoolyard now. He threatens you, tell Padilla, the prosecutor. You don't want that asshole on your back."

"Johnny or the prosecutor?"

Fran said, "You can't help it, can you? Your normal reaction is to be a smart-ass. I imagined coming back from Africa, all you've been through over there, you'd have changed, become more serious . . ."

Terry nodded, waiting.

". . . show a sense of responsibility, and gratitude. You know how much I sent you altogether, counting what I paid for the T-shirts? Over twenty thousand dollars. You write and tell me about the weather and, 'Oh, thanks for the money.' "

Terry said, "You wrote it off, didn't you, as a contribution?"

"That's not the point. What about the cigarette money? With the three trips you must've taken off with fifty grand, counting the Pajonnys' cut from the last one. You spent all that?"

Trying to find out if he had any money. Terry said, "Fran, I was over there five years." And that was all he wanted to say about it.

"I read one of your letters to Mary Pat, the one you opened up in a little more than usual, that had all the smells in it. I commented that you were starting to sound like your old self again. You know what Mary Pat said? 'Is that good or bad?' " Fran said, "You see what I mean?"

Terry wasn't sure, but nodded again, squinting just a little, showing Fran he was giving it serious thought, while Fran seemed to stare at him as long as he could before looking at his watch again.

"I gotta go."

Terry waited on the front steps until the Lincoln Town Car was out of sight. He went into the library, saw two numbers for Johnny on the message pad—his home and what looked like his cell phone—as he dialed Debbie's number. As soon as she answered Terry said, "He's gone."

Man, last night. Last night decided his future for him. It would have to come one day at a time, but the trip looked full of promise all the way.

Just talking about it, Debbie telling stories . . . First offering to twist one if he wanted. "A yobie? Sure, why not." She appreciated his name for it and said that's what she'd call a joint from now on, a yobie. See? Looking into the future together. They sat on her secondhand St. Vincent de Paul sofa toking and grinning at each other, sipping their drinks, getting high while they looked for a way to score off Randy. Now loaded. A fact she hadn't mentioned before. Married a wealthy woman, divorced, but left in good shape, with a few million and a restaurant downtown.

"We'll get to that," Debbie said. "I think I told you, the first time he asked to borrow money he showed me a picture of his boat?"

"The one he didn't own," Terry said.

"That's right, but what I didn't mention, it had my name lettered on the back end, DEBBIE, and under it, PALM BEACH. He said he renamed it because he was so crazy about me. And oh, by the way, could I spare a couple of grand."

"How'd he do it?"

"Wait. Okay, now this is later, after he wiped me out and took off. It's been a couple of months and I'm in Florida visiting my mother. I stopped by the marina Randy was always talking about, looked around and there it was, a forty-six-foot cutter named DEBBIE with PALM BEACH under it. I asked in the marina bar if anyone knew a guy named Randy Agley. The bartender goes, 'You mean Aglioni?' A salty old guy sitting at the bar goes, 'Randy, that's the creep went around taking pictures of the boats. We ran him off.' I asked if they knew where Randy hung out. The bartender tells me to try the Breakers, where guys like Randy troll for rich broads. The old guy says try Au Bar, he saw him there a couple of times. Okay, at the Breakers I find out Mr. Agley is not allowed on the premises and Au Bar isn't there anymore, it's something else. I thought I'd struck out. But then right after, I have my mom out to dinner at Chuck and Harold's, we're almost finished and there's Mr. Wonderful himself. He has a drink in his hand and his sights on two women at a table. They're dressed casually but you can tell they're Palm Beach, the hair, simple jewelry but the real thing. Randy waits till they've ordered their drinks before moving in, the cheap fuck. I'm watching— it's obvious they don't know him. He gives them some bullshit for a couple of minutes, something like, 'Didn't I see you charming ladies at the Donald's last week? No? Then it must've been . . .' He joins them. Pretty soon the women are laughing and he's not even funny, has no sense of humor at all. I used to throw lines at him, ideas, off the top of my head? Like I'd say, 'My boyfriend is so good-looking, when he goes out he has to wear women's clothes,' beat, 'or else he gets mobbed by babes.' Randy would think about it with a blank look on his face, then turn on this fake laugh that sounds like ha ha ha. He wasn't fun. He had no idea how to get into a goof."

"He joins the ladies," Terry said.

"And I'm with my mom. What do I do, warn the ladies? Pour a drink over his head and cause a scene? Not with my mom there. I told you she thinks she's Ann Miller? While I'm watching Randy, Mom's telling me how much fun she had making *On the Town* with Gene and Frank, but that cute Vera-Ellen was a pain in the ass the whole time."

Terry said, "I'd like to meet her."

"She's still there. What I ended up doing, I took Mom over to the table and said, 'Mother, this is Randy, the bullshit artist who stole all my money.' My mother says to him, 'How do you do, Andy, I'm pleased to meet you.' She thought he was Andy Garcia. I got her out, raced across the bridge to the nursing home—it's right on Flagler— dropped her off, and raced back to Chuck and Harold's. I was sure he'd still be there because he'd have to clear himself, make up a long, involved story. Did you see *My Dinner with André*, the snob who bores the shit out of Wallace Shawn for an hour and a half? That's Randy."

"He was still there."

"I checked to make sure, peeked in. Then schmoozed the valet parking guy to let me sit there and wait, double-parked. Randy comes out, finally, with the two ladies and stands there talking to them while they wait for their car. Randy, I was sure, parked on the street, he never spends his own money if he can help it. He gets the ladies into their car, still bullshitting them. They drive off and he walks along the streetside of the cars parked along the curb. I creep up next to him, my windows down, and go, 'Hey, asshole,' to get his attention. I told him I'd hound him, I'd keep showing up and make his phony life miserable until he paid back every cent he stole from me. But without any idea how I'd do it. He came around to my side of the car, the Ford

Escort, and tells me with his face in the open window, 'Don't fuck with me, kid. You're not in my league.' "

"That did it," Terry said, "calling you kid, huh?"

"That and his tone of voice, Mr. Fucking Superior. I see him walking away, across the street to where he's angle-parked against the median, Royal Poinciana Way, lined with palm trees. I had to go after him. I floored it. I saw his face as he looked back and saw me coming and I plowed into him, bounced him off a couple of cars and drove off."

"You left the scene?"

"That was my mistake, a premeditated hit-and-run, witnessed by everybody standing in front of the restaurant."

Terry was sympathetic. "That's a shame, have all those people watching. You hurt him much?"

"He had to have a hip replaced."

"I hear that's a common procedure now."

"He fractured his other leg, punctured a lung. There were lacerations, I think thirty-five stitches in his scalp. The state's attorney wanted to bring me up on attempted murder. I had a court-appointed lawyer who did what he could. He tried for man two, where I'd get maybe a year; we settled for aggravated assault, three to five."

"You poor thing," Terry said, slipping his arm around her shoulders. "Being locked up with all those offenders. It must've been awful."

She looked up at him with sad eyes, holding the yobie away from them, and he kissed her for the first time, a tender kiss, Terry seeing what it was like, then putting a little more into it to see where it would take him, then glad to feel Debbie getting into it with him. When they came apart he took the yobie from her and put it in the ashtray on the coffee table. But then when he turned to her again there was a different look in her eyes. Not quite sure about this.

He said, "I'm not HIV, honest."

"You swear?"

He raised his right hand. "Scout's honor."

"You don't have any, like, weird African diseases you might've caught?"

"Not even malaria."

She kept staring at him and pretty soon the look in her eyes softened. She smiled and he believed he was home.

He was.

They went in the bedroom and kept on kissing and now touching each other as they took off their clothes, Terry holding her from behind as she pulled down the bedspread. They left the lamp off but could see each other in the light from the hall, where the bathroom was. She said, "It's been so long for me." And said, "I know, it's like riding a bike."

Only a lot better. But Terry didn't tell her that. He wasn't a talker in bed.

After, when they were lying there in each other's arms, Terry said, "We were trying to remember what those crucified guys were singing?"

"*The Life of Brian,*" Debbie said, "yeah, what was it?"

" 'Always Look on the Bright Side of Life.' "

She said, "Right, and then all the crucified guys would whistle the refrain. Yeah, I can hear it." She was quiet, maybe thinking up something funny to say. Terry waited, then turned his head to see her looking down at herself, chin pressed against her chest. She said, "It's hard to tell when you're lying down, but you can see they're just starting to sag a little."

"They look okay to me."

"When you see them sitting straight up and the person's lying down? You know they're fake."

"Is that right?"

"You put on an act sometimes, don't you?"

"Like what?"

"Like you're this simple soul."

"I am."

She said, "Uh-huh. Are you hungry?"

"I thought we might twist one and go for seconds."

She said, "Oh my. Really?"

So they didn't get to Randy and how well he was fixed until the next intermission and were resting again, Debbie telling about her visit with Randy's ex, Mary Lou Martz. "See, she didn't change her name when she married Randy. She's always been Mrs. William Martz in Detroit society, a patron of anything that has to do with the arts—the symphony, the opera company, the art institute. She's active, and very popular, known to her friends as Lulu."

"You call her that?"

"I didn't call her anything. On the phone I told her about my experience with Randy and she invited me to her home in Grosse Pointe Park, a beauty, like a French château on Lake St. Clair. I was surprised she was so willing to talk about him. She was Miss Michigan first runner-up about thirty years ago, looks good, keeps in shape, has had a couple of lifts—"

"She told you that?"

"You could tell. I asked if Randy wanted her to sail around the world with him. She said it was almost the first thing out of his mouth. At some black-tie affair."

"The guy works hard, doesn't he?"

"Yeah, but you know what she said to him? 'Your yacht or mine?' Cool? She had her guard up and still fell for him. He told her he was writing a book on the conflict in the Middle East, having covered it during the past ten years for the *Herald Tribune*, living in Paris most of the time. Though he kept his boat in Haifa, Israel. Four months from the time they met, Randy supposedly hopping back and forth to the Middle East, they were married."

"How'd she get on to him?"

"Little things. He lived in Paris for years but didn't speak any French. He told her it wasn't necessary, everyone there spoke English. Lulu had been to Paris enough times to know that was bullshit. She wanted to hop over to Israel with him, take his boat out and cruise the Greek islands. Randy goes yeah, let's do it. Then he's gone for a week. The next time she sees him he tells her the PLO blew up his boat. They hate him and he's on their hit list. Tell a big enough lie you can get away with it for a while. But now he's running up charges, buys a new Jaguar . . . Lulu wants to know what happened to his money. He had told her he was given a two-hundred-thousand-dollar advance by a publisher, but it ran out as he worked on his book. Lulu said, 'What book? I don't see you writing any fucking book.' "

"That's what she said?"

"Words to that effect. He told her he'd had writer's block for the past year but believed he was about to break through and get going again. Lulu put a detective on him and that was that. But, it didn't happen soon enough. Because the marriage lasted more than a year, the prenuptial agreement kicked in and Randy walked away with his settlement, a few mil and the restaurant."

"Have you seen it?"

"Not inside. I don't want him to know I'm around just yet. Lulu won't go near it. She said if she knew how to make a bomb she'd blow the place up. With Randy in it."

"She wanted to get laid," Terry said, "and it cost her."

"She wanted to meet a nice guy, that's all, and have some fun."

"What was her husband's company?"

"Timco Industries. Automotive suppliers, they make fittings."

"Yeah?"

"You don't know what I'm talking about, do you?"

"Nuts and bolts."

"Connectors," Debbie said. "What they use when they're putting together subassemblies on a conveyor line. Like, you know, engines, transmissions, fuel tanks, they have to be connected on a line that's turning out a car every minute. You can't use a wrench, it would slow up the line. So Lulu's husband, Bill, invented a way to snap the parts together with a plastic fitting . . . and an O-ring for a seal. I remember it in case I want to use it sometime."

"That made him rich, a plastic fitting?"

"With the O-ring. Terry, ten million cars a year come off the line with her husband's patent holding them together. He sold the company so he could retire and play golf."

"And he died right after?"

"On the twelfth at Oakland Hills, a long five par."

"The company's Timco?"

"Automotive suppliers," Debbie said, "have names like that, Timco, Ranco, you never know what they do. I've done stand-up at dinners put on by suppliers you've never heard of and all those guys are millionaires."

Terry said, "Makes you want to go to work for a living, huh?"

They got up to grill hot dogs and an hour later were back in bed, all the lights off in the apartment.

Terry said in the dark, "What're you gonna do, slip and fall in Randy's restaurant?"

"I'm not," Debbie said, "you are. Fr. Terry Dunn, missionary hero from Rwanda, the sole support of hundreds of starving children."

13

THEY DIDN'T TALK ABOUT IT last night, in bed. He did say, "I walk in the restaurant and slip and fall. On what?" All Debbie said was, "We'll work it out." This morning sipping her instant coffee he said, "How do we work it out?" And she said, "What?"

Well, here she was now, looking up at the high-domed foyer, Terry watching her from the top of the curving staircase: Debbie in a dark skirt and turtleneck beneath the open raincoat, Debbie clickety-clicking across the marble floor, doing a tap routine in her heels.

"You know what I wanted to be more than anything? A chorus girl."

"Why didn't you?"

"I found out it was work. You know, to be any good and get in a show. I was a go-go dancer once, but only for a few weeks, when I was at U of M."

"I'd like to have seen that."

"You did. I didn't have enough tit to be a star. And really, to do it for a living you have to be on crack."

"Come on up."

She said, "Wait," and clickety-clicked over to take a look at the living room. Coming up the carpeted staircase she said, "It's o-*kay*, what I call four-star hotel decor, Mary Pat not taking any chances."

"Nothing from Taiwan," Terry said, "or India."

"Now you're making fun of my decor, Pier One kitsch and St. Vincent de Paul hand-me-downs." She reached the top and kissed Terry on the mouth. "What's your plan, throw me on a bed?"

"I thought you wanted to see the house."

"I do, and I won't make any more cheap remarks."

They came to the master bedroom, gold draperies, a tufted gold spread covering the king-size bed. Debbie looked in. "So this is where Fran and Mary Pat do it."

"We know they have at least twice," Terry said, and in the same moment wished he hadn't, sounding like a smart-ass for no reason. He brought Debbie along to the little girls' rooms.

She looked in at each one and said, "Cute."

Nothing about the dolls and stuffed animals.

"Remind you of when you were little?"

"I was more into dancing and playing doctor."

He said after a moment, "It's a nice place though, isn't it?" thinking of his brother who loved his home and was proud of it.

She said, "The house? Yeah, it's very nice. What else is up here?"

"The guest room, where I'm staying."

He showed her and she looked in at the twin beds with white spreads, a comfortable chair, Terry's duffel and athletic bag on the desk, no clothes lying about.

"You keep your room neat. There's a good boy."

"I don't have enough stuff to mess it up."

Now she said, "Terry, what is that?"

His machete, lying on the desk close to the duffel.

"For cracking open coconuts."

She went into the room and picked it up to heft it and put it down, not saying one word, and walked to a window.

"I've got the Rwanda pictures here," Terry said. He picked up the athletic bag and turned to the beds, but then walked up behind Debbie at the window. They looked out at a swimming pool covered in dark-green plastic, the rest of the yard, the leafless trees and shrubs stark, the dead look of winter holding on. He said, "Fran hangs a swing from that maple tree in the summer."

He turned and walked over to stand between the twin beds with the athletic bag, Debbie, still at the window, saying, "I should do a bit on winter in Detroit. Shit, if this is spring, I could do a whole set." Terry was taking the color photos from the bag now as she said, "I wish Randy lived in Florida. I think I'll move there after we score. You want to?"

Terry didn't answer, busy laying out photos on the spread; he wasn't sure what she meant. Did he want to move to Florida after? With her, or what? Now she was next to him between the beds, looking down at the photos. She asked how many he had and he said about two hundred. "These are the best ones."

"Are they all boys?"

"No, but that age, it's hard to tell them apart. Some of these kids are in orphanages, but they're not much better off than the ones that live in the street. They form families, an older girl maybe fifteen taking care of the little ones. They're on their own, they have to scrounge for food, clothes to wear . . . This kid's digging in a charcoal pit. He'll collect bits and pieces that haven't burned and sell them."

Terry handed Debbie a photo.

"Kids at a garbage dump looking for something to eat."

She said, "Jesus, Terry," and sat down on the bed behind her with the picture. She said, "But in some of the shots the land looks so green and lush, crops growing everywhere—"

"They're children," Terry said, "they're not farmers, with land. They're little Tutsis nobody wants. Here, a couple of ten-year-olds smoking cigarettes. They roll their own. This boy, he's thirteen now, killed a friend of his during the genocide. With a machete. They were eight years old at the time." Terry was saying, "What do you do with this boy?" and looked up.

So did Debbie. She said, "Did you hear that? Someone calling you?"

He was moving now, reaching for the machete on his way out of the room, Debbie behind him, Terry saying, "You left the door open."

"It was open when I got here."

In the hall they heard the voice again, calling out, "Terry, you fuck, where're you at?"

And he knew who it was.

At the staircase railing that curved around to the hall, they looked down at the foyer to see Johnny Pajonny looking up at them.

Terry said, "My man Johnny."

Johnny said, "Where's my fuckin money?"

It surprised her when he stopped to pick up the machete from the desk. Debbie, behind him, had put her hand out, almost bumping into him. She wondered if it was a reaction left over from Africa: you hear something, grab a machete.

Now she watched Terry going down the stairs with it, the blade about a foot and a half long, the carved handle a natural color of wood, Terry holding it pointed down, along his leg. Johnny saw it. She heard him say, "The fuck is that, a sword?" She heard Terry, on the stairs, say, "A machete," and as he reached the marble floor, "one I found in the church after they hacked to death seventy people, while I was on the altar saying Mass. There was still blood on it." Johnny said, "Jesus Christ." She watched Terry raise the machete, hold it by the blade and offer Johnny the carved wood handle. Taking it Johnny said, "Jesus Christ, they kill people with this?" "Chop their heads off," Terry said, "and their feet." Debbie started down the staircase, her hand sliding along the gold leaf railing. She saw Johnny look up, but only glance at her as he hefted the machete saying, "It's heavier'n it looks." He made a short hacking motion with it. "They actually killed people with this, uh?" And Terry said, "Right in front of me." Debbie paused a few steps from the floor, then remained there to watch.

It was a show. Johnny comes in yelling for his money and Terry meets him with a machete and tells about death in Africa.

Two buddies from cigarette-smuggling days. Terry in Levi's and a blousy white starched dress shirt that had to be Fran's. Johnny in a long black-leather jacket, collar turned up behind his thin dark hair slicked into a half-assed ponytail. He wasn't bad-looking. He was shorter than Terry, five eight or nine, one of those skinny tough guys with a slight stoop to his bony shoulders. He said, "You're a priest, huh? I don't fuckin believe it."

Which could mean, the way Debbie heard it, he did believe it. She watched Terry make the sign of the cross over Johnny, saying, "*In nomine Patris, et Filii, et Spiritus Sancti . . .*"

Johnny waved the machete at him, saying, "Get outta here, for Christ sake. I want to know what you did with my money, ten grand, and Dickie's."

"Dickie gave his to an orphanage."

It stopped Johnny and he got with it saying, "Oh, is that right? And who'd I give mine to?"

"Some lepers."

"Oh, some lepers."

"They bought booze with it," Terry said, "to relieve their suffering. I told them it was okay, you wouldn't mind. But then when the money started to run low they switched to banana beer."

Johnny said, "Banana beer."

Terry said, "You know when you change your oil and you see it drain out of the crankcase? That's what banana beer looks like."

"You try it?"

"I was never tempted."

"But the lepers drank it, huh?"

"They couldn't get enough. It took their mind off of being lepers."

Johnny said, "Terr, fuck the lepers. You spent my money, didn't you?"

Debbie watched Terry shrug, a helpless gesture, and hold up his empty hands.

"I was over there five years, Johnny. What do you think I lived on?"

"What do other missionaries live on?"

"Contributions. Don't you remember at Queen of Peace giving to the missions? You gave to the St. Martin de Porres Mission in Rwanda. You can deduct it on your income tax."

"You think I pay income tax?"

"If you ever do. You put down 'ten grand to the lepers.' Johnny, you kept me alive during those five long years. I was able to buy sweet potatoes, meat once in a while. Mostly goat, but that's all I could afford. If you can look at it as your gift to the mission, Johnny, then I can forgive you for what you did."

Debbie loved it. What a cool move, turning it around on Johnny, no match, Johnny frowning now.

"Forgive me, for what?"

"Dragging me into it, saying the whole thing was my idea."

"Man, you were gone. Me and Dickie're in the Wayne County jail, for Christ sake. That place is so bad you can't fuckin wait to get sent to prison. I'm telling you, man, almost six months they're trying to decide should it go state or federal."

"Yeah, but Johnny, I'm not off the hook. I gotta go down this afternoon and see the prosecutor about my indictment, Gerald Padilla."

"That's the same fuckin guy put us away."

"And now he's got a chance, because of what you told him, to put me away."

"But you're a priest, for Christ sake."

"Doesn't matter," Terry said. "I'm gonna have to tell Mr. Padilla you lied, all I did was drive the truck."

"Go ahead."

"Is that okay with you?"

"Tell him anything you want, I'm out, man."

Terry said, "Was it pretty bad?"

"What, Jackson? Live with five thousand morons screaming and fuckin with each other? Watch your back every minute you're outta your cell? You fuck—was it pretty bad. I ran a sports book in Four East, hired two of the biggest boon coons in the block keep me from getting robbed. I still got shanked, in the gut. Sewed it up myself."

"How's Dickie making it?"

"He practically lives in Five, the Hole, in and out on account of his attitude. Dickie keeps selling his radio to fish, new guys. Takes fifty bucks off 'em but never gives 'em the radio. I told him, 'You're gonna sell it to the wrong guy one of these days.' He says, 'Fuck it.'"

"Is he ever coming out?"

"That's a good question."

"How's Regina?"

"You know she's born again. She's got a bumper sticker now on the car says MY BOSS IS A JEWISH CARPENTER. You two oughta get together, sing some hymns."

"What about Mercy?"

"She's a senior at Wayne State, wants to get into computer programming."

"You never know," Terry said, "do you?"

Johnny said, "You never know what?"

On the way downtown, Debbie driving, she said, "Last night when we were talking about Johnny, I said I wouldn't want to owe him ten grand, and you said don't worry about it. I guess you knew you could handle him."

"Get him confused enough," Terry said, "he'll believe whatever you tell him."

"Like your being a priest."

"You could see he didn't want to believe it, but he does."

"Will you ever tell him you're not?"

"I don't know. Maybe someday," Terry said. "In the meantime let's keep Johnny in mind. We might be able to use him."

They had lunch at the Hellas Café in Greektown: calamari in olive oil, lamb shanks that Terry said tasted a lot like goat, and rice pudding Debbie swore was the best in town. The diners in the café wearing I.D. tags were jurors from Frank Murphy courtrooms, like tourists here for the first time, looking up wide-eyed when they heard *"Opa!"* and would watch a waiter present the flaming cheese dish to a table. They walked the two blocks from the Hellas past the back end of 1300 Beaubien, Detroit police headquarters, and past one of the newer county jail buildings to the Frank Murphy Hall of Justice, all criminal courtrooms and the offices of the Wayne County prosecutor.

Terry went in to ask about Gerald Padilla. He came out and said to Debbie, "He's either out to lunch or in a courtroom on four; he's got a trial going."

They took the stairs to the fourth floor and passed groups of people waiting along the corridor.

"It sounds like he's working me in during his lunch hour," Terry said, "so it shouldn't take too long. Get me out of the way and back to sending some poor asshole to the joint."

"Are you nervous?"

"Why? Fran says the guy's an usher at Queen of Martyrs."

"You're too much. Is it okay if I go in with you?"

"I don't see why not."

"Good," Debbie said, "I like to watch you."

It was another show.

Terry, with the black parka, his gaunt face, his beard, takes on the suit, a navy blue one, the prosecutor pushing his glasses up on his nose, a neat-looking gent who turns this way as Terry announces:

"Mr. Padilla? I'm Fr. Dunn, from Rwanda. Sir, I understand you want to see me."

From Rwanda. Like he'd come all the way from Africa for this, Terry's voice subdued but level, a touch of humility in his tone, completely at this guy's service.

Debbie hung back.

She watched the prosecutor drop papers on the table where he stood and come out through the gate in the railing to the rows of benches that were like church pews, Gerald Padilla saying, "Father, I'm so glad you were able to make it. I won't take up much of your time." He gestured. "Let's sit down, anywhere here, and get this business out of the way."

Terry moved into the second row from the railing, then half turned and extended his arm. "Sir, this is Miss Dewey, an associate of my brother Francis, here to represent me."

Making her a lawyer on the spot.

Padilla nodded as he took a long look, smiling in a nice way. He said, "Gerry Padilla, Miss Dewey, it's a pleasure. You're welcome to sit in, though I don't see that Fr. Dunn needs legal representation."

Debbie smiled. She said, "That's good to hear, but I'm really only his chauffeur. Fr. Dunn's been so busy working on mission appeals he hasn't had time to renew his driver's license."

Terry said, "Believe me, Gerry, I'm in good hands with this young lady."

Getting on a first-name basis right away.

But then he said, "I wish I could take her back to Rwanda with me."

Debbie said, "Father, please," sounding mildly shocked, but with a smile to show he was kidding and she was going along with it.

Padilla said, "I don't blame you, Father."

And she had to smile again, this time as Padilla winked at her—the rogue.

She sat in the same row but left space to show she didn't intend to become involved. Terry sat turned away somewhat, his back to her, while Padilla could look right at her over Terry's shoulder. Debbie kept her gaze on the judge's bench now, straight ahead, giving the prosecutor a good shot of her profile, her cute nose, the pert way she tilted her head as she gazed about, lips slightly parted. She could hear them okay.

From the start talking about Rwanda.

Padilla saying he had read an account of the genocide, a fascinating book with the chilling title *We wish to inform you that tomorrow we will be killed with our families*. Asking Terry if he'd read it. Terry saying no, Gerry, being there was enough, seeing dozens of his parishioners hacked to death as he watched from the altar. Padilla taking this in and then wanting to know why the victims accepted death in such a fatalistic manner. Terry saying they were a very serious people, Gerry, who bowed to authority and would always abide by the fact of whatever was happening to them. Terry saying nonetheless he knew in his heart they were martyrs, welcomed by Our Lord that very day into Heaven.

Nonetheless?

Padilla would raise his head to steal a glance this way and Debbie would show him a solemn look, almost but not quite sorrowful. Now the prosecutor was asking about the Rwandan legal system's ability to deal with the more than one hundred thousand alleged perpetrators being held in prisons, saying he'd read about a system of tribunals on the village level they might try in order to speed up the process, the prosecutor saying he believed it was called Gacaca. Terry saying yes, it was being considered, "But if you don't mind my correcting you, Gerry, it's not pronounced *ka-ka* in their language, Kinyarwanda, but *cha-cha*, like the dance. So it's Gachacha." Gerry Padilla was smiling, shaking his head . . .

As Debbie, smiling back at him, was saying to herself, I've got to get out of here.

She took the elevator down to the main floor and stepped outside the front entrance to have a cigarette. It was cold out here, bleak, a few other smokers waiting to go in. Jurors coming along St. Antoine, back from lunch, got Debbie thinking about a jury bit. She heard her voice playing it to herself:

"I served on a jury once. It was a murder trial, like *Twelve Angry Men* only this one was eleven pissed-off guys and me. They all wanted to convict and I was the holdout. They'd say, 'The guy was caught with the fucking gun in his hand. Why can't you see that?' And I'd go, 'But he couldn't have done it.' Beat. 'He's so cute.' "

Work on it. You can't vote to convict. You can't even kill a fly. Why not? Because you are a fly. A fly on the wall. Buzzing around, buzz buzz—it's what you see out of your huge fly eyes. "I've been walking around on dog shit out in the yard. Hmmmm, why don't I take a stroll on that lovely lemon meringue pie? My purpose in life is to be annoying, fuck with people and get them waving at me and cursing. Oh, there's a couple getting it on. Why don't I land on—"

Her phone rang.

"—that big white butt."

Her cell phone, a faint sound coming from her handbag. Debbie got it out and for the next few minutes listened to a lawyer, a good friend of hers, answer a question she had left with his assistant two days ago. As she listened she said, "Yeah?" a number of times. She said, "Oh?" thinking oh no. She listened and said, "Oh," a few more times. Listened again and said, "No, I'm outside, on Frank Murphy's front steps," and looked up at the building against a dead-pale sky. "I'm with a friend, a smuggler." Had to explain that, then listened for more than a minute and said, "Get out of here. Really? You think he could be called up?" She said, "Ed, I appreciate this more than I can tell you. And I'll think about what you said, I promise." She said, "Anytime. Give me a call."

Not more than a few minutes later Terry was coming out of the building, a happy Saint Francis in his beard and parka, grinning at her.

"I'm off the hook."

"Did you ever get around to the indictment?"

Terry hugged her. "We ran out of time. He told me not to worry about it—I must have enough on my mind with the business of saving souls."

"Saving your ass," Debbie said. "What did you do, call him 'my son' a few times?" Debbie talking, filling in, still in her mind with Ed Bernacki, a lawyer who gave her confidential information with confidence, but seemed hesitant this time. She was anxious to tell Terry what she'd learned and would watch him to get his reaction. But it wasn't something to talk about here.

Terry was saying his very dear friend Gerry Padilla had turned out to be a good guy. "He even gave me a hundred bucks for the orphans. A check."

"Made out to you?"

"No, I had him make it out to the Little Orphans of Rwanda Fund. I've already opened an account; Fran took me."

She said, "That's where you want to put the check?"

"Yeah, and get a drink."

She saw him looking down St. Antoine now, toward Greektown, and said, "There's nothing much around here. Why don't we go back to your brother's house? We can get comfortable—if you catch my drift."

It put a smile in his beard. "Anything you say."

Which was just what she wanted to hear.

14

IT WAS FRAN'S LIBRARY THAT reminded her of the home where she grew up: the distressed paneling and the sets of leather-bound books no one had ever read. She told Terry and it led to a short version of her life:

Really, a lot like the home she left to go to Ann Arbor and only came back for holidays and the summer her mom and dad divorced and that was the end of pre-law and the idea of following her dad into what was possibly the world's most boring fucking profession. She never really wanted to be a lawyer. Switched to psychology, hated it and switched to English Lit, since she'd be reading anyway, she might as well get credit for it. Dug Restoration comedy, nutty stuff like *Love in a Tub*, and thought she might want to act. No, dance. In a chorus line. Do funky Bob Fosse numbers in a derby. No, do stand-up comedy because her friends thought she was funny and Goldie Hawn became her idol till she trimmed her goal to a comedy tap routine, telling jokes while clickety-clicking. Shit, but that was vaudeville. Strip and tell jokes. That was burlesque. There was good money in go-go dancing, dirty guys stuffing your G-string with dollar bills, but it was too scary, crack a major threat. So after her dad's funeral, where she met the legal assistant who'd become his second wife and liked her and agreed to stay in touch, and her mom moved to a condo in Florida, pre-Alzheimer's, she never went back to go-going, saved the tap shoes she finally gave her mom, took the advice of her dad's second wife and went to work in the murky fringes of law doing investigations, stand-up on the side, "Minding my own fucking business when that snake slithered into my life, cost me three years and all my money."

Terry said, "You've done a lot without really doing anything, haven't you?"

"All I want now," Debbie said, "is a normal life."

He went out to the kitchen, came back to the library with a bottle of beer, a double Scotch neat and her vodka on a silver tray. They sat down in the sofa to talk, Debbie saying, "There's something I better tell you."

"You're married," Terry said.

"No, I'm not married."

"Well, since you're telling me everything there is to know about you, were you ever?"

"I came close, but realized in time the guy was a control freak. He'd try to tell me how to dress, how to fix my hair, how much makeup to use. He'd buy me tailored outfits, a polo coat with the little belt in back? I looked like I was from Grosse Pointe. He was a doctor, so my mom loved him. The whole time I went with Michael I think he laughed maybe twice and we saw one movie."

"What was it?"

"Rain Man." Debbie said, "You're acting frisky 'cause you're off
the hook. If you'll shut up for a minute and drink your drink—" This
time he didn't interrupt and she said, "I've been in touch with a friend
of mine, a lawyer I've done investigations for, Ed Bernacki. I asked if
he knew anything about Randy."

"Why would he?"

"Ed's big time, he knows what's happening downtown and likes to
gossip, as long as it isn't about his clients. His law firm represents the
two top guys in the Detroit Mafia. Or I should say the alleged Detroit
Mafia. When Ed Bernacki uses the term he always qualifies it with, 'If
in fact such an organization exists.' He got back to me while I was
waiting for you, outside the Frank Murphy."

"Why didn't you mention it then?"

"I didn't want to talk about it on the street or in some bar or while
I'm driving. It's something we have to discuss. Then you decide if
you still want to help me."

Terry said, "Randy's in the Mafia? If such an organization in anyone's wildest imagination exists?"

"You got by in Africa," Debbie said, "on Scotch and that smarty-
innocent attitude, didn't you? Like nothing really bothers you." She
said, "No, Randy's not in the Mafia. But he has a silent partner, a guy
who does exist and you'd better believe it, who is. Right at the top.
Randy only acts like he's in the mob. It's his new thing. He even has
a gangster for a bodyguard, a guy Ed says is called Mutt, or the Mutt.
And do you know where Randy got his bodyguard? From Vincent
Moraco."

Terry said, "Oh."

"Oh is right. When you were in the cigarette business didn't you
see a Mrs. Moraco to get paid?"

"Yeah, but I never believed she was Vincent Moraco's wife. He's
an older guy and she was pretty young."

"You knew Vincent?"

"I'd hear about him from Johnny, he had the connection."

"Well, listen to this," Debbie said. "I tried to get Bernacki to represent me on the assault thing? He would've got me off with time served, three months in the lovely Palm Beach County Stockade 'cause I couldn't raise the bond. But Ed was busy with racketeering indictments. That was three years ago and they've finally come to trial, here in federal court—the Tony Twins, Anthony Amilia and the underboss Anthony Verona. They could get like twenty-five to life if convicted."

"Those guys've been around forever."

"Both in their seventies," Debbie said. "There're six defendants on trial, the Tonys and some other guys I've never heard of. But Verona has a heart condition and may not stand trial."

Terry said, "I'm beginning to see where you're going with this."

"I thought you might," Debbie said. "It turns out cigarette tax fraud is on the RICO indictment, going back five years." She took a sip of vodka, giving herself a few beats before springing the punch line. "So then I wondered if they might call you as a witness."

He said, "Testify against the mob in federal court."

Looking at her with that quiet gaze.

She wanted to kiss him. "You're a cool guy, Terr, even if you did see it coming."

He said, *"Witness for the Prosecution.* That wasn't a bad movie, Charles Laughton, Marlene Dietrich . . . But this sounds a little different. You told Bernacki I was in the cigarette business?"

"He asked what I was doing at the Frank Murphy. I told him and that's when he told me cigarette tax fraud was on the indictment, going back to when you were involved."

"He said I could be called?"

"Well, actually," Debbie said, "I brought it up. I asked Ed if it was a possibility, and he said if you haven't been subpoenaed by now the chances are you won't be. Ed says the U.S. Attorney refuses to give him their witness list, afraid Ed's clients might get to them. If you want, he'll find out if you're on the list."

"You gave him my name?"

"No, I wanted to tell you about it first."

"See if I'd panic?"

"I know you better than that."

"But you're not sure. What do you think I'd do if I was subpoenaed? Leave town?"

"I don't know, would you?"

He kept looking at her in his quiet way, but didn't say anything and she didn't have a clue as to what he was thinking. She said, "I mentioned it so you'd know, that's all, in case you are called. But the chances are you won't be, so why don't we forget it, okay? What we have to talk about is Randy's situation. If he's in tight with gangsters—and Ed says he's starting to act like one—you might want to forget the whole thing. I wouldn't blame you if you did."

"You tell Bernacki what you're up to?"

"Only that I want to get my money back."

"What'd he say?"

"Forget about it. Write it off to experience."

"Well?"

"You know I'm not gonna back off," Debbie said, "whether you're with me or not." She watched Terry finish his drink and wipe the back of his hand across his mouth.

He said, "I decide to walk away, you'll slip and fall all by yourself?"

"I'm not sure what I'll do."

"Have dinner there and get food poisoning?"

"That's not bad."

"Throw up on the table?"

They were playing again, back in business.

"Or, once a day walk in the door and throw up," Debbie said, "till people stop coming and his business falls off. His restaurant business."

"Or," Terry said, "you try the direct approach, ask Randy to pay what he owes you."

Debbie said, "Now why didn't I think of that?"

"How much you make a year?"

"Why?"

"Come on, tell me."

"Never less than fifty thousand."

"That's not bad, but let's make it sixty-one thousand. Times three, that's a hundred and eighty-three grand you didn't make while you were locked up. Add that to the sixty-seven he ripped off, he owes you two hundred and fifty thousand. Can you slip and fall and win an award like that?"

"You figured that out in your head?"

"Stay with me. Can you win that much in court?"

"Not unless you break your back and you'll never walk again. You could even get a lot more."

"But two-fifty, does that sound about right, being realistic, something he can handle without too much trouble? We split it, you still get back almost twice what he scored off you."

"But when we take this direct approach," Debbie said, "and get thrown out on the street—"

"Okay, let's say I do slip and fall in his restaurant, injure my back. We can begin by threatening him with a lawsuit. He says no to the two-fifty, we show him how he can write the entire amount off on his income tax."

"Wait a minute—how?"

"By making the check out to the Little Orphans of Rwanda Fund, a charitable write-off."

She watched him take a sip of beer, from the bottle. "You've been working this out, haven't you?"

"It's what priests do mainly, figure out how to raise money. Buy a new organ, repair the roof of the church—"

"He still won't pay."

"Maybe—"

"I know he won't."

"Let's talk to him and see what happens."

"He'll sic the Mutt on us, that thug he's got working for him."

Terry said, "Now we're getting to what I know something about."

It scared her a little, the way he said it.

Later on Terry left in Fran's car to pick up his suit. Debbie offered to take him, but he said he wanted to try the Lexus. He'd already tooled around in Mary Pat's Cadillac and thought they'd take it downtown tomorrow night to see Randy. Terry said he liked to drive. Not having a license or knowing exactly where he was going didn't seem to bother him. He said don't worry, he'd find it, a giant mall on both sides of Big Beaver, right? Debbie told him it was called Somerset Collection, very upscale, Tiffany, Saks, Neiman Marcus, no Sears or JC Penney . . . He said right, and drove off. Confident.

No longer coming off as a simple soul. Confident in a very low-key way, not trying to be cool and yet he was.

Debbie went in the kitchen and took one of Mary Pat's casseroles out of the freezer, in a hard-as-a-rock plastic bag, CHICKEN DELIGHT neatly handprinted on the bag in green Magic Marker. Yeah, well, we'll see. Debbie turned to place the casserole on the counter and saw the machete lying there. This morning they'd brought Johnny out to

the kitchen for a cup of coffee, Johnny still holding the machete, playing around with it, swiping it in the air. Terry told him he was going
to cut himself and he laid it down. They stood sipping coffee and
talking, Terry telling about the piles of machetes you'd see, hundreds
that were confiscated: in the kitchen talking about the genocide the
same way she and Terry had stood talking about it in her kitchen, last
night. Terry telling about the guys, the Hutu thugs, in the beer lady's
house . . . No, get it right, in the words she told him she'd never
forget.

They were sitting at a table in the beer lady's house drinking banana beer and I shot them with my housekeeper's pistol.

Sitting there. He said not giving them a chance to make a move.
Just walked in and shot them? He said no, they exchanged a few
words.

But I knew going in I was gonna kill them.

Telling her that in the same quiet way he had told her a little while
ago:

Now we're getting to what I know something about.

She thought about it making herself a drink while hot water from
the faucet ran on the plastic-covered casserole in the sink.

It scared her, even though there was no reason to think he'd want
to do it again. Or that he liked doing it. Or the time would come when
he'd have to do it. What bothered her was the fact he had lived for
years among people who had killed their neighbors because they were
told to and the victims had accepted being killed. He had said to her,
"How do you understand that . . ." Like saying it had nothing to do
with reason. Why had he brought the machete home? He said as a
memento. She told herself not to assume anything. She wasn't even
that sure what he meant by "getting to what I know something

about." It could mean talking his way out of a tight spot, the way he handled Johnny Pajonny, turning the situation around on him. Randy tries to get tough, Terry talks him out of doing anything drastic.

Except Randy wasn't like Johnny.

And Terry . . .

She heard the garage door open, raising automatically on its tracks, then heard it closing as the door to the kitchen opened and Terry came in pulling his new black suit out of the Brooks Brothers hanging bag, held it up for her to see, proud of it—she could tell—and asked how she liked it.

. . . Terry wasn't like anyone she'd ever met in her life.

"You have to admit, Mary Pat knows how to cook."

"Casseroles," Debbie said, "are easy. Throw a lot of stuff together and shove it in the oven."

"How was the food inside?"

"For lunch, macaroni and cheese, cole slaw, rice pudding and three slices of plain bread. Everything looked alike." She said, "You didn't eat insects, anything like that, did you?"

"You only ate the ones flew in your mouth," Terry said. "Listen, I'm gonna call Johnny, see if he wants to go with us tomorrow."

Debbie said, "Why?" because there was no obvious reason to have him along.

All Terry said was, "I think he'd enjoy it."

15

RANDY BECAME A GANGSTER ABOUT two months after
opening the restaurant, still into a Pierce Brosnan phase, custom-
tailored dark suits and a hint of Brit nonchalance in his speech. His
response to problems, a minor fire in the kitchen: "Oh really? Why
don't you see Carlo about that?" Carlo his manager–maître d' with
thirty years in the business and a small percentage of the restaurant
profit as incentive. Randy loved being Randy's, always ready with car
talk visiting tables, business trends he got out of *Automotive News*,
motoring fun and gear ratios from *Automobile*. That part, for a world-
class schemer, was easy. Being on his feet most of the day was the
killer, but worth it. Randy's had opened big and was the place to be.

Hour Detroit magazine said: "Filling the gap left by the old London
Chop House—still mourned by those who feel fine dining should allow fine diners to be seen to their best advantage—Randy's is clubby,
polished and features a floor plan that encourages seating elitism.

Booth No. One is back downtown and, not incidentally, in a place un-
rivaled for fabulous food, pricey booze and a wine list that's the Yellow Pages."

Randy had the review framed on the wall near the entrance. The
rest of the walls were gathering caricatures of Detroit celebrities,
most of them famous names who'd died or left town: Joe Louis,
Gordie Howe, Lily Tomlin, Tom Selleck, Henry Ford II, Jeff
Daniels, Iggy Pop . . . Carlo was responsible for refinements. The ci-
gar room with its own bar. The personal lockers with nameplates for
cognac and expensive whiskeys purchased by the bottle. Godiva
mints in the dish by the entrance. Ice in the men's room urinals, newspaper pages from the business and sports sections taped to the wall
above each one. "So they can read while they piss," Carlo said.
"These are busy men dine here."

Randy said, "But not in the women's?"

"Women don't read on the toilet," Carlo said. "They have hairspray on the sink and a colored woman helps them pin things that
come undone."

Randy's change from sophisticated Brit to cool gangster began to
take place on a Monday night about ten. (They were closed Sundays.)
Randy was talking to his little maître d' at the end of the bar near the
entrance. Carlo glanced up and seemed momentarily startled, then
looked aside as he said to Randy, "Be careful of this guy. Be nice to
him." Now Carlo raised his brow in pleasant expectation and stepped
past Randy saying, "Mr. Moraco, is so good of you to come in. I believe only your first time, no? Shame on you."

There were two of them. To Randy, a couple of guys off the
street. But if he had to be careful—Carlo's warnings always to
be trusted—let's see what we have here. A couple of mob guys?
Quite possibly. The older one with sleepy eyes, dark suit and shirt, no
tie but buttoned up all the way, steel-gray hair cut very short, this

would be Mr. Moraco. Randy saw him as a dedicated soldier, but lacking the polish of an officer, more like a thirty-year noncom, though not a mob soldier, Moraco would be at least a capo. Betcha. The other guy was the soldier, about five eight, maybe thirty, one of those street tough guys in a bomber jacket and Banlon shirt, open. He could be a fighter, a pro boxer Moraco had brought along. The guy, though, did not look at all Italian.

Moraco said something as he came past Carlo looking straight ahead—thin nose, not a bad-looking guy, mid-fifties—and Randy stuck out his hand.

"Mr. Moraco—"

He took hold of Randy's fingers, squeezed and let go, saying, "Mr. Agley, how you doing? I'm Vincent Moraco," and stopped there, turning to look over the room. "Not bad for a Monday. I thought you had a trio."

"Thursday through Saturday," Randy said.

Vincent Moraco was nodding. "Good bar business. You have any girls come in?"

"Young ladies? Yes, of course. But it's not a pickup bar, if that's what you mean. We get quite a nice crowd every night, fortunate to have General Motors only a couple of blocks away, in the RenCen."

"What I'm gonna do," Vincent Moraco said, "is line you up with some high-class girls, dress nice, fit right in. They come in ten o'clock on, every night. Saturday guys're here with their wives or girlfriends, so maybe only one will come in, make the guys from out-of-town happy. The girls have a drink at the bar, they're seen and they leave. But not with a guy. Any guy comes up to them, they're waiting for somebody, their husband. The guy keeps trying, becomes a problem"—Moraco half turned, his sleepy eyes moving to the soldier—"the Mutt here tells the guy in a nice way to get lost. The guy gets tough about it, the Mutt takes him outside."

"The Mutt," Randy said, "and you go by Vincent or is it Vinnie?"

"Stay with Vincent you'll be okay. The Mutt's also your body-guard, so you pay him."

"How much?"

"Five a week, cash."

"I'm not sure I need a bodyguard."

"You not sure 'cause you never know, that's why you need one. What you do, let your good customers with house accounts know the girls are here. Maybe three or four will come in, but not at the same time, so it don't look like a whorehouse."

Randy glanced over to see Carlo watching, Carlo nodding toward Number One, called a booth but actually a banquette, and Randy said, "Why don't we sit down and have a drink?" His first step in becoming a mob guy.

Moving to the booth, Vincent Moraco motioned to the Mutt to join them. The waitress, in her tux, was there before they were all seated. "At Randy's," Randy said, "every waiter in the place is yours. Cindy here is my star. Cindy only takes care of this booth, Number One. She needs help she's got it."

Cindy took their orders and left.

Watching her go the Mutt spoke his first words, saying with a country accent that turned Randy's head to look at him, "Man, she could sell pussy 'long with the others, you know it?"

Randy had to ask him, "Where you from?"

"Indiana," the Mutt said. "You know where Bedford's at? On U.S. Fifty?"

Randy made a decision. He said, "Mutt, I don't need a Hoosier hotshot fucking with my staff. You got it?"

The guy seemed surprised. Vincent Moraco said, "He knows his place."

And Randy's role was established. He was accepting the arrangement—since he didn't see that he had a choice—but would remain the boss here. It was Randy's second step approaching gangland.

"The way it works," Vincent said, stirring his Canadian Club and Coke, "your good customers from GM, Ford's, Compuware, call you over to the table. 'Say, Randy, you happen to know that redhead sitting at the bar?' You look over. 'Oh, you mean Ginger? You like to meet her? She staying at the hotel 'round the corner.' Then you say, 'We have a special arrangement, you want to party over there with Ginger, I can put it on your tab, here.' After that they know they don't have to carry extra cash with them, it's house-account pussy. The wife sees the bill, 'Jesus Christ, you buying drinks for the fuckin house?' What she don't accuse the guy of is getting laid."

"How much a trick?"

"Five."

"They're all the same?"

"Stand 'em on their heads . . . Yeah, all're five a trick."

"What about all night?"

"A grand, anything over an hour. The girls with baby-sitters get another two bills from the guy, over and above the tip."

"What if the customer, after he's down for one—"

"Wants to go again? The girl calls you and you put it on the guy's account."

"What's the girl get?"

"Three bills. There's a table of guys, out-of-towners here for a convention at Cobo, like the Society of Automotive Engineers, and they all want a piece of the action? The girl stays there at the hotel. You get the relay team going it makes it easier."

"The girl does everything the guy wants?"

"As long as it don't leave marks. The guy wants her to piss on him, or take a dump on a glass-top coffee table while he's underneath looking up?" Moraco shrugged. "If she has to go, no problem. She don't, I don't know. Maybe the guy calls down for some prune juice."

Randy looked off at Cindy in her tux to get the picture out of his mind. He said to Vincent, "What's your take?"

"So you don't have to keep books, a flat eight thousand a week."

"Based on what?"

"An average night. Say four girls turning two tricks each, then times five nights, Monday to Friday, what's that?"

"Twenty thousand."

"They make twelve, we take eight. You pay every Saturday, keep anything over eight for yourself."

"What about slow nights?"

"It's up to you to bring in the business."

"What if all the girls don't show up?"

"It can happen, say illness in the family."

"But you get your eight grand even if the girls don't make the nut."

Vincent said, "You have a problem with that?"

"I want to be sure I have it straight," Randy said, a sleepy look coming into his eyes as the image of Pierce Brosnan faded out and Lucky Luciano, without the pockmarks, faded in to take his place. "What you're telling me," Randy said, "the girls could all quit and become stockbrokers, you still get your eight a week."

Vincent was nodding. "As your partners."

By the end of April, nine months into the arrangement, Randy's mob connection had cost him $116,200 out-of-pocket. He still saw himself as a wiseguy, but no longer on the level of a Luciano. Christ, Luciano would've had Moraco whacked by now and taken over the girls.

Carlo was threatening to quit, not happy about some of the clientele, these goombas who'd show up, no reservation, and squeeze into Booth Number One without asking. The linen service, owned by Moraco's boss, cost twice what it should. And the Mutt, the Mutt was five bills a week down a rathole. What did he do? The girls, the ones who showed up, didn't need protection.

Randy had never been curious about the Mutt until one Saturday, just before Vincent Moraco arrived for his free lunch and the eight grand, he had a talk with him, standing at the end of the bar.

"Tell me," Randy said, "what you do exactly."

It brought a frown. "My job? I keep an eye on you."

"For Vincent?"

"He don't talk to me either. I watch out for you 'cause I'm your bodyguard. But what you could say I do is no more'n fuck the dog, 'cause you don't gimme any jobs to do."

Randy said, "Like what?"

"Like throwing the drunks out, the ones get loud and cause a commotion."

"Most of them are friends. What else?"

"What bodyguards do. Some guy's bothering you, I teach him a lesson."

"Well, I do have someone bothering me."

"Gimme his name, I'll tell him to leave you alone."

"Vincent Moraco."

That might've been too blunt, or too much all of a sudden for the Mutt to think about. He nodded, staring off, but after a moment said, "Mr. Moraco, huh?"

"I want you to be at the meeting," Randy said. "Listen to what I tell Vincent, keeping in mind who pays you."

———

Signed celebrity photos—not the caricatures—looked out from the walls of Randy's office, done in browns, recessed lighting and a lot of chrome. Vincent Moraco was seated across the desk from him, the Mutt over to one side, beneath a black-and-white photo of Soupy Sales.

"First of all," Randy said, "you realize that what my customers are paying to get laid appears on the books as profit, restaurant income."

Vincent said, "Yeah . . . ?"

"It means I'm paying taxes on income that isn't income, over three hundred grand in fuck money I can't write off."

Vincent said, "You look at it like you laundering the money."

"Yeah, but people who do that are paid a fee, they get something for the service, the risk they take."

"You need a bookkeeper know what he's doing."

"That's only half the problem."

"Yeah . . . ?"

"You base your cut on four girls a night, but only two show up, once in a while three. And there aren't that many relay teams or all-nighters."

"You have to understand," Vincent said, "you don't get this class of girl off the street. You know who some of the best ones are? College girls. They work hard to pay for school and make something of themselves."

"But two, at the most three girls," Randy said, "even with Ph.D.'s and working their asses off, won't come close to making the nut."

"Why? You having trouble bringing people in? Business falling off?"

"Leveling off. Carlo said you have to expect that. No matter how well you open, after a while it's bound to settle down. We do okay all week and still go crazy weekends."

"So what're you trying to say?"

"I just told you, the way it is doesn't work. Either put on more girls and turn the place into a brothel that serves food, or cut back on your take. You're not gonna make a cent if we have to close."

"Cut it back to what?"

"Four, at the most. I'll do business with you, Vincent, but I can't pay you out of restaurant receipts and stay open. Your take's drawn from my personal account."

"The dough," Vincent said, "you fucked that widow out of? I know how much you got, Randy. Everybody knows."

Randy had to ignore that one, let it pass. He said, "Up to right now, today, I'm out about a hundred and fifty thousand. And do you know what I get for that, Vincent?" Randy paused, playing his role. "I get to watch you eat lunch."

For the first time in nine months Randy saw Vincent Moraco smile. He watched Vincent look over at the Mutt and now the Mutt was smiling.

"You hear what he said?"

"He gets to watch you eat?"

Vincent said, "Mutt, you're a stupid fuck, aren't you?" He pushed out of the chair, still smiling a little, and said to Randy, "Lemme have the envelope and I'll get out of your way."

"Mutt, what was the main idea you got from the meeting?"

Mutt had to think about it, half closing his eyes, the brow above ridged with scar tissue.

Randy was patient. He said, "Mutt, I'm paying that man out of my pocket. You ever hear of a business partnership that works like that?"

"He don't care about you."

"What happens if I stop paying?"

"The first time you're late? Somebody shoots out your windows. That's what they do to bookies they don't pay their street tax."

"What if I said no more pussy on house accounts and stopped paying altogether?"

"I 'magine you'd have a fire. Have to shut down."

"What would he do to me?"

"You're paying him out of your cookie jar anyway, I 'magine he'd keep after your money."

"What would you do, go back to work for Moraco?"

The Mutt grinned. "That was funny what you said about watching him eat. I mean I wasn't laughing 'cause he was. I have no respect for Mr. Moraco and he knows it. Not being one of them's why he put me here."

"Why'd he hire you in the first place?"

"I was at Southern Ohio Correctional, the prison? There was an old boy there I looked after, saw no harm came to him. I got my release, it was Mr. Rossi set it up for me to come work here in De-troit."

"So Moraco hired you," Randy said, "out of respect for this Mr. Rossi."

"Yeah, but I never kissed Mr. Moraco's ass like he wanted, so we didn't get along too good. I started out driving for Mr. Amilia. It was the first time I had to wear a suit of clothes."

"The boss himself, uh?"

"Yeah, but he said I drove too fast. So they put me on the street. You know, lean on the bookies, make sure they pay their street tax. I'd do a shylock collection if the guy fell behind."

Fascinating. Randy leaned forward, resting his arms on the desk. "What would you do?"

"You mean get him to pay? Stop by his home, meet his wife, talk to 'em. If there was a second time I'd catch him away from home and body-punch him good, break a couple of ribs."

"What if he was a big guy, two hundred pounds?"

"I can hit," the Mutt said. "I lifted weights and got into boxing again at Southern Ohio. Got pretty good."

"Why'd you go to prison?"

"I was in a bar fight and shot a fella, Bellefontaine, Ohio. I was working at the ski area there, making snow."

Randy said, "They ski in Ohio?"

"They got a hill there. This fella in the bar gimme a smart mouth, looking for it. I hit him with a Bud Light. He come out with a pistol and I took it off him and he got shot as we tussled."

"You killed him?"

"Yeah, but the witnesses, fellas that worked at the ski area? They said he started it, so it wasn't called murder. I did forty months. Mr. Rossi said I coulda done 'em standing on my head. Oh, and I killed another fella while I was inside, shanked him out'n the yard, but nobody saw it. Two hundred convicts out there, nobody saw it."

"Why'd you kill him?"

"Teach him a lesson. He's one of the fellas leaning on my friend Mr. Rossi."

"Have you done anything like that for Moraco?"

"One time, yeah. Was a Chaldean bookie lived over by Dearborn? I was only the driver, but this Tootsie Roll they hired got nervous or something, I don't know. I took his pistol and shot the Chaldean through the heart. I still only got my wages."

"Moraco didn't respect you for that?"

"I told you, I don't respect him, and he knows it."

Randy said, "Mutt, you've been here nine months, and you know something? You've never told me your real name."

"You never asked. It's Searcy J. Bragg, Jr."

"Where'd you get Mutt?"

"When I was at Southern Ohio my cellmate's name was Jeff? He was a big tall fella, so I got called Mutt. You get it? He was hurt pretty bad, some boys come after him during the prison riot? You might've heard of it. Left the place a mess, I'm telling you."

"You don't mind being called Mutt?"

"It's okay."

Randy eased back in his chair, got comfortable and locked his fingers behind his head. "Well, Searcy—"

The Mutt stopped him. "I like Mutt better'n Searcy. How'd you like to be name Searcy?"

"I think I'd change it."

"When I was fighting I was called Banger, Banger Bragg, but I never much cared for it, either." He raised his right fist to show B-A-N-G tattooed on his knuckles. "My right hook's my banger."

Randy started over. "Well, Mutt, we're in some kinda fix here, aren't we?" Randy's voice taking on the trace of an accent it never had before. "How to deal with Mr. Moraco. You know something? I think he's skimming offa that eight grand, keeping maybe half of it for himself. See, with his boss in federal court— You know about that, don't you, the trial going on?"

"Yes sir, it's in the newspaper."

"But Moraco isn't on trial, is he? Why you suppose he wasn't brought up?"

"I guess 'cause he's smart," the Mutt said, "never talked business anyplace they coulda hung a wire. Not even in his car. They say the gover'ment's still trying to put something on him."

"So while he's walking around free," Randy said, "I don't imagine Mr. Amilia's paying much attention to him. Old Tony's got his own problem, how to stay out of jail." Randy paused before he said, "Just out of curiosity, how much do you normally charge to take somebody out?"

"Kill'm? I don't have a set price," the Mutt said. "How much is it worth to you?"

Randy was ready. He eased forward in his chair to rest his arms on the desk and look directly at the Mutt.

"I can go twenty-five."

"Twenty-five what?"

"As much as you make in a whole year, twenty-five thousand dollars. Cash or check."

"Okay."

"Really?"

"Yeah, I'll do'er."

Randy sat back, but then came forward again.

"How?"

"I prefer to shoot him."

"You have a gun?"

"I can get one. After, I'll have to take off, as they're liable to find out was me."

Randy said, "Yes, I would, too." He waited a few moments and said, "Well . . ." and waited again.

"One time," the Mutt said, "I thought I'd try stickin' up places, see if I was any good at it? So I went in a—it was like a drugstore only it sold all kinda stuff. I went up to the girl behind the counter and said, 'You see this?' and opened my jacket."

"You exposed yourself."

"I showed her the pistol tucked in my pants. She looked at it, then looked up at me and said, 'Yeah?' "

"I said, 'Aw, fuck it,' and left. That girl was too dumb to rob." He paused again, said, "Okay then," got up and walked out.

Randy watched him, fascinated.

16

CARLO SAW THE BLACK LEATHER jacket sliding into Booth Number One, looked past to the reservations stand where Heidi should be—no Heidi, nobody—and got to the booth as fast as he could make his way through the tables.

"Sir, I'm very sorry but this booth is reserved."

The one in leather, his hair pulled back severely into a ponytail, said, "That's right, garson, I reserved it."

"Sir, I know the party—"

"What's the name?"

"I know them personally, they come here—"

"It's after ten. Don't look like they're gonna show."

"Sir, I'm very sorry, but you must have a reservation. Fortunately I can seat you, if you would come this way."

"No, this works for me," the one in leather said. "Don't worry about it." Now he looked up, his face becoming more pleasant. "And here's the rest of my party."

Carlo turned to see a young lady in an inexpensive raincoat and a priest. A priest? Yes, helping her off with the coat and Carlo was confused; he couldn't see this one in the booth in the company of a priest. He said, "Father, how are you this evening? I'm afraid we have a misunderstanding about the table."

The priest said, "No, it's fine," handing him the raincoat. "Check this for us, would you, please?" He turned to the table where the young lady in her plain black sweater and skirt was already sliding in.

Carlo said, "Wait, please," wanting to ask, Who are you people? Now she was seated and he turned again to the priest, who seemed patient, reasonable, and said to him, "Father, I'm very sorry to tell you this booth is reserved for another party," Carlo sounding disappointed. "I wish with all my heart I could say yes, please, stay here. But I cannot. I have a table over there—you see it?—and a very nice one closer to the music. You can listen and enjoy as you dine." He heard the one in leather call it "elevator music," and the young lady, looking around, say, "It's cooler than I thought it would be. Fran's fulla shit, it doesn't look like a men's club." The leather one said a friend had told him there were ice cubes in the urinals, and the young lady said, "Doesn't that make the drinks taste funny?" Carlo heard the priest say, "You sure you want to stay here?" The leather one answered him, "We're here, okay? And we're fuckin staying here." He said, "She wants to piss off the management." Then looked up to say, "Garson, you want to get us some drinks?" Carlo thinking, No, get the Mutt. But then heard the young lady say, "I just want to see how Randy handles it," and Carlo began to think their sitting here had a purpose.

He said, "Excuse me, please," and left.

Debbie said to Johnny Pajonny, "How do you know his name's Garson?"

Terry said, "He means *garçon*."

Carlo came along the back hall past the rest rooms to Heidi from behind, Heidi standing in the doorway to Randy's office. He said to her, "Dear, would you mind going back to work?"

"Would you mind," Heidi said, turning, moving past him, "if I went to the little girls' room once in a while?" This big blonde, confident, able to turn it around because she would sleep with Randy when he wanted her.

Randy was reading a newspaper open on his desk. He looked up at Carlo. "The trial is in recess till next week on account of Tony Amilia's prostate. It says he appears, though, to be in good health"—Randy looked down at the paper again—"and is 'the best dressed of the defendants, always in a business suit and tie. The others on trial often wear jogging suits and sneakers.' Classy old guy with a déclassé outfit," Randy said, looking up again. "I am no longer gonna worry about those punks. Bunch of losers. What's the problem?"

"People have sat down at Number One and won't get up. I tell them it's reserved, they don't move."

"In what name?"

"Mr. Moraco, for four."

"What time?"

"Ten o'clock."

"Tell Mr. Moraco you had to give up his table because he's late. If he complains, tell him tough shit."

"Can I quote you saying it?"

"Tell him anything you want."

"I think the ones sitting there know you. One is a priest."

"I don't know any priests."

"The other one says the young lady with them wants to piss off the management. But she says oh no. She says, 'I just want to see how Randy handles it.' "

"That doesn't mean anything. What's she look like?"

Carlo shrugged. "Cute, but common. Probably a very nice young lady."

"Then why would I know her?"

"What do I do, please, when Mr. Moraco comes?"

"Let him work it out."

"I mentioned the one is a priest?"

"Carlo, if you can't do your job—"

"Yes?"

"Look. If Moraco wants them to move to another table, they'll move to another table. What's the problem?"

Cindy, who worked the first booth and didn't care who sat in it, brought menus and served their drinks, Johnny swigging his beer out of the bottle now as they studied the caricatures of famous native Detroiters, Debbie spotting them, Johnny questioning, Terry biding his time.

"Sonny Bono."

"You sure?"

"Who else looks like that? There's Lily Tomlin, Tom Selleck in the Tigers baseball cap. The girl next to him is . . . Pam Dawber."

"It's Marlo Thomas. I know she's from Detroit."

"It's still Pam Dawber. *Mork & Mindy,* I never missed it, I wanted to look just like her."

"You didn't come close," Johnny said. "There's—Jesus Christ, is that Ed McMahon? He's from here?"

"I see Diana Ross," Debbie said, "Smokey Robinson . . . Michael Moriarty—I loved him on *Law & Order*. And there's, my God, Wally Cox."

"The one next to him," Terry said, getting into it, "you know who that is? Seymour Cassel."

"Who the fuck's Seymour Cassel?"

"He's good, he was in . . . something about a Chinese bookie. Okay, and the one next to him you should know. David Patrick Kelly."

"Never heard of him."

"Pat Kelly, he was three years ahead of us at Bishop Gallagher. He was in that movie with Nick Nolte and Eddie Murphy, *48HRS*."

"Which one was Kelly?"

"Guy's running down the street, Eddie Murphy opens the car door and knocks him on his ass? That one."

"Look," Debbie said, "sitting at the bar, Bill Bonds."

"The anchorman? That's not his hair," Johnny said.

"Anyone who watches TV knows that."

"I mean that's not the rug he always wears."

Debbie called the maître d' over and asked him. Carlo looked toward the bar. He said, "Yes, Mr. Bonds and his wife. They come here often."

"He's drinking?"

"Only Perrier."

Right after that Johnny spotted Ted Nugent's picture on the wall. "I know it's him, 'cause there's a hack in Four East looks just like him."

Debbie said, "Were the hacks at Jackson stupid?"

"You gotta be stupid to be one, don't you?"

"Where I was they'd never get the count right the first time. Never."

"I know what you mean, you can stand there all day while they do their recounts."

Terry said, "Isn't that Alice Cooper?"

They went right on talking.

"You had women guards, didn't you?"

"Some, mostly men."

"They hit on you?"

"I didn't have any trouble. But it was going on, yeah, some of the girls doing it for favors, preferential treatment."

Johnny said, "There's one over at the bar, the redhead? I wouldn't mind her doing me a favor."

"If you like whores," Debbie said.

"Come on—"

"Go ask her."

Johnny looked past Debbie to Terry. "You think she's a whoer?"

Debbie said, "What're you asking a priest for? How would he know?"

"Well, how do you know?"

"I heard there were call girls here, and that redhead is my idea of a chick who does it for money."

Johnny said, "I'm gonna go check."

They watched him walk over to the bar buttoning his jacket, touching the collar to make sure it was up and his ponytail hooked over it. They saw the woman turn as he reached her and cock her head to one side to adjust her earring. They saw Johnny ready to take the empty stool next to her. The woman said something to him and now Johnny was talking, gesturing, laying his hand on her shoulder.

They saw the guy with the crew cut coming along the bar.

They watched him walk up to Johnny—both about the same height, but Johnny lacking the guy's solid build—and say something to him. Johnny shrugged, gestured with his hands, nodded as he looked this way, toward the booth.

Debbie said, "What's he doing, inviting them over?"

No, Johnny was coming back alone. Sliding into the booth he said, "That bouncer, he walks up, he goes, 'Angie, this guy bothering you?' She says to me, 'This is my husband,' the fuckin bouncer. You believe it?"

Debbie was still looking at the redhead and the guy with the crew cut. "He's her pimp, you dummy."

Now Johnny was looking over. "Oh, he is? You ever see a pimp dresses like that?"

"What'd you say to him?"

"I told him I was with a priest, so he wouldn't get the wrong idea. The guy has scar tissue up here, over his eyes."

Terry said, "He must've got hit a lot."

Now Debbie was asking Johnny about the green outfit the girl at the bar was wearing and what her earrings were like. Terry's gaze wandered off . . .

Came to a man who reminded him of his uncle and saw Tibor sitting there in a checked sport coat, a young lady with him, their waiter pouring red wine. No, it wasn't Tibor. Tibor's drink was bourbon, Early Times, managing somehow to buy it or have it shipped to him, Kentucky bourbon in Rwanda, and always had a supply. Tibor would sip it through crushed ice packed in the glass, a little sugar sprinkled on top. For his sweet tooth, because he couldn't find chocolate candy that he liked. A half-dozen bottles left when he died. Early Times in a wooden case with words in Kinyarwanda stenciled on the side. Terry drank three of the bottles during the first year, different times when he ran out of Johnnie Walker and didn't feel like driving all the way to Kigali. Bourbon was okay, it did the job. But Johnnie Walker red was his favorite because he admired the look of the square bottle with its smooth, rounded edges and neat red label, seeing it as a work of art sitting on the old wooden table, a warm, amber glow in the last light of day. The black label, more expensive, looked almost as good. There was a bottle in the kitchen, up in a cupboard, saved for a special occasion that never came. He would bet anything Chantelle had sold the leftover fifths of Early Times by now. Unless she tried the whiskey and liked it. She would weave when she was high, walking to the house, but still with grace, her hips moving in the *pagne* that fell to her ankles. Her voice would change, too, become higher and inquiring, a hint of irritation asking him to explain what she didn't understand. And in the dark under the netting she would rest her stump on his chest and he would cover it with his hand.

Johnny had his hand in the air to bring the maître d' over.

"Yes?"

"You see what time it is? Going on eleven."

Carlo waited.

"Where're these people suppose to have a reservation?"

"When they come in," Carlo said, "you will be the first to know."

Debbie said, "We'd like another round and we'll order."

"Of course."

"Wait. Is Randy here?"

Carlo turned, looked over the room and came back to them. "I don't believe so. You wish to speak to him?"

"Maybe," Debbie said, "I'm not sure."

"May I give Mr. Agley your name?"

"You just said he isn't here."

"So I can tell him when he comes."

Johnny said, "Tell him Fr. Dunn wants to hear his confession."

Debbie shook her head. "I'll let you know." Carlo walked off and she put her hand on Terry's arm. "I was thinking I might talk to him first, before we get into it with him. You know, see what he's like now."

"What was the last thing he said to you, 'Don't fuck with me'?"

" 'Don't fuck with me, kid.' That was the second to last thing he said. His last words were 'You're not in my league.' But," Debbie said, "maybe he's changed. You know, now that he's got what he wants."

Terry said, "You told me he's a gangster now."

"Shit. I forgot. But he did like me, I know that. We had a pretty good time, at least at first."

"I bet he's here," Terry said. "You want to see him, go ahead."

She said, "Yeah, I'm gonna do it," and nudged Johnny with her elbow. "Move, so I can get out." She said to Terry, "If the waitress comes I'll have the bluepoints, a house salad, the Coho salmon in the paper bag and another Stoli. I'll see you."

Johnny slipped back into the booth, picked up his menu and said, "I'm gonna start with the jumbo shrimp cocktail. I like surf and turf but I don't see it here."

Cindy came by to take their orders and he asked her about it, how come no surf and turf? She said, "Sir, you can have anything you want."

"And you'll charge me anything you want, huh?"

Terry waited while they went around and around on what Johnny might like put together. When his turn came Terry gave her Debbie's order and said, "I'll have the same," keeping it simple, "but instead of the Johnnie Walker, lemme have a double bourbon this time over crushed ice. Early Times, if you have it."

17

DEBBIE STOOD JUST INSIDE THE office while Randy put on his act, looked up as she came in, got the right expressions in his eyes, pleasure in one, surprise in the other—she could hear herself delivering the line onstage—and he froze the look; next, he arched one eyebrow quizzically—the word that would come to mind when he used to do it. First, I must be seeing things. And then, Can I believe my eyes? Now he'll laugh this low chuckle and begin to shake his head.

He did that, audibilizing the eyebrow thing with "I can't believe it." Then serious, ad-libbing, "God, but it's good to see you."

It was the last part that got to her. She didn't believe him, but so what? It still made her feel good. Gave her confidence a boost.

She watched Randy get up, come from around his desk and put his arms out toward her. Now she was supposed to rush into them. What she did was walk past him and sit down in the chair facing his desk.

And what Randy did, he stepped back until he was against the desk, raised his right leg and laid his thigh on the surface, his crotch aimed at Debbie, the bulge telling her he was still stuffing his Jockeys. When they were living together she caught him one time—they were getting ready for bed—pulling a pair of socks out of his undies and said, being stupid back then, "You're bad," and he cocked his head at her and winked. Well, not this time, you phony baloney, but then couldn't help saying, "You still think that works?" and could kick herself for letting him know she'd noticed.

Randy grinned. He did that a lot, sleepy-eyed, and said, "You missed me, didn't you?"

She decided at that moment to quit screwing around and said, "No, I didn't, Randy. I knocked you on your ass with a Buick Riviera." Used to saying it that way.

And the cool son of a bitch said, "Oh? I don't recall you driving a Buick. I thought it was a Ford Escort."

It made her mad and Debbie had to take a few beats to get her insides to calm down.

She said, "Why don't you quit trying to be so fucking cool all the time? What're you now, a gangster? You quit sailing around the world? You were always someone else, like you wanted me to think you had a secret life. You did, but you know what I mean. You'd be gone for a few days, I'd ask where you were and you'd go, 'Sorry, babe.' You'll never know how much I hated being called babe. I'm not a babe, Randy."

"Why didn't you tell me? I mean that you hated it."

"Because I was stupid. I actually thought I was in love with you."

"Maybe you still are, deep down."

"Don't, okay? You'd go, 'Sorry, babe, but there's a reason I can't tell you at this point in time.' Like one of these days you'd tell me you were with the CIA. Why don't you just try to be yourself?"

Randy said, "I'm whoever I am," making it sound like something he was told on a mountaintop.

He could wear you out. Debbie said, "Randy, that is so fucking dumb, 'I'm whoever I am.' You want to appear wise, you keep your mouth shut. I'm serious. You don't have to base your whole life on bullshit."

Now he was giving her his sincere look, hands folded on his thigh. He said, "Why do you care?"

Sounding as though he was serious, so she went along with it, watching her step though. She said, "Do you like being an asshole?" See if that would nudge him.

He let his breath out in a long Randy sigh, staying in his serious mood. "I am sorry for the way I treated you. Really. Even at the time, when you trusted me to invest your money—it was the first time in my life my conscience ever gave me a hard time."

"But you took it."

He said, "Yes, I did," looking past her and sounding contrite.

"Well, would you like to give it back?"

"It's been on my mind," Randy said. "Not while I was lying in the hospital, in pain, but since then."

"While I was in prison," Debbie said.

"The thing is, I want to make it up to you."

She said, "What does that mean?"

And the fucking maître d' came in the office saying, "Mr. Moraco is here."

They started on their appetizers without Debbie: Johnny dipping his giant shrimp in the cocktail sauce, Terry dealing with his oysters. He heard Johnny say, "Jesus, there's Vincent Moraco," and Terry looked up.

"Which one?"

"The little guy, with his wife."

"That's not the one used to pay us."

"The one paid us was his girlfriend. She said she was Mrs. Moraco so nobody'd argue with her or fool around. Understand? Or you'd be fuckin with Vincent Moraco himself. I heard the feds're looking for the girlfriend, but she's disappeared."

"They call you?"

"No, but some other guys making the same run I heard were sub-poenaed."

"What about the other guy?"

"Vito Genoa. He's the enforcer. Mr. Amilia's take-out guy."

"They're watching us eat," Terry said.

"I know they are. Don't look at 'em."

Too late. Terry nodded to the three standing with the hostess, and smiled. The Moracos and Vito Genoa, looking this way as the host-ess was talking to them, did not smile back. Now the maître d' was there, taking over, talking maître d' talk to them, schmoozing them over to the bar.

Johnny was saying, "Remember we use to go sledding at Balduck Park? Genoa was the guy use to come by there, act like he was king of the fuckin hill."

"He went to Queen of Peace?"

"No, he was from over in Grosse Pointe Woods. He was gonna wash my face with snow and you jumped him. We were about ten, he was twelve or thirteen, big for his age."

Terry said, "He beat me up."

Johnny said, "And I got a concussion of the fuckin brain, but he never bothered us again, did he?"

"How do you know this is the same guy?"

"The name, Gen-oh-a. High school he was All-City in football two years, with his picture in the paper." Johnny saying, "He's put on a good fifty sixty pounds since then," as Debbie came back and he had to get up.

She slipped into the banquette saying, "I almost had him. I got him to say he'd make it up to me, and that fucking maître d' walked in." She said, "There's Randy, coming along the bar. See him? What's your first impression?"

"He looks like a guy runs a restaurant," Terry said, "and eats a lot. He fills out that suit."

"He's put on some weight," Debbie said, "but the style is still there, the pose."

They watched him reach the Moracos and Vito Genoa, Randy already saying something to them as he walked up, taking Mrs. Moraco's hand now, still talking, making her smile, the two guys looking at him now not happy, and now Randy was gesturing, shaking his head, acting helpless.

"We're in their booth," Debbie said, "and he's telling them there's nothing he can do about it."

"Maybe an hour ago it was their booth," Johnny said, "not now. Any restaurant, a busy night, they'll hold your reservation fifteen minutes, that's it. You show up late, get in line, man, it's the way it is."

They watched Moraco turn from Randy to say no more than a few words to Vito Genoa and the guy was coming this way, looking right at them.

Debbie nudged Johnny. "Tell this bozo what you just said," and all Johnny could say was, "Shit," without much behind it.

Terry watched Genoa stop in front of Johnny. He placed his hands flat on the table to lean in and get close. Now he took one of Johnny's giant shrimp and popped it in his mouth. Johnny didn't say a word.

Terry said, "Vito? I'm Father Dunn."

Genoa turned his head. Now he brought his hands from the table to stand erect.

"What parish you in, Vito?"

Genoa didn't answer, taken by surprise, or maybe thinking about it. What parish was he in?

"I remember when we were kids you were in, I think, Star of the Sea. Am I right?"

He still didn't answer, maybe wondering what's going on here? Who's this priest?

"You remember Fr. Sobieski, your pastor? He's been there a long time, hasn't he? I've been serving at a mission in Africa, Vito. Rwanda. I was there when over a half-million people were murdered in three months time. Some shot, most of 'em hacked to death with machetes." He paused.

Genoa stared at him.

"A week from Sunday," Terry said, "I'll be at Star of the Sea, make an appeal for the mission. See if I can raise enough to feed my little orphans, hundreds of 'em, Vito, their moms and dads killed during the genocide. You see their little faces—it tears at your heart."

Vito Genoa finally spoke. He said, "You don't get up right now, Father, I'm gonna drag you across the fuckin table."

It was in Terry's mind that if the guy dragged him across the fuckin table it would mess up his brand-new suit and he'd have to get it cleaned and pressed. On the other hand, if the guy did drag him across the table, in front of a roomful of witnesses, he wouldn't have to slip and fall to threaten Randy with a lawsuit. The opportunity was waiting for him. He would have to put aside the urge to get up and punch the guy in the mouth. He was the victim here.

He said to Genoa, "Vito, you'd lay hands on a man who's an ordained minister of your Church?"

"I gave up going to church for Lent," Vito said. "I won't need to till it looks like I'm gonna die. Okay, then I'll cash everything in at once, tell you all my sins and ask to be forgiven."

"That's presumption, my son. And presumption itself is a sin. You can't win, Vito."

"You either. Move."

Terry said, "I'm staying," and waited to get dragged across the table.

But what Vito did, he came around to Terry's end of the banquette, put his hand on Terry's shoulder and pinched that muscle between the neck and the shoulder blade, kept pressure on it, and the sudden pain, Christ, made his arm go limp. He tried to twist away, but the guy's fingers were clamped on tight. Debbie was yelling, "Leave him alone," trying to hold on to his arm as the guy took hold of the front of Terry's suit and pulled him up out of the booth by his lapels. Now he was patting Terry on the shoulder, straightening the front of his suit, Vito saying, "That wasn't so hard, was it?"

Terry had to agree, it wasn't. It needed to be a lot worse and he needed witnesses. So he said to Vito, up close, eye to eye and in a low voice:

"You pinch, huh? Why is that, Vito, 'cause you're a fuckin guinea faggot with no balls?"

Said it and got what he wanted, the body punch, Vito driving a fist into him with weight behind it and it rocked Terry, punched the air out of him, hunched him over to grab hold of his stomach—Debbie screaming now—and he couldn't get his breath, couldn't straighten until the guy brought up his knee to catch him in the chest, the guy's thigh ironing his face and Terry went down, landed flat on his back and lay there gasping, trying to suck air into his lungs.

He saw Debbie close to him pulling his collar off. It didn't help. He saw Randy looking down at him and then away, Randy saying to somebody, "Tony's gonna hear about this. Get him out of here." Now a guy with a crew cut—it looked like the bouncer who told Johnny the hooker was his wife—had Terry's coat open, his belt loosened, and was pulling on the waist of his pants, lifting Terry's back from the floor, up and down, telling him to take short breaths, in and out. Telling him, "You took a shot, you know it?"

They were in Randy's office now in lamplight, Debbie helping Terry into the leather chair facing the desk, Randy watching.

"I want to know what he said to Vito Genoa."

Debbie's back was to him, hunched over Terry, touching his hair, his face, their voices low as Terry asked if Johnny had got into it. Debbie said no, he was still at the table. Terry said good, lying back to rest his head against the cushion. Debbie straightened. She took the chair beneath Soupy Sales and got out her cigarettes. Randy remained on his feet, restless. He turned to Debbie.

"He said something that pissed Vito off."

Debbie said, "You mean it's okay then to beat him up, a priest, a man of God—"

"Just shut up. I want to know what he said."

"Ask him."

"Who is he? What're you doing with a priest?"

"He's a very dear friend of mine."

"You never told me about any priests."

"What're you talking about—I went to Catholic schools, didn't I? I told you, he's Fr. Terry Dunn, he's a missionary from Africa." She looked over at Terry and said, "Father, how's your tummy? Does it still hurt?"

Terry turned his head on the cushion. "Not too bad. But when I move, oh boy, it's like somebody's sticking a knife in my back. From the way I hit the floor. I don't think I'll be able to say Mass tomorrow."

Beautiful. Just right. Debbie wanted to kiss him but had to hang on to her anguished look. She said, "I think you should go to a hospital."

It hooked Randy. He turned to her saying, "Shit," and moved about without going anywhere. He seemed to be thinking for a moment, plotting, and said, "Who's the other guy?"

"Father's friend Johnny. They were altar boys together at Queen of Peace." She looked at Terry again. "Randy wants to know what you said to that man."

Terry turned his head on the cushion. "I asked him what parish he was in. He didn't say, but I thought maybe he was in Our Lady Star of the Sea." Terry groaned and closed his eyes. "Oh, boy, I never had a pain like this before."

"He has to leave," Randy said, turning to Debbie. "Where's he staying?"

"With his brother, in Bloomfield Hills."

"Oh? The brother must do pretty well."

"He does, he's a personal injury lawyer."

Randy said, "Fuck!" turning away again.

"Or," Debbie said, "we can settle it right here."

She watched Randy put on a half-assed sly look, narrowing his eyes. "That's why you took the booth, isn't it? You set the whole thing up."

"Right," Debbie said. "I found out a couple of gangsters had reserved the booth, so we took it with the idea of pissing them off and Fr. Dunn would be injured." Beat. "I hope not seriously."

"Jesus Christ," Randy said, "come on—when did you start hanging out with priests?"

"While I was inside, Randy, I saw the light and was saved. You know who my boss is now, a Jewish carpenter."

Randy said it again, "Jesus Christ—"

And Debbie came back with "My Lord and Savior." She said, "Randy, did you know there was a well-known TV anchorman sitting at the bar? Carlo pointed him out to us. Bill Bonds with his wife. You must know him. Carlo said he was drinking Perrier and saw the whole thing. Of course, everyone in the place saw it if they weren't blind. You want to settle or go to court?"

Randy took his time. Debbie believed he was facing the fact of the situation now, a priest assaulted in his restaurant, and knew she was right when he said, "How much are we talking about?"

She said, "Two-fifty."

"And you didn't set this up."

"I swear, Randy, it was our Savior looking out for us."

"All right, if you want a carpenter for a lawyer, bring him to court." Randy paused, getting that narrow look in his eyes again. "You said, '. . . looking out for us,' didn't you? What does his falling down, maybe drunk—I don't know—have to do with you?"

"Fr. Dunn and I are going in together," Debbie said. "The settlement includes the sixty-seven thousand you stole and said you'd pay back."

"When did I say I owed you anything?"

"Randy, see if you can keep your mouth shut for a minute. I'm gonna tell you how you can give us two hundred and fifty thousand dollars, feel good about it, and be able to write the whole thing off."

Johnny stayed at the table trying to look innocent. Debbie's idea. He was innocent. Shit, he didn't do anything. Still, the two mob guys gave him the stare before they left. Now Johnny had to get the waitress over and ask when he was getting his dinner. She said oh, she thought he wanted to wait for the others. He didn't like sitting here alone, people watching him, talking about what they had seen, so he went over to the bar where the bouncer was hanging out: standing with his arm on the bar as he looked out over the room. Johnny took a stool next to him.

"You see what happened?"

" 'Course I did."

"Why'd you let him deck the priest? You're the bouncer, aren't you?"

"I'm Mr. Agley's bodyguard. One of those two fellas was here? He loaned me to Mr. Agley."

"You're a mob guy, uh?"

"I told you what I do."

The Mutt raised his hand to look at his watch and Johnny saw the tattoo on his knuckles, B-A-N-G.

"You ink that tat yourself?"

The Mutt raised his hand again. "This? No, I had it done. I was a fighter."

The tattoo was crude and ugly enough for Johnny to ask, "Your cellmate letter it?"

"Guy in the yard. How'd you know?"

"Takes one to know one," Johnny said. "I did mine in fuckin Jackson, biggest walled prison in the U.S. Where'd you?"

"Southern Ohio."

"For what?"

"Killed a guy. Shot him."

"That what you are, a hit man?"

"You could say, on the side."

"Yeah? You've whacked guys?"

"Three so far. Was a truck driver, a convict and a Chaldean."

"You aren't Italian, are you?"

"Hell no."

"Or from around here. How'd you get hooked up with those guys?"

"I had a letter from a important man—"

"In the joint?"

"Yeah, saying to hire me."

"What do they call you?"

"Just Mutt, mostly."

Johnny believed it. This guy was dumb as a fuckin stump. He said, "I'm Johnny, I worked for 'em five years ago. Ran cigarettes up from Kentucky."

"Any money in that?"

"There was at the time. You ever see the big boss, old Tony?"

"I drove for him one time, but he don't come in here."

"He's got a piece of it, doesn't he?"

The Mutt shrugged.

Johnny said, "I knew a guy at Jackson was a hit man. He got ten grand a pop."

"Shit, I get more'n that."

"You must be good at it. What kind of piece you like to use?"

"Different ones."

"You say you took out a truck driver, a convict and one other guy?"

"A Chaldean. Guy wouldn't pay his street tax."

"You didn't shoot the convict."

"No, I shanked him."

"So you only actually shot two guys."

"Yeah, but I got one coming up."

"Yeah? You need a driver?"

"I doubt it."

"The hitter I knew at Jacktown always used a driver." Johnny waved the barman over and said, "Lemme borrow your pen."

The Mutt said, "I was thinking of going to the guy's house."

Johnny wrote his phone number on a cocktail napkin saying to the Mutt, "I wouldn't. What if other people're there, the guy's wife? You want to pop her, too? You also got neighbors looking out the fuckin windows." He handed the Mutt the cocktail napkin. "Here. Case you want to get in touch with me sometime."

The Mutt was looking at the phone number now. He said, "For what?"

"Get together and tell stories," Johnny said. "Didn't you use to talk to cons in the yard, hear their stories, what they did, how they fucked up? There was a con at Jackson had pulled over a hundred armed robberies. He'd tell where it was, how much he scored, the times he fucked up, had close calls, scrapes he got into. We'd listen 'cause this guy was funny, he knew how to tell a story and would have us all laughing. Guys'd come up to him and say, 'Hey, Roger, tell us about the time you robbed that Safeway store.' They'd already heard it more'n once, but it didn't matter, it was still funny." Johnny was grinning now and it got the Mutt to grin a little, Johnny saying, "Like we're out'n the fuckin yard, huh?"

The Mutt said, "I do the next fella you can read the story in the newspaper."

"When do I look for it?"

"Next couple of days or so."

"I was wondering," Johnny said, "you ever get to make it with those whoers that come in?"

18

"TONY AMILIA HAS PROSTATE CANCER," Terry said,
holding the newspaper open in front of him. "But they caught it
early, so the odds are he won't have surgery because of his age. By the
time it would kill him he'd already be dead from something else. So
if he's convicted it won't keep him out of prison."

"I'll bet he walks," Debbie said, "or gets probation and has to pay
a fine. He was brought up ten years ago on practically the same allegations and got off."

They were in Fran's library reading the combined Sunday edition
of the *News* and *Free Press*. A special section summarized the trial,
with sidebars that described the personal lives of the defendants and
a brief history of organized crime in Detroit, going back to the Purple Gang in the 1920s.

Debbie said, "Did you know they were a Jewish gang?"

"I knew they weren't Mafia." He turned from the paper to look at

Debbie on the other end of the sofa, newspaper sections on the cushion between them. "Where'd they get the name, the Purple Gang?"

"They were described as 'colorful,' and some guy they'd leaned on said, yeah, purple, the color of rotten meat, and it caught on." She looked at him to ask, "How's your back?"

"It really is a little stiff."

"I loved what you told Randy—like someone sticking a knife in your back."

"We had him going."

"But he'll never come up with the two-fifty, and he knows we'd never score that much in court."

"He thought we should sue Vito Genoa."

"Yeah, go after a Mafia hit man."

"If that's what he is," Terry said. "In the movies they're always sending to Detroit for a hit man, like they're sitting around waiting for calls. Guy picks up the phone, 'Hit man, can I help you?' I just saw a mention of it." Terry's gaze scanned the spread he held open. "Here it is, three people found murdered and decapitated. The two accused hit men were brought here from San Diego. If we're supposed to have all these hit men, why send away?" He lowered the paper to his lap. "Johnny was talking to that guy he thought was a bouncer? That's Randy's bodyguard, the one you were talking about they call the Mutt. He told Johnny he's sort of a hit man, does it on the side. He says he's killed three people and has a contract to do another one."

"Why would he tell Johnny that?"

"That's what Johnny said. You can tell a con inside, but not some guy comes up to you at the bar. He says the guy's too stupid to be trusted with a contract. The only thing Johnny wanted was the phone number of that redhead he was talking to at the bar. Her name's Angie."

"He get the number?"

"Yeah, but he wouldn't tell me."

Debbie didn't bite, still looking at her section of the paper. They had spent the night in Fran and Mary Pat's king-size bed, getting even more serious and sweaty than any of the times before, here or other places. She took offense when he said, "Honey, you could be a pro," turning away from him saying, "Thanks a lot." He tried to make peace telling her it didn't come out right. "I meant it as a compliment." She rolled back to him saying, "I'm better than any pro, Terry, I'm emotionally involved." Being in bed with Debbie was an experience he could take with him and look at for as long as he lived. There was a tender moment, seeing her face in the soft light from the window, when he'd almost said he was in love with her.

"What I'm thinking," Terry said, "if the Mutt's as stupid as Johnny says he is, and then you read the wiretap conversations, the two mob guys in the car . . . ?"

"I haven't come to that yet."

"Even their attorney refers to them as nitwits. He told the jury they learned to talk tough watching movies like *The Godfather* and *Mean Streets*."

"But they're really nice guys."

"Yeah, they can't help it if they've got this image from the movies and people are intimidated by it. There could be some truth to that, you listen to the tapes. The FBI bugged their car and you hear the two guys. They're parked across Michigan Avenue from a party store that fronts a sports book. They refer to the owner of the place as a camel jockey, so he's from the Mideast, maybe a Chaldean. They're gonna shoot out the store window, so the guy must owe them money. But it's raining and neither one of these enforcers wants to get out of the car. The one guy says, 'Can't you hit it from here?' And the other guy says, 'There's too fuckin many people on the street. Look at 'em, walking around. Who the fuck says Detroit streets aren't safe?'

They're driving back to the east side and get lost. 'Where the fuck's Ninety-six? It's suppose to be right here.' There's more of the tape, the same ones talking about what would happen if Tony Amilia got whacked. They sound like kids trying to act tough."

"Did they shoot out the window?"

"Not that time. Some of the bookies, witnesses at the trial, said yeah, they'd get threatened but never worried about it too much. They said it's not like you used to read about Gotti and the New York mob."

"They're referred to as the 'quiet mob,'" Debbie said. "Tony Amilia has never been convicted of a crime; he's a family man, fifteen grandchildren; gives to charities, a major contributor to Boysville; minds his own business, Mayflower Linen Supply, and lives quietly in Grosse Pointe Park. I just saw a picture of his home." Debbie turned through the pages of the section until she saw it again and handed the paper to Terry.

"Windmill Point Drive," Terry said, looking at it. "Houses used to be a million and up along there, right on the lake. They're probably more now. It goes, up the shore, Grosse Pointe Park, Grosse Pointe, Grosse Pointe Farms and Grosse Pointe Woods off the lake, across the freeway from Harper Woods, where I grew up. Right below Harper Woods—give you a tour of the east side—is Copland, where a lot of white Detroit cops live. Fran says they're talking about changing the rule and they won't have to live inside the city limits anymore. Most of the mob guys, outside of Amilia, live north of the Pointes, up past St. Clair Shores in Clinton Township."

"The feds would love to confiscate all their properties," Debbie said, "their cars, whatever they own, based on what they've made illegally over the past ten years or more. Twenty million. Which doesn't sound to me like there's a lot of profit in racketeering."

"A couple mil a year," Terry said. "That's not bad."

Debbie said, "Tony makes out, he takes his cut off the top. But what do all the guys under him come out with? Even saying no more than ten or twelve are 'made' members of the mob. I just read there've never been more than twenty-three 'made' guys at any given time here, going back to when they started, in the thirties."

"What a lot of people can't understand," Terry said, "is why they're coming down so hard on illegal gambling in a city where it's always been accepted. I remember when I was a kid, one of the ushers at Queen of Peace was a numbers runner. We've always had racetracks, for years a state lottery, now we've got casinos. What's the difference?"

"But there are bad guys in the mob," Debbie said. "You should know."

"That's right, and there're postal clerks and kids in school who shoot their friends. I'm not defending what the mob does, but they're so low-key you hardly know they're around." Terry kept going. "You said something that interested me before, about Tony Amilia." He paused and said, "I wonder if we could arrange an audience with him, an official visit."

"Why?"

"I wonder if you might be able to work it through your lawyer friend. What's his name? Bernacki? I'll tell you what I have in mind. You like the idea, I think you'll want to give him a call."

He watched her look out the window at the gray morning and turn back to him again.

"You want to talk to a mob boss—"

"Who's known as a generous benefactor."

"Ah, you go in as Fr. Dunn."

"Of course."

"And tell him," Debbie said, "about the little orphans of Rwanda."

———

Ed Bernacki's office in the Renaissance Center looked down on the Detroit River and Canada across the way, the casino over there in Windsor the only bright spot on the riverfront. He said, "It's Sunday. How'd you know I was here?"

Debbie told him she'd called his home first.

And Bernacki said, "I've got to be more careful who I give my numbers to." He listened to her explanation of why they wanted an audience with Mr. Amilia, and said, "Okay, you want to know what I think? It's not a bad idea. Still, I don't think Tony'll go for it. He won't see it's that important to him. What he's trying to do is avoid any kind of publicity."

"Even when it makes him look good?"

"The press can turn it around, editorialize, say it's fairly obvious why he's doing it. But, I'll speak to him. Maybe Tony will agree, but I have to tell you, I doubt it. One thing for sure, he won't see you at his home. No one steps inside the door but family and close associates."

Debbie said she didn't care where they met.

"I'll get back to you," Bernacki said, and phoned Tony Amilia at his home in Windmill Point that was swept once a week for bugs.

Bernacki asked Tony how he was doing on this gloomy piss-poor Sunday morning, and the man's voice, low and slow, said, "It's funny you should say that. You know what I do all night? Piss. I get up four, five times. Have this tremendous urge, go in the bathroom and the piss dribbles out. It stops and then starts again. I'm in there so long Clara will call out to me, 'Are you all right?' Sometimes it comes out in two streams. I'm thinking, The hell's going on? You ever have that happen, two streams? During the day, in the morning, it's almost as bad. I quit having my coffee in the morning or I'd be pissing all over the courtroom. Which isn't a bad idea. Show 'em what I think of their fuckin case. Ed, I get the urge, I think I'm gonna piss for twenty minutes, it dribbles out. I said to Clara, 'I piss more'n the amount of liquids I take in.' Explain that to me."

"It's a symptom," Bernacki said. "It means your prostate's swollen and impedes the natural flow of urine."

"But why do I piss more'n I drink?"

"That's just the way it seems to you."

"Sometimes there's blood in the piss. My urologist says don't worry about it, you got cancer, what do you expect? Guy's got the bedside manner of one of those Big Four cops, used to drive around in a Buick with their fuckin shotguns."

Bernacki said, "I can understand you sound more concerned with pissing than your trial."

"Fuck the trial. The feds're playing with themselves."

"Tony, I want to talk to you about something that could get you favorable press, which you could use right about now. There's a priest named Fr. Terry Dunn, from Africa, who'd like to talk to you."

"Jig?"

"He's white, a missionary."

"They all come with their hand out. How much's he want?"

"It's a pitch," Bernacki said, "but has an interesting twist to it, an idea you might go for."

"All right, what is it?"

"I'd rather you hear it in person."

"The phone's okay."

"They hang wires, Tony, outside the house. You know that. Listen, why don't I set it up? Instead of hearing it twice, you hear it directly from Fr. Dunn. Today, so we don't mess around trying to pick a date that's agreeable."

"A mick priest, he's got his fuckin hand out. That, I'm sure of."

"As I say, there's an angle you might like."

"You're absolutely sure of this guy?"

"A man of God, Tony, vouched for by someone I trust all the way."

"All right, I'll set it up and let you know. Hey, and tell him to bring some holy oil. He can give me the last rites ahead of time, get it out of the way."

19

THEY WAITED IN A PART of the restaurant that could be closed off for private parties: Tony Amilia and his lawyer, Ed Bernacki, at a round table that would seat ten, covered with a white tablecloth. On it were dishes of olives, several bottles of Pellegrino, a pot of coffee, glasses and cups, ashtrays, one in front of Tony sipping coffee and smoking a cigarette. Bernacki was next to him and they'd talk, but never loud enough for Vincent Moraco, standing by the table, to hear what they said. Vincent, buttoned up in his dark suit and shirt, moved to the open doors of the section. From here he could look through the empty restaurant to the entrance where Vito Genoa was waiting for the priest.

Vincent had asked Tony, "Who we meeting?" Tony said, "A priest." He asked him, "What priest?" thinking of the one from last night, and Tony said, "A priest, okay?" Tony with one foot still in the Church from going to his grandchildren's baptisms and First Communions.

Twenty years ago Vincent would never've asked the boss—a different boss then—who they were meeting. He never spoke unless he was spoken to first. Now it didn't matter. You couldn't say old Tony was one of the boys, like you could bullshit with him; still, you could call him Tony and you could piss and moan about the trial fucking up business. All Tony'd say was wait, they'd be back running things again. Just before the trial, Tony said to him, "How come you weren't indicted, Vincent?" sounding suspicious, but never coming out and asking had he made a deal with the government. Vincent told him, the main reason, he never talked to those street assholes. Even in a car he never said a fuckin word about business—and thanked Almighty God he hadn't the one and only time he went to the courtroom, sat with the visitors, and they played the tapes they got off the bugs in the cars.

The two yahoos talking tough. JoJo and that fuckin greaseball Tito, both of 'em now federal witnesses. He asked Tony, after, if he wanted 'em taken out and Tony said, "What do those two fuckups have to tell? The only thing they have is hearsay, or my word against theirs. Ed'll ask 'em on the stand what kind of deal they made and that will be that."

The tapes were identified as the rainy day they were across the street from the bookie joint on Michigan Avenue and wouldn't get out of the car. They're talking—you could tell their voices—JoJo the Dogface Boy, they called him, saying "What do you think would happen if old Tony got whacked?" Tito, who doesn't know shit, says he doesn't know, but then asks, "Who'd take over?" JoJo says, "That's what I'm talking about. It's how you move up in the crew. The way Gotti did it in New York when he took out Castellano. New York, they know how to do it. Here, you sit on your dead ass." Tito's voice: "You want to whack out Tony?" JoJo: "All I'm asking is what would happen."

Bullshit. He was thinking about it or he wouldn't mention it to Tito. Some of the other guys could be thinking about it, too.

That time when he spoke to Tony about taking the yahoos out and Tony said no, he spoke up to him. He said, "Tony, people hear what's on those tapes—those assholes can't even drive home without getting lost—people will lose respect for us, think we're a bunch of morons." Tony said don't worry about it and went to take a piss. The old man a boss in name only now. He's convicted and goes away, the door'd be open and Vincent believed he could walk right in. Tony doesn't go to prison, then you have to wait for him to piss himself to death, or, as the two morons were saying, somebody whacks him out. If that ever happened and who knows?—then he'd walk in and take over. The first thing he'd do, keep Randy's eight K a week for himself and become Randy's full-time partner, hang out at the restaurant, let people see him, know who he was. He believed rich broads especially liked to meet gangsters, flirt with a guy known to be dangerous. Wear a tux. Fuckin Tony lived like a mole, stayed in his hole till he had to go to court. He wouldn't say what this meeting was about. Only that it was a priest coming. It had to be the same one from last night who called Vito a guinea faggot. The guy had nerve for a priest.

They came over 10 Mile to Kelly Road, Debbie driving, turned right and there it was. "La Spezia." Terry said, "Closed on Sunday."

Debbie said, "Not if this is where Tony wants to meet. What time is it?"

"Four-twenty."

"Perfect. Ed said don't come before a quarter after." Turning into the lot she said, "There's a guy at the door who looks like your friend."

They parked in front of the place, its low-sloping roof and A-frame facade making her think of a ski lodge. She waited for Terry to get his bag of photos from the backseat and together they approached Vito Genoa holding the door open.

"How you doing, Father?"

It reminded Terry to hunch over a little more, show a stiffness in his neck as he turned his head. He said, "I think I'll live."

Following them inside Vito said, "You shouldn'ta said that to me."

Terry kept his neck stiff and turned his body to say, "Now you tell me."

They came through the empty restaurant, white tablecloths and place settings in the gloom, and the neat little guy Debbie recognized from last night, Vincent Moraco, motioned to them to approach the round table. She saw Tony Amilia in a blue warm-up jacket watching them as Ed spoke to him, Tony nodding. She didn't know if they were supposed to sit down at the table. It didn't look like it, because now Ed was looking at them—his expression solemn, he could be at a wake—and said, "You understand this is not a social occasion. I've told Mr. Amilia who you are, so go ahead, tell us what you have in mind."

Terry stepped up to the table with his athletic bag, zipping it open, and Ed said, "Father, you're gonna make the presentation?"

He didn't get a chance to answer. Vincent Moraco appeared next to him, took the bag from him and felt inside. He placed it on the table and said to Terry, "I'm gonna have to pat you down, Father, since we don't know you." Vincent's tone pleasant enough. "You could be some guy dressed like a priest."

Terry turned to him holding his suitcoat open. He said, "I understand. Go ahead."

Debbie kept her eyes on Tony, his face and balding crown tan from a winter in Florida. He wore tinted, wire-frame glasses and could be taken for a retired business executive, a former CEO now taking it easy.

Vincent Moraco stepped aside and now Terry began bringing out his photos, reaching out to lay them in rows across the middle of the table.

Debbie watched Tony lighting a cigarette, talking to Ed now, showing no interest in what Terry was doing. She wanted Terry to notice and hurry up, get on with it. He looked up, finally—

And said, "I'm sure you've seen pictures of homeless kids before, orphans with no one to take care of them. These kids represent thousands just like them, left on their own to search through garbage dumps for food, because their parents were murdered, most of them cut down with machetes. In my church in Rwanda are forty-seven bodies that've been lying there since the day I was saying Mass and saw them killed, slaughtered, many of them having their feet hacked off, something that was done by the Hutus all over Rwanda during the genocide."

Terry placed his hands on the table to take his weight, resting for a few moments before straightening again, slowly, to show his pain.

"I came here to visit parishes and raise money for the kids. But now I can't because of an injury I sustained last night when I slipped and took a fall in a restaurant called Randy's."

Debbie kept her eyes on Tony and Ed. No reactions. Terry was putting them to sleep.

She stepped forward saying, "Father, sit down, please, before you fall down," pulled a chair out and got him seated, Tony watching now, more interested.

"If you'll allow me to make the pitch," Debbie said to him, "I'll cut right to it." Tony seemed to give her a nod and she kept going. "I'm

involved in this, too. If you want to know why, it's because that cocksucker who owns the restaurant conned me out of sixty-seven thousand dollars and refuses to pay me back."

She had Tony's attention.

"The next time I saw the son of a bitch I hit him with my car, in
front of witnesses, and drew three years at Sawgrass Correctional
in Florida. I get my release and find out Randy's loaded, won millions in a divorce settlement and owns a successful restaurant downtown. I decided to go after him. I brought Fr. Dunn along—Father's
a friend of the family—with the hope that he could possibly get
Randy to look at himself, recognize what a fucking snake he is and
do what's right."

Tony was holding his cigarette in front of him, the ash so long it
was about to fall off.

"My plan, Mr. Amilia, was to ask Randy for two hundred and fifty
thousand, half for Father Dunn's children, the other half representing double what the snake owes me, to make up for money I was un-
able to earn while I was down those three years." Debbie cleared her
throat and said, "You mind if I have a glass of water?"

Tony didn't answer. He looked at Vincent Moraco. Vincent came
over, picked up a bottle of Pellegrino and poured her a glass. Debbie
took a long drink, paused and took another one. She said, "Thank
you," and got back into it.

"Something happened last night at the restaurant that changed our
plan. We were evicted from our table by two of your men. It upset Fr.
Dunn and he said something he's sorry for now. He called your Mr.
Genoa a faggot. Mr. Genoa naturally resented the remark and decked
Fr. Dunn, injuring his back. Let me say, in Fr. Dunn's behalf, he
spoke up because he resented our being removed from the table by a
party an hour late for their reservation." As Tony Amilia's gaze wandered over to Vincent, Debbie said, "Fr. Dunn's a man of God, but

he's also a stand-up guy. You have to be to run a mission in central Africa, up against street thugs killing people at will."

Debbie picked up the glass and took a sip of water.

"So the meeting with Mr. Agley, which followed, took a turn. Now we included a personal injury settlement, which we believed Mr. Agley would understand and prefer to going to court. I suggested to him how he could make things right and he told me to get lost. Actually, what he said to me was 'Don't fuck with me, kid. You're not in my league.' Well . . . I'm going to anyway. May I sit down?"

It would give her the table to hold on to.

Tony nodded, unaware of the cigarette ash on the front of his warm-up jacket.

She took the chair next to Terry's, put her hand for a moment on his shoulder and got ready.

"What I'd like to propose, Mr. Amilia—if you were to get the two-fifty from the snake, and make out a check for that amount payable to the Little Orphans of Rwanda Fund, you could write the entire amount off on your income tax. And, the press will see you as the savior of Father's orphans, the publicity coming at a time when you need it the most."

There was a silence in the room.

Tony continued to stare at Debbie, but said nothing. It was Ed Bernacki who broke the silence.

"If the check goes to the orphans, Deb, how do you get yours?"

"Ed, I hope you don't think Father would cheat me out of my share."

"All right, and how does this timely publicity get in the paper?"

"I'll make sure it happens. If Mr. Amilia is willing, with a photo of him handing Father the check."

"You don't think the intention would be obvious, coming at this time?"

"Why? Mr. Amilia is well known for his charitable interests. His being on trial right now, facing some rather absurd allegations, is beside the fact. His generosity speaks for itself."

Ed smiled. "You're laying it on pretty thick, Deb."

Her face remained solemn. "I can't help it, Ed, if it's how I feel."

Again a silence, everyone waiting for Tony the boss.

Finally he said to Terry, "Tell me something. These guys that cut off people's feet—why do they do that?"

20

MONDAY MORNING TERRY WOKE UP first, left Debbie in the king-size bed asleep and went downstairs to get the paper and put the coffee on.

Last night Debbie sat by the phone waiting for Ed Bernacki to call and tell them Tony said okay, Debbie full of confidence. "I know he will. Why wouldn't he? He's got the clout. All he has to do is tell Randy to give him the money." As they were leaving the restaurant yesterday Ed walked them out and she asked him what their chances were. Ed said he didn't have an opinion. "Tony's predictable in certain areas but this isn't one of them. You have to let Tony make up his mind. He says no, you forget about it, you don't try him again."

"If it doesn't work," Terry said last night, "then what, go back to Randy?"

Debbie said, "He'll do it. Didn't you notice? Tony likes me."

He brought Debbie a cup of coffee and sat looking at the little scam-
mer sleeping like an angel. He could imagine keeping it going, living
together. The idea of getting married had not come up. She'd said one
time she never planned on having kids and he said, "Why not?" He
said he'd always imagined having a family, three or four kids, and she
said, "Why didn't you? Instead of trying to fake out your mother all
those years." They could go round and round on that one: he wasn't
ready, hadn't met the right girl, never had a job he liked—all those ex-
cuses. There was no question in his mind Debbie could be the right
girl. Christ, look at her. And she was funny. How many girls were
funny? But that was the reason she wanted to be an entertainer and
why he couldn't see her keeping house. So there you were.

He said, "Deb?" Tried it once more and she opened her eyes.

"Did Ed call?"

"He's probably in court."

"He'll call when they break for lunch."

"My brother and the family'll be home this afternoon. They get in
about four."

Debbie said, "We'll have to change the bed. No, we'll have to do
the sheets and put the same ones back on. And the towels. Then what
do we do? You stay and I move out? Unless you set Fran straight,
then you can move in with me, we can play house."

It was funny that she said it that way. He nodded to the coffee on
the nightstand.

She picked it up, smiling at him. "You know what you are, Terry?
A saint. I said that to your brother one time while you were still in
Africa with your orphans, and your housekeeper with the cool skirts,
I said, 'Maybe he's a saint.' Your brother said, 'I wouldn't go that far.'
And then he said, 'But who knows?' See the impression you make?
You are, Terry, a very thoughtful person."

It didn't make him feel any different than he already felt, sitting there in a bedroom that wasn't his, on the verge of . . . whatever happened next, looking at a girl he slept with and believed he loved, experiencing tender feelings, but without that urge to take it further. There were similar times, moments, when he was with Chantelle in Ah-fri-ca and wondered what would come of it. Chantelle was beautiful, but not funny, though maybe she was funny in Kinyarwanda, something he would never know.

Debbie was sitting up now sipping her coffee. She said, "We get the check we'll have to open an account—"

"I told you, I already opened one," Terry said, and saw her eyes change. "Right after I got here Fran took me to Comerica. We can put it right in there, the Little Orphans Fund."

"Yeah. I forgot. I thought we'd be opening a joint account."

"What do you think I'm gonna do," Terry said, "withdraw it when you're not looking?"

She smiled. "That means you believe we're gonna get it."

She kept her cell phone turned on all morning and into the afternoon. It rang at one-fifty.

They were in the bedroom again with the clean sheets, Debbie trying to remember how they were tucked in and folded back when they pulled the covers down last night and jumped in. She moved to the window with her phone and stood looking out at the road, the shrubs and trees just beginning to show buds, Debbie taking it as a sign.

"Deb?" Ed's voice.

"What did he say?"

"He'll do it."

"Did you have to sell him?"

"You did that, kiddo. He likes you. He said to me after you left, 'How about her calling Randy a cocksucker?' He loved that."

"I thought he would, that's why I said it. Tapes, they're always calling guys that. So now what happens?"

"Once he has it in his hands I'll call you. Or somebody will. It can't take more than one visit. Those guys, I'm telling you—"

"Ed, why do you represent them?"

"I'm a lawyer. Didn't you know that?"

"Come on, tell me."

"All right. One, the cases are dynamic, you get a lot of press. Two, they pay on time. And three, they're fun to watch. Look at 'em all on TV in sitcoms—I get to see the real thing. Now, with the trial? I'm practically living with them. You know what I mean. If you know you're not gonna get hurt they're amusing guys to be around. If you're not laughing with 'em you're laughing at 'em, either way. I'll see you, and congratulations."

Terry was poised by the bed, still holding his side of the sheet. "When do we get it?"

"In a day or two. He has to have it in his hands first, Tony does."

"Well, you did it. If you'd left me up there I'd still be making the pitch and they'd all be asleep."

Debbie said, "I told you he liked me."

Angie answered the phone. She said, "Just a minute," and brought the portable into the bedroom where Vincent Moraco was pulling on his pants. He always left his shirt and socks on, though never seemed in a hurry. That was the problem this afternoon, trying to get him out of the apartment by six.

"Who is it?"

"I think it's Vito."

Vincent took the phone. It was Vito, Vito saying Tony wanted to see him right away. "He couldn't find you," Vito said. "I told him I bet I know where he's at. So, how was it?" Vincent hung up on him.

"Tony wants me."

Angie glanced at the clock. Five past six.

"Well, you better get going."

She wore a big loose white cotton sweater that hung down to cover her panties, pink ones. From there on were the whitest legs Vincent had ever seen in his life, like fuckin marble. Except they were always warm you ran a hand up them.

"You got somebody coming, haven't you?"

"Honey," Angie said, "I work. If I don't have somebody coming, you don't get your free ride."

"Who is it?"

"What difference does it make? A guy."

"One you got through Randy's?"

"I think so."

"Then two bills of it's mine."

What a prick. She'd bet anything he still had his First Communion money.

Vincent left.

A few minutes later Johnny Pajonny walked in.

"Yeah, now I remember," Angie said. "I was hoping it was you. Let me have your coat."

Johnny said, "I think I passed Vincent Moraco down the lobby, but I didn't look at him good."

"It's better you don't," Angie said, "he'll give you that 'You lookin at me?' I think it was in a movie."

Vincent had to stand around in the front hall waiting for Tony to see him, Vito saying Bernacki was in there. Vito went outside and

Vincent picked up thinking about the guy in Angie's lobby again, pretty sure now it was the other guy in their booth last night, with the priest, had the same leather coat on. The guy looked familiar, the face going back a few years to that cigarette business they were in, but Vincent couldn't put a name with the face.

Now Ed was coming out with his briefcase, giving him a nod. Vincent entered the study and approached Tony sitting at his desk that looked like a fuckin gold and red wedding cake—Tony saying one time Louie XIV used to have one like it—the red leather surface clean as usual except for papers directly in front of him.

"Go see Randy," Tony said, "and come back with a check for two-fifty."

Vincent couldn't believe it. "You serious, you giving 'em the money?"

What he gave Vincent was a hard stare, and shoved the papers across the desk toward him. "Have him sign this. It's a loan agreement."

"Tony, we own the guy. It's like you're taking it from yourself."

"What's he give us a week?"

Vincent said, "Five grand," without hesitating, even knowing what would come next.

"I thought we talked about eight."

"What he's got going there won't take the load. I settled on five with him, like the bookies."

"He's been paying it the past nine, ten months?"

"From what the girls bring in."

"It's enough to cover the five?"

"That's the figure I gave him. I don't ask what it comes out of. If he has to dip into his personal finances, well, that's how it goes." Vincent said then, anxious to change the subject, "You want to give this mick priest a quarter million to spend on a bunch of nigger kids?"

"The little girl gets half," Tony said. "You were there, you don't remember that?"

"Okay, but what do we care if Randy at one time or another fucked her over? You're giving 'em dough that's sitting there waiting for us to dip into whenever we want."

Tony kept staring at him. Without looking at the phone he reached over and put his hand on it.

"I call Randy right now and ask him how much he pays a week, he'll tell me five grand?"

Vincent hesitated. He wasn't ready for it and, Christ, he hesitated a moment too long, old Tony staring him down. What Vincent did was shrug and say, "Yeah, five," trying to sound a little surprised. Now he said, "I already told you that," with an edge, like he felt Tony was questioning his loyalty.

Tony's hand came away from the phone. He said, "Vincent, go get me the two-fifty."

21

RANDY DIDN'T SEE A PROBLEM with the priest. He gives
it to his brother to bring suit, then months of depositions, court dates
set and postponed for one reason or another, by then, or long before
then, the guy's back in Africa. Debbie, he knew he could handle. If
he got sixty-seven grand out of her once—he'd forgotten it was that
much—he could give her a few grand to calm her down and then play
with her, massage her ego, laugh at her jokes, even get her back if he
felt like it.

Ideally, the Mutt would get to Vincent this week, before Saturday,
and that would be the end of the eight-grand payoffs, at least till Tony
realized it wasn't coming in and by then he could be in some federal
lockup doing twenty years. That was the hope. Randy believed the
Mutt would make good and whack Vincent out because he was moti-
vated, he hated Vincent; but the Mutt, being stupid, would probably
fuck up and get caught, by either the mob or the cops, more likely by

the mob, unless he made the hit and took off, no time for good-byes, or to get paid. Randy did not believe the Mutt would try to implicate him. If he did, Randy was ready to act astonished and simply deny it.

He sat at his desk in soft light reading the latest review of the restaurant in *Hour Detroit*. Ambience, excellent. Service, very good. Food . . . and the Mutt walked in.

"You want to see me?"

"Hey, come on in and sit down. How's it going?"

"Okay."

The Mutt closed the door, came over to the desk and took a seat.

"Anything you want to tell me?"

"About what?"

"You're getting ready to do the deed, aren't you?"

"Oh. Yeah, you bet. What I'm doing is working on a plan, decide where's the best place to do it. I was thinking go to his house, only his wife'd be there, and I don't want to have to do her, too. If you know what I mean."

"I know exactly what you mean," Randy said, maintaining a soft approach now that he and this redneck retard were pals.

"I'd like to catch him like someplace having his supper."

"You don't mean here."

"No, some Italian restaurant, he's sitting there, has his napkin stuck in his collar—"

"A mom-and-pop place," Randy said, "that's been in the neighborhood for generations. Known for good basic pasta dishes, checkered tablecloths. Like in the movies."

"Yeah, like that."

"There aren't any," Randy said. "Detroit, for some reason, is not big on good Italian restaurants. There're a few . . . No, I was thinking the best way to do it, you follow him. You see him get in and out of his car. The right moment comes, you pop him and drive away. You do have a car?"

"I got the pickup I drove here. She needs a new batt'ry, I'm always having to jump her. What I been thinking of doing, go to Sears and get a new one."

"Or you could steal a car, just for the job. I understand," Randy said, "that's often the way it's done. You know, in case someone gets the license number."

"That's a good idea."

"Have you ever stolen a car?"

"When I was a kid—they called it joyriding. Yeah, we'd get us a car and go on up to Indianapolis and drive around in it. But what I was thinking," the Mutt said, "I could get me a driver. It would, you know, free me up. I wouldn't have to find a place to park when I go to do it."

"Ask one of your buddies?"

"I don't have none here. But I know a fella's done some time'd go for it."

Randy didn't like the sound of that one bit. He said, "Mutt, I can't see you needing help, like it's your first time and all," Randy getting a hint of down-home drawl going. "Hell, you get a pistol and shoot the guy. Do a drive-by, you don't need an assistant for that."

"I could."

"You did get hold of a pistol?"

"Not yet, but I will. I'm told there's nothing to getting a gun in this town."

Randy said, "Mutt? Let's do it before this Saturday. Okay?"

"Yeah, well, I'll get on it." The Mutt stood up and was about to go; he turned to Randy again. "You never said when you're gonna pay me."

Randy looked a little surprised, to show innocence. "I thought when the job's done. Isn't that the way?"

The Mutt said, "Well, most times—"

Randy stopped him. "Mutt, hold it."

The door opened and Vincent Moraco walked in. Mutt stepped aside as the capo approached the desk and Randy said, "Hey, Vincent, we were just talking about you."

Debbie was in the kitchen making grilled cheese sandwiches when the phone rang. Not hers, the one on the wall, so she let Terry get it, Terry in the library with the paper open looking up movies. A few minutes passed before he came in the kitchen.

"That was Fran. They're staying another day, be home tomorrow at four."

Debbie said, "What about the bed?"

"That's right, we sleep in it we'll have to do the sheets again."

Debbie said, "What if that's all we do, sleep in it, and in the morning we make the bed, good as new."

"Not do the sheets."

"Who's gonna know?"

"Just sleep in it."

"Sweetheart, we can fuck anywhere."

Now Vincent was in the chair at the desk facing Randy and the Mutt was over sitting under Soupy Sales. Randy thought Vincent might ask what they were saying about him, and then thought, No, not Vincent, he would never show he cared. No, he started right in.

"Tony wants you to give him two hundred fifty as a loan." He held up the papers. "You sign these, so Tony can turn around and give the check to the girl you fucked over. Tony says let that be a lesson to you."

Randy narrowed his eyes, but it didn't change anything. "How did she get to him?"

"With the priest. They got a religious shakedown going. She made the pitch."

"She tried the same game on me, I threw them out. She sold Tony Amilia?"

"He likes little broads like that."

"Come on—he's seventy-five years old."

"Hey. Tony wants it, he gets it."

"Okay. He makes out a check to this fund for the little orphans in Africa, writes it off . . . When does Tony repay the loan?"

"It's in here." Vincent dropped the papers on the desk. "You sign all three copies."

Randy looked at the papers, a promissory note, without picking them up. "Twenty-five years 'at a rate agreed upon—' I'm giving it to him."

"With a check," Vincent said, "out of one of your personal accounts."

"I don't have that much in one place."

"Write the check."

Randy had to think. He said, "Or," and paused. "What? I mean isn't there a way to get around it?" He said, "After all—"

And the answer came from the Mutt, over against the wall. He said, "Hell, whack him out, the guy that's getting the check. Then you won't have to."

There was a silence. Not a long one. Vincent picked it up saying, "Sure, that's the first thing you think of, but you got to look at it good, think it through."

The idea, coming the way it did, got Randy sitting up straight. It was in his mind to wonder why Vincent would go for it, but he said, "What's to think about? Christ, just do it."

Vincent said, "I'm talking about how, you fuck."

"Get a guy who knows how."

"Not anybody from the crew, no way."

Randy's mind was racing now. "Run him down. Hit him crossing the street with a truck, hell, anything, a Buick Riviera."

Vincent turned to look over his shoulder at the Mutt. "He's done it, the farm boy. Tell him to go take a guy out. The Mutt says okay, goes and does the guy. Hey, Mutt?"

The Mutt said, "You bet," and looked at Randy looking at him, the two making eye contact for the first time since Vincent walked in. What surprised Randy was the calm expression on the Mutt's face. The Mutt got it—accepting a contract from a guy he had a contract to take out. If that wasn't cool . . . And if Vincent had confidence in him, Vincent a made guy, into this kind of thing, then maybe the Mutt wasn't as dumb as he looked. Man, this was weird. It allowed Randy to settle back.

He said to Vincent, "He can handle it?"

"I told you, he's done it."

Turning to the Mutt again, "What do you say?"

"Yeah, I'll do'er. But now which person was it again?"

"The priest."

The Mutt said, "Oh," hesitated and said, "I guess it's okay, I'm Baptist."

"Then it's a deal," Randy said. "Do'er."

"Yessir, but who's gonna pay me?"

Randy said right away, "Vincent will take care of you," knowing he'd get an argument.

Of course, Vincent saying, "You're the one out the cash."

"But you have more to lose than I do," Randy said, "if Tony finds out." He could stare back at Vincent now—fuck him. He could say, "I wondered, Why don't you want Tony to give them the two-fifty? And then I realized, shit, you think of it as yours. It's where the eight yards a week comes from. I wouldn't be surprised if you're skimming off the top. Tony goes away you can keep the whole thing, even raise it, uh? Take whatever you want. The restaurant business, hell, it's just a front. What I am really is a fucking bank."

Vincent listened, sat there watching him. Didn't get excited or do any more than stare with his sleepy eyes. No, he seemed quite calm—and that did begin to work on Randy's central nervous system and tighten him up. He was pretty sure he was right; but, shit, he might've gone too far.

Randy felt the need to add then, with a slight smile, "But who's complaining?"

Vincent got up from the chair to stand over the desk. "Sign the papers and cut a check."

Randy said, "Why? You don't need it now, do you?"

"I go back to Tony I got the check in my hand he sent me to get. Understand? Write the fuckin check."

Randy signed the copies of the promissory note. He brought a checkbook out of the desk drawer, made a check out to Tony Amilia in the amount of two hundred and fifty thousand dollars and laid the check on the papers. He watched Vincent pick it up and fold the papers with the check inside. No thank-you or anything.

What he did say, "You and I're gonna have a talk, smart guy." Turned and said to the Mutt on his way out, "Do the priest right away."

He was through the door before the Mutt came out of his chair and started after him.

Randy called out, "Where you going?" But the Mutt was already gone.

He caught up with Vincent in the restaurant and followed him out to the street. Vincent turned to him now.

"What?"

"How much you paying me?"

It took him a minute to say, "Twenty-five."

"Twenty-five what?"

"Hunnert—the fuck you think?"

Now the Mutt had to think a minute. "Okay. And I need a pistol, a clean one."

"I'll see what I can do."

He started to turn away and the Mutt said, "You better pay me when you gimme the pistol as I'll be taking off soon as I'm done."

"I said I'll see what I can do."

"You have to do better'n that," the Mutt said. "You want the priest done or not?"

Now Vincent gave him a look that reminded the Mutt of his mom, the times he'd forget and say "shit" in front of her and she'd call him "young man" and threaten to wash his mouth out with soap, but never did. These people were like her, they liked to try and scare you. Vincent gave him the look but then said, "Stay around here. I'll call you." See? They got by on dirty looks.

22

TUESDAY MORNING TERRY WAS UP, Debbie still in bed: Terry coming through the dining room with coffee for Debbie, heading for the foyer. He glanced at the window as the limo was turning into the drive, 11:15 A.M., Fran back from Florida with the family a good five hours before they were supposed to arrive. Terry placed the mug of coffee on the dining room table, flew across the foyer and up the stairs two and three at a time. He was going to wake Debbie up with the coffee and tell her she slept like a teenager. What he did instead was get close to her face and say, "They're back." It opened her eyes. "Fran, the whole family, they're here." He heard her say, "They can't be," but that's all. Debbie was cool, rolled out of bed in her T-shirt and they tugged and smoothed and tucked the covers together; Terry ran out to the hall and was on the stairs as the front door opened, the two little girls running in, stopping as they looked up and saw him.

Jane the older one and Katy still a baby the last time he was here; the girls would be eight and six now. Coming down the stairs he said, "Hey, girls, you remember me? Your uncle Terry."

Mary Pat was behind them now, looking a little surprised but okay, so far. Fran came in with the luggage, placed the bags on the floor looking at Terry but didn't say anything until Terry said, "You're early," and Fran said, "Yeah, we decided to get going. You take the one o'clock flight, the one I told you we'd be on, it only gives you a couple hours in the morning, get any sun . . . Hey, I called Padilla. He said you had a good talk and he's, you know, satisfied."

"Yeah, he seemed like a nice guy."

Mary Pat hadn't moved, staring at him, Mary Pat in a long black coat with some kind of black fur collar, her blond hair in the same suburban bob he always pictured when he thought of her. She said, "How are you, Terry?" sounding like she wanted to know. But then as he was saying "Fine, good to see you, Mary Pat," she said, "Girls, your uncle Terry is now Fr. Terry, Fr. Terry Dunn. He's become a priest." She gave each of the girls a push and they came over to hug him, putting their arms around his hips and his legs until he got down with them and they each hugged him around the neck. He gathered them to him, his hands feeling their small bones. The older one, Jane, said, "We know where you were. You were in Africa." He said, "Yes, I was, and if you'd like, I'll tell you about it and show you pictures I have brought with me." He wanted to be natural with them and not sound like he was talking to children, but he did, talking much too slowly, picking the words. He said, "Listen, you little cuties, we'll sit down later on, I'll show you a bunch of little African kids and tell you what they do . . . you know, how they live . . ."

Fran saved him. He said, "So you did take pictures."

"Yeah, a lot."

He straightened and the girls were moving around him, going up the stairway and he wanted to stop them, but there was nothing he could say. They would go upstairs, run into Debbie—

Mary Pat said, "Is that your coffee on the table?"

It brought him around again, thinking fast. "Yeah, I was coming from the kitchen when I saw the limo pull into the drive . . ." Thinking too fast—why was he coming down the stairs—if the coffee . . . It didn't matter. The girls were on their way down the staircase now and Mary Pat and Fran were looking at Debbie standing at the top in her sweater and jeans.

She gave them a nice smile. "Well, hi. You must be Mary Pat. I'm Debbie Dewey." She was coming down the staircase now. "You know I do investigative work for Fran every once in a while? I stopped by to pick up Father and he offered to show me the house I've heard so much about, and I love it. You have excellent taste, Mary Pat." She was down to the foyer now saying, "Well, hi, girls," and offering her hand to Mary Pat, Fran saying, "Yeah, this is the Debbie I've told you about," Debbie saying to Mary Pat, "I finally get a chance to meet you." They shook hands, Debbie saying now, "I was going to take Father to visit parishes, line up a few Sundays when he can make his mission appeals, the Little Orphans of Rwanda Fund. But, listen, you probably want to visit, I'll get out of your way," but then took time to bend over, hands on her knees in front of the little girls. "Hi, I'm Debbie. Let me guess, you're Jane, right? Hi, Jane. And you must be Katy. Hi, Katy. You both have lovely bedrooms, neat dolls."

Terry watched with a smile fixed to his face. She didn't know how to talk to kids any more than he did. He said, "I'll get your coat," and started for the hall closet.

"I think it's in the kitchen," Debbie said.

Now Terry was heading toward the dining room. "That's right, you came in and we made coffee . . ." He picked the mug up from the table telling himself to keep his mouth shut, for Christ sake, Mary Pat following him now as far as the dining table. He got the raincoat from the kitchen and was back in time to see Mary Pat inspecting the table, rubbing the tips of her fingers over the place where the mug of hot coffee had been sitting on the polished surface. She didn't say anything. Not until she was in the foyer again and Terry was helping Debbie on with her coat.

"I wondered whose car that was in the drive."

Debbie said, "Oh." She said, "Oh, yeah, that's mine. Well, listen, it was really a pleasure meeting you."

Terry watched Mary Pat, the suburban lady pretty cool so far, meeting Debbie, not making an issue of the stain on the table, Mary Pat telling Debbie it was nice to have met her, too, and Debbie was out.

Fran got out next. He said every day you stay in Florida more work piles up. He said he had a pile of work to do, a pile of work.

That left Terry with Mary Pat and the luggage.

She said, "You want to help me up with these?"

Three nylon hanging bags and two backpacks, he slid them from his shoulders to the carpeted bedroom floor and stood waiting for Mary Pat to look at the bed. He knew he was acting like a teenage kid—a girl upstairs and all of a sudden the family walks in—but couldn't help it; there was no way to explain the situation, the bed most of all. He watched Mary Pat walk past the bed to a matching white love seat and chair, a low table between them, in the window alcove. There were plants on the table, plants all over the house, he'd forgot to water. Mary Pat sat down in the love seat looking at the plants, then motioned to him.

"Shut the door and come over here. I won't hurt you."

He could hear the girls down the hall as he pushed the door closed. He started toward Mary Pat and she said, "Do you have a cigarette?"

He raised both hands to touch his T-shirt. "Not on me."

"Look in the top drawer of the dresser, the one close to you. There should be a pack in there."

He opened the drawer, felt around among panty hose and brought out a pack of Marlboro. "There's an ashtray in there, too."

"And there should be a lighter, a pink Bic. Bring everything."

He handed her the cigarettes and lighter and placed the ashtray on the table. "I didn't know you smoked."

"You thought I made casseroles and cookies and went to PTA meetings. Fran thinks all I do is vacuum the kitchen floor."

"Do you?"

"Not more than twice a day."

"Does it need it?"

She smiled at him. "Does it matter? Sit down, Terry. Would you like a cigarette?" He shook his head and she lit one with the pink Bic. She said, "You never know what to say to me, do you?"

"We talk."

"Not really. How was Africa?"

"It wasn't too bad."

"See what I mean? You spent five years in Rwanda and it wasn't too bad. What wasn't, the food, the incidence of disease? Did you like living there?"

"I was comfortable."

"Did you drink much?"

"No more than I did before."

"Were you bored?"

"Sometimes."

"No more than you ever were at home, uh? When aren't you bored, Terry?"

"Does Fran know you smoke?"

"Of course he does. I hide it from the girls."

"What if they come in?"

"The door's closed. They know they have to knock first, see if it's okay." She drew on the cigarette. "I'm gonna knock on your door, Terry, and ask you a question. I hope you'll be honest with me."

He was going to wait, but then said, "There's never been anything between Fran and Debbie, if that's what you're worried about."

"Oh, for God's sake, I know that. Fran's conscience would drive him crazy. Terry, he's president of the Dads' Club at school. He's the youngest member of the Knights of Columbus in the Archdiocese of Detroit. His buddies are like veterans left over from some war long past, even the uniforms look ancient."

"He's got the admiral's hat, and the sword? He never mentioned it to me."

Mary Pat drew on her cigarette. She waited.

"All right, what's the question. You want to know if Debbie and I slept in your bed?"

"I knew someone did as soon as I walked in the room. But even before that, seeing little Debbie at the top of the stairs, and all that cheerful chatter—"

"I'm not good at that," Terry said.

"No, you never were. But there's more to it," Mary Pat said. "Sleeping in my bed with a woman is one thing . . . Did you change the sheets?"

"Not yet."

"But a priest sleeping in the bed with a woman—you could never admit to that, not with all your years of Catholic schools, the idea would be shocking, scandalous." She drew on her cigarette and said, "You're stuck, Terry. You have to tell me the truth."

"I have."

"Nothing but the truth, so help you God. You're not a priest, are you?"

He shook his head. "No."

And remembered Debbie asking if he felt better now, and he did. But then saw where this was going, Mary Pat saying, "It's still a sin, I suppose, but not as serious as breaking a vow? You have to remember I was a good Presbyterian before I met Fran and became a convert. And the way they're relaxing the rules, I'm not sure what's a sin and what isn't anymore. Debbie of course knows you're not a priest."

"She guessed the same as you did."

"Terry, I didn't guess, I know you. You're not selfless enough, or that security-minded or devoted to your mother."

"You told the girls I was Fr. Terry."

"Maybe for a moment I believed it. Then Debbie appeared, little sleepyhead trying to look innocent."

"Fran believes it."

"He wants to more than anything. Then he doesn't have to worry about you ending up in jail. But deep down? I'm not so sure." She said, "I loved little Debbie calling you Father. 'I'm taking Father to visit parishes so he can make his mission appeal, for the little orphans.' The bed still warm. You and the Deb are hot for each other?"

"That's where we are right now, yeah."

"You did do it in my bed."

"Only once."

"Five years in Africa, you come back—"

"Maybe twice."

"Terry . . . ?"

"Another time where you're sitting." He believed he saw Mary Pat move her butt on the love seat, squirm, just a little. "Once in the library, the other times at her apartment, and that's all."

"I admire your restraint," Mary Pat said. "Tell me, if you're not a priest, what are you?"

"I guess I'm back to whatever I was."

"Terry, don't act dumb, okay, or innocent—'back to whatever I was'—you're a crook, admit it. You're gonna put on your Roman collar and con parishes into giving you money. Isn't that what you are, Terry, a con man?"

"That was the original idea," he said, serious, telling his sister-in-law of all people what she wanted to know and looking at it himself, hearing himself. He said, "But now we have a benefactor," Terry smiling just a little, seeing Tony Amilia sitting at that table in his warm-up jacket. Mary Pat might think that was funny, too, if he told her. And maybe not. She wasn't smiling.

She said, "We. Debbie's in it with you?"

"She's helping out."

"Con one person now, this benefactor, instead of a bunch of people sitting in church?"

He didn't have to answer that one. The girls were banging on the bedroom door, calling their mom. Mary Pat said, "Let them in, will you?" stubbing out her cigarette, then waving her hand in the smoke rising from the ashtray.

Terry walked over and opened the door and the girls looked up at him, hesitant. He started back to his chair and now they came in, Jane saying, "We can't find our backpacks."

"They're right there," Mary Pat said. "Uncle Terry brought them up for you." She said, "Girls, come here for a minute." They came over to their mother's side of the table, the six-year-old, Katy, pressing close to her and Mary Pat brushed the girl's hair from her forehead. "Tell Uncle Terry what you want to be when you grow up." She had to be coaxed. "Tell him, honey, he'd like to know."

"I want to be a saint," Katy said.

"Like the one you're named after," Terry said, "Saint Catherine?"

"Which Saint Catherine?"

He had to think. "Saint Catherine of Siena?"

"She's okay. She was a mystic and could see guardian angels. My favorite is Saint Catherine of Alexandria, virgin and martyr. They put her on a spiked wheel, only it broke? So they cut her head off."

Mary Pat said, "Katy loves martyrs."

Terry said, "You know what they did to Saint Agatha?"

"Is she the one, they cut off her boobs and threw her in a burning fire?"

"Hot coals," Terry said.

Katy was edging around the table toward him. "Do you know any more?"

"How about Saint Sebastian?"

"He was stuck with arrows."

"Katy's into saints," Mary Pat said. "She picked it up from Jane who got most of them off the Internet—they're little cyber Catholics—but now Jane's into serious tennis, USTA competition, ten-and-under age group. She started last year when she was seven, lost her first couple of matches and hasn't lost since. Jane's now regional champ," Mary Pat said, touching Jane now, fooling with her hair. "Aren't you, sweetheart?"

She said to Terry, "You know who I want to play? Serena Williams, she won the Open."

"Isn't she a lot older than you are?"

"Yeah, but when I'm her age? She'll only be like twenty-four or -five." She turned to her mom then. "How come you said he's Uncle Terry instead of Father?"

"I thought he became a priest," Mary Pat said, "but he really didn't. He was kidding."

Jane said, "Oh," and walked away from them. Katy caught up with her and Jane said, "You're not suppose to call him Father anymore," and Katy said, "I know." Mary Pat waited until they'd picked up their backpacks and were out of the room.

"You see how easy it is? No big deal. Uncle Terry isn't a priest. Okay. They think you're just a good guy who knows something about saints. Nothing wrong with that." She said, "Do you realize this is the first time we've talked?"

"Mary Pat, you could've been a good prosecuting attorney."

"I could've been good at a lot of things. I chose to marry your brother and have children and be a homemaker, and that's what I am. If you want to be a crook, Terry, that's up to you. I won't pry anymore or get in your way. I just want to ask you one more question. Maybe two."

"Go ahead."

"Does she really like the way I've done the house?"

"Debbie? She loves it. It reminds her of the home she grew up in. What's the other question?"

"Will she stick by you, Terry, if you fuck up?"

23

THE MUTT CAME IN AT noon. He stuck his head in Randy's office, said, "It's all set for tonight," and started away.

"Wait a minute—Mutt? What's all set?"

The Mutt appeared in the doorway again. "I'm gonna do both of 'em tonight. Mr. Moraco first."

"Where?"

"I don't know yet. I'm waiting to find out where to meet him. You know, so he can gimme the gun and my money."

Randy was standing at the desk in his shirt sleeves, dark shirt, light-colored tie. He sat down. "You don't have a gun?"

"I guess I didn't tell you. Mr. Moraco's giving me twenty-five to do the priest and he'll furnish the gun. That's the deal. So I'll have me one by then."

Randy said, "To do Vincent."

"Yeah, once he gives it to me."

Randy took his time. "You're gonna use the gun Vincent gives you to do Vincent."

"I may as well, huh?" And said, "Well, I'll see you" as he started out.

"Wait."

The man's simplicity was overwhelming: this little Hoosier, bless his heart, standing there with his muscles and scar tissue waiting now to be dismissed, hat in hand—Randy was thinking—if he had a hat.

Randy said to him, "Mutt? Be careful."

Midafternoon Johnny Pajonny was waiting for him at the bar. The Mutt had called saying he wanted to talk to him. Johnny asked what about, and the Mutt said, "You know. Remember what you mentioned the other night?" He wouldn't say more than that on account of the phone might be bugged. It was pitiful the way this guy's mind worked. Johnny assumed it was about the whoers. After the Mutt had fixed him up with Angie, Johnny said he'd be interested in trying some of the other girls. He had a deal going: he'd told Angie he was a mob guy and expected the usual mob discount on the three hundred she ordinarily got, so he only had to pay her a bill and a half—

There he was now, the Mutt coming out from the back of the restaurant, but then the bartender said something to him as he was going past and the Mutt went back to the other end of the bar and picked up the phone. After a minute he was waving to the bartender—he needed a pen. Now he was writing something down—back at the end where the waiters got their drink orders filled.

Johnny was pretty sure Angie liked him and didn't mind the discount. She was so good it was quick anyway. He could always go back; but why not try another one of the whoers and go for the mob discount? That's what he thought this was about.

The Mutt walked up to him and said, "I'm gonna take you up on your offer."

Johnny hadn't offered him anything, so he wasn't sure what the guy meant. He said, "Yeah . . . ?"

"You offered to drive for me."

Johnny said, "Lemme get a drink," and ordered a vodka tonic, giving himself time to readjust his mind, switch from thinking about whoers to contract hits, and talk to a guy Johnny believed might never've even fired a gun before outside of a single-shot .22 down on the farm, shooting squirrels and chipmunks. He would accept the Mutt having shanked some con in the yard, and maybe, just maybe, he might've shot a guy in a bar fight as they tussled. But a real contract? Look at the guy. It didn't seem likely.

"You're saying to me you have a contract to make a hit and you want me to drive the car."

"Two," the Mutt said.

"Two what?"

"I got two contracts, both for tonight."

Johnny got his drink and took a good sip. "You have a car?"

"Don't the driver supply the car?"

"You think I'm gonna drive mine? No, the way it's done, the hitter supplies the car. Otherwise it doubles the risk for the driver. First, for boosting a car, and second, I could go down as an accessory. No, I'm sorry, I can't help you."

"All right, I'll get a car," the Mutt said.

Now Johnny hesitated. "Say you do, where you want to go?"

The Mutt took a cocktail napkin from his shirt pocket, unfolded it and looked at his handwriting. "Franklin Street between St. Aubin and Dubois. You know where that's at?"

"Yeah, but there ain't nothing there, it's all warehouses and old empty buildings. Let's see, outside of some bars, the Soup Kitchen's close by there."

"He said that, the Soup Kitchen was on a corner down there, not too far."

"What's the guy gonna be doing, sitting in his car waiting for you?" It didn't make sense.

But the Mutt said, "I guess."

"What time?"

"Eight o'clock. He said sharp."

"The guy that gave you the contract."

"Yeah. You want to drive me?"

Johnny gave himself more time saying, "It depends on what you're paying."

"Well, I'm not sure, tell you the truth."

This guy had no idea what he was doing. Still, it didn't sound like he was making it up, so Johnny pried some more. He said, "You want to negotiate driver pay based on what you're getting? That's one way it's done."

"They're paying twenty-five each—"

"That's right, you got two contracts."

"Twenty-five hunnert for one, twenty-five thousand for the other."

Johnny said, "Uh-huh." This guy was pure idiot. Get him to explain that. But then thought, No, don't. Ask him . . . Johnny said, "You get half down?"

"The twenty-five hunnert I'm getting up ahead, the whole thing. But I haven't got none of the other one, the big one."

Johnny said, "Mutt, the way it works, the only way it works, you get half down or you don't do the job. Otherwise you could get fucked over real good. You know what I mean? No, the first rule of this kind of business, Mutt, you gotta get half down."

The Mutt said, "Okay then."

Johnny took time to light a cigarette and sip his vodka tonic. "All right, here's the deal. I come by here . . . No, I better not. Lemme think . . . Where you have to go for the other one?"

"I don't know yet."

"Mutt, I hate to say it, but you don't sound like you know shit what you're doing."

"I need to find out where to go, that's all."

Jesus Christ. Johnny took another sip of his drink. "I'll tell you what, you get hold of a car and come by the MGM Grand—you know where it's at?"

Mutt squinted, like he was trying to picture the place.

"The gambling casino, Mutt, you can't fuckin miss it, over by the Lodge freeway? That'll be your test, to find it. You pull up to the main entrance there at half past seven with five grand in your hand, slide over, you got yourself a driver."

"I'll be there," the Mutt said.

The guy was an idiot, but so what? He'd have the five or he wouldn't.

Randy looked up from his desk to see the Mutt back again, the Mutt saying he forgot to mention he was supposed to get half the money down on the contract and could he have it now. But not sounding convinced that he should, still hat in hand.

"You want to make sure you're paid," Randy said. "I can understand that, but you're a little late for it to do you any good today."

"Why's that?"

"The banks are closed. You won't be able to deposit the check until tomorrow anyway. Why not wait and get the full amount, twenty-five big ones paid to the order of Searcy J. Bragg, Jr."

"I also forgot to tell you," the Mutt said, "I want it in cash, twelve thousand and five hunnert dollars."

"Well, now, that's not possible."

"Cash, or no deal."

Randy stood up and pulled the pockets out of his pants. He saw the Mutt grin and told him, "You have me at a disadvantage. Where'm I supposed to get it if the banks close at four?"

"You lock your door," the Mutt said, "it's a woman or it's money business."

"And what's that, a Hoosierism?"

"Heidi or some woman's in here with you or you're getting money out of the secret place you keep it. You pay my wages in cash, you pay Mr. Moraco his end in cash, and you said when you gimme the job, you said cash or check."

Yes, he did say that; but Randy's plan from the beginning was to give the Mutt a check and stop payment on it as soon as the Mutt took off. Since it was hardly something he could explain, Randy said, "All right, I'll give you your check."

"I want cash."

"I can write you a check, Mutt, for the entire amount, right now."

"Cash or no deal."

Randy took his time. "Has Vincent paid you?"

"For the priest? Tonight he's gonna."

"How much?"

"I told you before, twenty-five."

"Really? I know you said he's getting you a gun—"

"You don't believe me," the Mutt said, "call him up. Pay me first, it'll be the last time you ever hear his voice. And never again have to watch him eat."

It gave Randy a picture of Vincent Moraco, a dinner napkin tucked in his collar, head lowered over his free lunch, and it was enough to get Randy to change his mind, stop his quibbling. He said to the Mutt, "You're right, you're doing me an enormous favor and should have your money whatever way you want it. I have to confess, Mutt, at times I tend to lose sight of main objectives and become niggardly over details."

The Mutt said, "You do?"

The machete was still in the kitchen, where Johnny had been playing with it.

Mary Pat asked Terry why he'd brought it home and he told her it was a reminder. She said she wouldn't think he would have to be reminded of an experience so horrifying, all those poor people murdered. He said he found the machete in the church, the place where it was used, and it brought back to him parts of the scene in detail that were like—what do you call it—tableaux, hideous moments caught in stop-motion, silent, without the screams, the din of voices. She didn't ask about the details, so he kept them to himself. He told the little girls the knife was used to cut sugarcane and hack stalks of bananas from the trees.

And he'd left the canvas bag of photos in the kitchen.

When they were ready to look at the pictures he placed them on the butcher-block table, displaying all of them except a stack bound with green rubber bands he dropped back in the bag. The girls climbed up on stools to have a look, got interested, knelt on the stools to get closer, over the photos, and began asking questions. What's he doing? Looking for scraps of charcoal so he can sell it or make a fire. Why? So he can have something to eat, roast an ear of corn. Why doesn't his mom do it? He doesn't have a mom, he's an orphan. What's an orphan? You know, Mom told us. I forget what one is. A kid who doesn't have a mom or dad. They let him play with fire? He's not playing, he knows what he's doing. Rwanda, you grow up in a hurry or you don't make it. The ones here're at the orphanage, playing some kind of game. What's he doing? That's a girl. How do you know? She's wearing a dress. It doesn't look like a dress. How come they don't have any hair? They shave it off so they won't get, like, bugs in their hair. What kind of bugs? Any kind, Africa, I never saw so many bugs in my life. On the wall, they look like wallpaper designs moving. He looked over at Mary Pat, at the sink rinsing lettuce. What's he doing? That's a garbage dump and he's looking for food, anything he can eat, even if it's, well, a little rotten. Won't he get sick? Probably, if not from that from something else. Why doesn't he go to the store? He's poor, he doesn't have any money. Why doesn't his mom go? He doesn't have one. I explained that, these kids're orphans. Why? I just told you, they don't have parents. Why not? Oh. The parents died, so most of the kids don't have a place to live. Mom said that's why you came home, to get money from people for the little orphans.

He looked over at Mary Pat again, Mary Pat looking back at him this time. She said, "Why don't one of you girls get the atlas? Show Uncle Terry where he lives?"

Katy wanted to get it so they let her, and while they were waiting the phone rang, the one on the wall by the sink. Mary Pat got it and turned to Terry.

"Your fund-raising partner."

———

"What're you doing?"

"Showing my pictures to the girls."

"Does Mary Pat know?"

"Everything. I mean every thing."

"What'd she say? . . . Oh, you can't talk, can you? Listen, Ed Bernacki called, we're going to see Tony. And guess where?"

"I don't know."

"His house. You remember Ed told me no one gets in his house except family and goombas? We're going to his house. Oh, and you're being picked up."

"You're coming by? When?"

"No, they're sending a car for you, seven-thirty."

"Why?"

"Ed says we're seeing him, I don't ask questions."

"Are you being picked up?"

"Yes, we both are."

"Then why don't we go together?"

"Maybe we are, but the way Ed said it, it sounded like we're being picked up separately."

"Why can't you get picked up and then you come over and pick me up?"

"Maybe that's what'll happen."

"Can you check with Ed, tell him we want to go together?"

"What're you worried about, you nitwit, he's giving us the money."

The girls, head-to-head over the atlas open on the counter, were looking for Rwanda, Katy saying, "Mom showed us where it is." Jane saying, "It's hard to find. It's suppose to be right here . . . somewhere."

"It's hard to find," Terry said, "even when you know where it is. You see Lake Victoria? Rwanda's a half inch or so to the left. The one that's mostly green, and it is, the whole country's like a big vegetable garden."

"Aren't there any wild animals?"

"There isn't room for them, it's almost all farmland, except here in this corner where the gorillas live, up in the mountains."

"We saw gorillas in a movie. A lady was talking to them. She said you have to be real quiet or the gorillas get mad, like they think you might hurt them."

"That's the way gorillas are," Terry said, "you have to be careful around them." He looked up to see Mary Pat on the other side of the table, watching him. He said to her, "We're meeting our benefactor later on this evening. Anthony Amilia. You know who he is?"

She hesitated before saying, "Of course I do," turned to the sink again to gather the lettuce in a dishtowel and carry it to the refrigerator. When she looked at him again, all she said was, "Does Fran know?"

"He left, I haven't had a chance to talk to him."

"Will you call him?"

"If you want me to. I was hoping he'd be home before I left."

"Terry, Fran and I don't keep secrets from one another. I called him after we talked this morning."

"You ratted me out, huh?" She didn't smile and he said, "You know I would've told him the whole story. The only reason I haven't, Fran was still talking to the prosecutor about me, even after I got home. I felt he couldn't in conscience do that unless he believed I was a priest."

She said, "Being deceitful doesn't bother you?"

"Not too much, no. You think I should've gone to prison instead of Rwanda?"

"I have no idea," Mary Pat said, "what you did in Rwanda, besides take pictures of kids."

"I thought I did okay," Terry said, "considering. I said Mass once in a while, always Christmas and Easter. I heard Confession every week. I asked my housekeeper one time if she thought I was doing any good. She said I could do better."

For a moment there Mary Pat looked as though she might be in shock, speechless. He knew, though, it wouldn't last.

He said, "Things aren't always what they seem, are they?"

24

THE MUTT WAS LATE PICKING up Johnny. Seven-fifteen, when he stepped out the front entrance of Randy's, was a busy time, parking attendants in their red jackets jumping in cars to gun 'em out of there. The Mutt said to one of 'em, "Hey, boy, bring Mr. Agley's Caddy you come back, hear?" Shit, it must've taken him fifteen minutes, pulled up in the car and the Mutt said, "What's wrong with you, taking so long?" This Tootsie Roll sassed him, saying, "I couldn't find it, boy." And the Mutt remembered Randy telling him one time to quit calling the parking attendants "boy," saying, "Colored guys don't like it, they hear it as a term of disrespect. You didn't call 'em 'boy' in prison, did you?" The Mutt said he didn't call 'em nothing, as he never had a reason to speak to any of 'em. Then, to make it worse, he couldn't locate the entrance to the goddamn MGM Grand gambling casino on the first pass and had to go around again, the freeway right there messing him up. He thought Johnny would be sore 'cause he was late. Uh-unh . . .

Getting in the car as the Mutt slid over Johnny said the only thing he needed to know, "You got it?"

The Mutt handed him a fat wad of bills and Johnny had to face the fact the guy was serious, there was a hit going down and he was driving the fuckin car. Johnny took time to open the wad and riffle one end. All hundreds. He said, "Well, all right," to get himself with it, show the Mutt he was cool. "What time you got?"

The Mutt had to work his watch out of the sleeves of his leather coat and his bodyshirt. He held it close to the Cadillac instrument panel, in front of the digital clock, and said, "A quarter of."

They were moving now, making their way through the west side of downtown, Johnny thinking, Lafayette or Fort Street over to Woodward, hang a right to Jefferson . . . He said, "Where'd you get the Caddy? Man, it's still got that new-car smell in it."

"It's Randy's."

"Jesus Christ—he know you took it?"

"I asked was he going anywheres, he said no."

"You realize if somebody at the scene, anybody, a witness, spots the license plate the cops'll trace it back to him?"

"I was Randy I'd say the car was stolen."

"What if they trace it to you?"

"I'd tell 'em Randy don't allow me to drive the car. Anybody says I took it's a liar, wanting to get me 'cause they say I disrespect 'em calling 'em 'boy.' "

"The fuck're you talking about?"

"It don't matter."

Johnny said, "Lemme guess. Randy's the one gave you the contract."

"That's right."

"But has no idea you took his car."

"What he don't know won't hurt him, will it?"

"Randy get you the gun?"

"The one I'm gonna use? I don't have it yet."

It got Johnny agitated again and he had to stay cool. "What're you talking about? We have to stop and pick it up?"

"Uh-unh, the guy I'm supposed to hit? He's giving it to me."

Johnny couldn't think of the next question 'cause there were too many next questions. In a way then he changed the subject, asking the Mutt, "Who's this you gonna hit? You know him?"

"Yeah, Mr. Moraco."

And Johnny said, "Jesus Christ—hey, come on."

"Randy hates him."

"I imagine, yeah, if it's worth twenty-five grand have him taken out." Big numbers, Johnny feeling the wad in his pocket, making a big-time move with this goofball calling the shots. He said, "And it's Vincent giving you the piece to use?"

"Yeah, for the other one."

"That's right, I forgot."

"We keep going after this one's done."

Johnny's brain was still trying to handle the idea, Jesus Christ, of driving this hayseed to hit Vincent Moraco. "But he doesn't know, Vincent doesn't—no, there's no way."

"What?"

"Or he wouldn't be giving you the fuckin gun."

"'Course not, he don't suspect shit."

Johnny was learning you had to pay close attention to what the

Mutt said and ask the right question. Then it made sense, even if you still couldn't fuckin believe it.

They were on Jefferson now heading east past the Renaissance Center's cluster of glass towers, the city's skyline. It was a nice evening, fifty-five degrees out. Johnny settled down. He was here, he might as well go through with it. Christ, five grand—it couldn't take that long. He wouldn't have to get out of the car . . .

"Okay, you're gonna clip Vincent Moraco."

"Yes sir, shoot him in the head, make sure."

"He hands you the gun and you pop him."

"I collect my money first."

"Mutt, you want to make sure the gun's loaded."

"That's a good point. Man, I don't want to shoot him and all I hear's click click. Yeah, that's a good thing to remember, check it first."

Johnny thinking, The fuck'm I doing here?

Terry in his black suit and Roman collar, ready to go, stood at the front window in the living room, anxious. Fran, coping with his mountain of work, called to say he wouldn't be home before eight. The girls'd had their supper and were in the library watching MTV. Mary Pat was in the kitchen. When the Chrysler Town Car pulled up to the front door Terry checked his watch. It was seven thirty-five. He saw Vito Genoa get out and come up on the stoop to ring the bell. Debbie wasn't in the car. In the foyer Terry called, "I'm going now," and Mary Pat came out through the dining room. She asked when he'd be home. He said he had no idea. Mary Pat said he should've eaten something. He said he still wasn't hungry. Vito Genoa nodded to him as he came out. Terry asked if they were picking up Debbie. Vito said another guy was getting her. Terry said he wondered, wouldn't it have been easier if one car picked them both up. Vito said easier for who? Terry sat in back during the forty-minute ride down and over freeways to the east side and the Pointes. He made conversation.

"You know why I thought you were in Star of the Sea parish?"

"You went there?" Vito looking at the mirror.

"I went to Queen of Peace. But you remember Balduck Park and the hill? Used to be full of sleds and toboggans in the winter? You and I were in a fight there one time."

"Yeah?"

"I was eleven, you were a couple years older."

"You saying I started it?"

"You did it all the time, picked on kids smaller'n you were. Vito, you were a big fuckin bully."

It got Vito looking at the mirror.

"Me and you had a fight, uh? Who won?"

"I gave you a bloody nose, but you hit me till I couldn't get up."

"That was you, uh? I remember that one."

"You get in a fight," Terry said, "I remember how much your hands hurt, after."

"Yeah, your fuckin hands. You learn to carry a sap."

"I remember later on seeing your picture in the sports section, when you were at Denby and made All-State. What were you, a defensive tackle?"

"Linebacker."

"Right. You must've got some offers."

"Couple. But I wasn't going nowhere."

They rode in silence for a while.

"You're one of the defendants in the RICO trial?"

"I been out on bond three years while they fuck around."

"How's it going?"

"Nowhere. We're gonna walk."

The cigarette business came to mind and Terry almost mentioned it, but then thought, Why? You trying to get this guy to like you?

There was a silence again. Moving east in the dark, headlights approaching out of the distance.

"So you live in Africa, uh?"

"Five years."

"I wouldn't want no parts of fuckin Africa you give it to me."

"Parts are pretty nice. Except for the bugs. I had a hard time getting used to the bugs, giant ones, every kind of bug there is."

Vito's eyes showed in the mirror.

"When you going back?"

"I think pretty soon."

Vito said, "I think so, too."

Terry hesitated. He said, "Oh?" and sat in the dark, waiting for the man's eyes to appear.

Debbie worked hard to get her driver to talk, a young guy who wore sunglasses at night. Great.

"How long've you been with the mob?"

He had to think about it before he said, "What mob you talking about?"

"How about the Detroit mob? Since that's where we are."

"Why you want to know?"

"I'm making conversation." Asshole. "You ever been to prison?"

Now he had to think that one over before saying, "That's my business."

"I'll bet you never have."

"I don't plan to."

"I have," Debbie said. "Aggravated assault with a deadly weapon.

I put a guy in the hospital." She waited. "You want to know what I hit him with?"

"What?"

"A Buick Riviera."

"Yeah?"

"He was my ex. I was in Florida visiting my mother and I saw him crossing the street right in front of me. He's over a year behind on child support and had no intention of ever paying up."

"You run over him?"

"He got caught underneath the car and I dragged him about a hundred feet."

"Yeah?"

"I said to the arresting officer, 'But the light was green. I had the right of way.' He shouldn't have been crossing then."

"Not if you had the green, no."

"They bring the guy to the courtroom in his body cast and I was fucked."

"Yeah?"

"I was down three years. Ask me if hitting him was worth it?"

"Was it?"

"No. What's your name?"

"Tommy."

"Don't ever go to prison, Tommy, if you can help it."

There was a silence for a while.

"What's it like being a gangster?"

Johnny told the Mutt his dad used to work down here at Eaton Chemical, gone now; they made dyes and different dry-cleaning products. Man, it was dark down here, huh? The whole area gone to hell, the warehouses, you couldn't tell if they were shut down or

doing business or what. They turned onto Franklin, creeping, following the headlight beams along this street where Eaton Chemical
used to be. Johnny said his dad'd come home his hands'd be all
stained. Once he got burned pretty bad with acid. On his arms. He
said, "Okay, you ready? Keep your eyes open."

The Mutt said, "I been ready."

"There's a car up there. What time is it?"

"I just told you. Ten past."

"We go by, take a look."

Johnny eased down on the accelerator, speeding up to about
twenty-five as they passed the car, parked there with its lights off.

"It's him," the Mutt said.

Johnny looked back. "There two guys in the car."

"Yeah, he's got some guy driving for him."

"You said he'd be alone."

"I said what he said, meet him here, and he is, he's here, ain't he?
Like he said."

"What about the other guy?"

"Too bad," the Mutt said. "I didn't invite him."

"I don't like it," Johnny said, slowing down to turn right at the
next street. They turned right three more times, Johnny keeping it at
fifteen miles an hour, till they were back around on Franklin. Man, it
was dark.

The Mutt said, "Pull up behind."

Johnny said, "I'm not getting too close. I'm leaving room we have
to pull out quick." He crept up to about twenty feet away before stopping. He could see two guys in there, the driver's head turned, looking back this way in the Cadillac's headlights.

"Cut the lights," the Mutt said.

"I want to see what you're doing," Johnny said. "You never know,
this kind of deal."

The Mutt got out and Johnny watched him walk up to the passenger side of the car and stand there at the window talking to Vincent, Vincent handing the Mutt something he put inside his leather coat. That would be the twenty-five hundred. Now they were talking again. Now the Mutt was holding something, looking at it. Johnny believed it must be the piece. Now Vincent's hand came out the window. He took the piece from the Mutt, brought it inside the car and handed it back to him. The Mutt turned with it now, Jesus Christ, aiming it this way in the headlights, then turned again to the car and that's when Johnny heard the shots, *pow-pow*. Loud, Jesus, and then two more, *pow-pow*, quick ones, the Mutt holding the piece inside the car to shoot the other guy, the driver. Johnny thinking now, Okay, let's get the fuck outta here. But now the Mutt was walking around the back of the car looking this way and motioning—like he was trying to tell what he was doing, which told absolutely fuckin nothing— as he went around to the driver's side, opened the door and the guy's body started to slide out. The Mutt hefted him back in, then stuck his head and shoulders in there over the guy, and when he straightened up Johnny could see the Mutt had a gun in each hand, aiming 'em both this way and grinning in the Cadillac's headlights. Johnny pulled up next to him.

"Get in the fuckin car, will you?"

The Mutt got in and Johnny took off before the door was closed, Johnny looking at the dark, dead street in his rearview mirror, nothing coming behind them. He said, "Jesus Christ, who was the other guy?"

"I never seen him before," the Mutt said, "some fella. He's the first one I done I didn't know." And said, "No, I take that back. I didn't know the Chaldean I did, the fella I told you ran a book? I never knew his name."

"What'd you take the gun for, wasting time like that?"

The Mutt held up a .38 with a short barrel in his right hand. "Mr. Moraco gimme this snubby saying it's loaded, but they's only five bullets in it. I asked him did he have any more. He says if I needed more'n five shots I was the wrong guy for the job and should give him his money back. I said to him, 'Yeah, but I have to use some of 'em now,' and shot him in the head. Then I had to shoot the other fella and that left only one load, see, for the next job. So I was hoping the driver had a gun on him and he did, this one, a automatic."

"That's a Glock," Johnny said, "you got more'n you need in there, like fifteen shots."

"Okay, Randy said get on Seventy-five and take it north to Big Beaver. You know where it's at?"

"Yeah, it's like Sixteen Mile Road. Then what?"

"Take a left on over to Woodward. I got to look at the directions for the rest."

"We're going out to Bloomfield Hills?"

"Yeah, he's staying out there with his brother."

Johnny braked, hit the pedal hard, rubber screamed on the pavement, the Mutt threw his hands out holding the guns, his hands hit the glove box and he dropped both of the guns. Johnny held on to the steering wheel looking at the Mutt bent over feeling around on the floor.

"Terry Dunn's the hit?"

The Mutt, still down there, said, "Yeah, the priest. Turn the light on."

"You can't do Terry, he's a friend of mine."

The Mutt came up holding one of the guns, the snubby, saying, "Hey, I can't help it, I got paid to do him."

"He's my friend, Mutt," Johnny looking straight ahead now, past his knuckles on the steering wheel to traffic going both ways on Jefferson Avenue, maybe a hundred feet away. He said, "Jesus Christ," shaking his head.

The Mutt said, "You driving me or not?"

"You can't do this one, Mutt. Pass on it—he's leaving anyway, going back to Africa."

"You driving me or not?"

"No, I'm not driving you—you crazy?"

"Then gimme my money back."

"Well, shit, I drove you this far."

The Mutt put the gun on him. "Gimme my money back."

Johnny got the wad out of his side coat pocket and handed it over. The Mutt took it still pointing the gun at him, Johnny watching him now, watching the gun, the guy making up his mind, Christ, and right on the edge of what he was going to do. Johnny slipped his hand from the steering wheel, the left one, and laid it on the door handle. He said, "Okay, then the deal's off, you got your money . . . You find your other gun? Look under the seat."

The Mutt reached down between his legs, head bent, and Johnny shoved against the door, going out as it swung open and the window shattered with the sound of that .38 going off inside the car and Johnny was running back down the street into the dark, thanking Jesus, Mary and Joseph it was the snubby the Mutt picked up off the floor, one shot left in it, and not the other one.

By the time the Mutt had the Glock in his hand his ears were ringing, he couldn't hear nothing, he couldn't see nothing looking through the rear window at the dark street back there. No sign of Johnny, so no sense in chasing after him. What he should do, the Mutt decided, was get on the freeway and head north. Get to the priest before Johnny called him up and said he was coming.

25

VITO BROUGHT TERRY INSIDE. HE said to a young guy in sunglasses standing in the hall, "Put your car around back." He said to Terry, "Wait in there."

The living room. Debbie turned from the fireplace as he went over to her. "You been here long?"

"A few minutes. Tony stuck his head in and said hi."

"He did?"

"I was surprised, too. He said, 'Be with you soon as the photographer gets set up.'"

"We're gonna have a ceremony, huh, the presenting of the check?"

Debbie's gaze drifted off. "What do you think of the decor? Nothing's been changed or moved in forty years. Fake logs in the fireplace."

Terry put his finger to his lips and Debbie hunched her shoulders and made a face. Terry stepped in close. "The room could be wired. I mean by Tony, so he can hear what people think of his house. They don't like it, he has 'em whacked."

"It's lovely," Debbie said out loud. "They have some beautiful pieces." Then dropped her voice. "Like my grandmother's place."

"Mary Pat wanted to know if you liked their house. I told her you loved it. Then she asked, did I think you'd stand by me if I fucked up. Would you?"

"What kind of a question is that? Of course I would. But how can we fuck up? We've got it made."

"That's what I told her."

"She guessed about you?"

"She knew. She said for whatever the reasons guys become priests, I don't fit any of 'em. She called Fran and told him. He didn't get home before I left, so I haven't talked to him yet." Terry said, "On the way here," and paused to glance at the door.

"What?"

"Vito asked when I was going back to Africa. I said I think pretty soon, and he said, 'I think so, too.' "

"Yeah . . . ?"

"Like they're gonna make sure I go back. I told Vito I flew out of Congo-Zaire with a guy who smuggles in guns. Vito wanted to know if there was any money in it. I explained to him I got the hop to Mombasa, and then bought one-way tickets after that 'cause I was low on money. So I don't have a return ticket back. And Vito said don't worry about it."

"What's that mean?"

"What I just told you, they're gonna make sure I go back and spend the money on the orphans." He watched Debbie thinking about it.

She said, "They're not gonna send a guy with you, are they? We could meet somewhere like Paris—why not? And play it from there."

"Yeah, we could."

Vito appeared in the doorway motioning to them. They crossed the front hall with him to Tony Amilia's study.

Debbie looked at the ornate seventeenth-century desk—Oh, my God—and gave the mob boss a perky smile. She said, "Mr. Amilia, I can't tell you how much we appreciate what you're doing."

Tony was standing now, wearing a dark suit and tie for the photograph. He said, "We're ready, let's get it done," and turned to the photographer testing his strobe, bouncing the light off a white umbrella on a stand. He looked over and said, "Hi, I'm Joe Vaughn," and edged toward them to shake hands, a young guy in his thirties, Tony Amilia's height; he seemed pleasant but maybe a little nervous. He said, "Father, if I could get you and Mr. Amilia to stand right against that wall—"

Debbie moved aside. She watched Joe place them in front of a commemorative plaque mounted on the wall:

> **The University of Detroit Mercy honors**
> **Anthony Amilia as a patron member of the**
> **Ignatian Circle in recognition of his**
> **generous financial support and dedication to**
> **higher education in the Jesuit and Mercy traditions.**

"You see this?" Tony said to Debbie. "I went there when it was just U of D, before they went in with this other college and tacked the Mercy on. I don't think it helps the basketball team, you're

U of D Mercy Titans. I was there they played football, Oklahoma, Kentucky, some good teams." He looked at the plaque again. "I want it to be part of the picture, show I do this kind of thing and it's not fake photography. Joe'll give it to the *News* and the *Free Press* and they'll run it. Joe takes my family pictures, different events, birthdays."

Debbie heard Terry say he went to U of D, too, but Tony didn't comment. He said, "Come on, take the picture."

Joe said, "You want the check in the shot, don't you?"

Tony motioned to Vito. "On the desk."

Vito brought Tony the check and Debbie watched Terry trying to read the figures, Terry smiling, taking the end of the check between his fingers as Tony presented it and then pulled it away from him.

"You don't need to touch it I'm handing it to you. All you have to do is look grateful. Joe, take the picture."

"I want to shoot a Polaroid first," Joe said. "See what we're getting."

"You're getting me and him and the check's what you're getting. Now take the picture."

Joe went to work shooting, the flash popping, Joe getting warmed up, five shots in the camera, and Tony said, "That's enough. Vito, help Joe with his equipment. Pack it up out'n the hall." He walked over to his desk with the check.

Debbie said, "Well, that was quick. We are grateful, Mr. Amilia, more than I can tell you."

He was looking at Terry. "All right, Father, you all set? Vito's gonna take you back."

Debbie said, "Well, if that's it," standing at the desk now, waiting for Tony to hand her the check.

He turned to her saying, "Father's going home, you're staying awhile. I want to talk to you."

Debbie said, "Would you mind if Father waited? So we can go back together?" She beamed a smile at him. "We're pretty excited."

Tony said, "Do what I ask, all right? I would like you to stay."

She gave him a cute, wide-eyed shrug, all innocence. "I just thought it might be easier—"

The man's expression did not change. He'd spoken and that was it, end of discussion. Debbie said, "No, if you want me to stay, I'd be happy to." God, overdoing it. She heard Terry, behind her, thank Mr. Amilia.

He said, "I'll call you later, Deb."

And she turned in time to see him going out the door, Vito closing it behind them. She thought of what he'd said in the other room, about their making sure he went back to Africa.

The first thing Tony said was, "Don't be nervous. Come on over here and we'll sit down, have a talk."

He brought her to a grouping of white leather chairs around a slate cocktail table, a phone there, a floor lamp turned low, but she didn't sit down right away. Debbie walked a few steps past the chairs to a glass door that looked out on water, the wide expanse of Lake St. Clair narrowing in the dark to enter the Detroit River. She stood close to the glass, hands shielding her eyes against the light in the study, to see what was out there. Nothing. Gray shades of night. His voice asked if she wanted a drink. She said without turning to him, "I don't want to put you to any trouble."

"Yes or no."

"Okay, but only if you're having one."

"I don't think I will, Miss Manners, so you don't get one."

Even as he said it she was thinking, Do you hear yourself? He even caught it. She remained at the glass door looking at nothing, into herself in the dark, wanting to get back to being herself and stop acting cute and so fucking grateful. She'd gone over the top thanking him and that was enough. Now there was a pinpoint of light out there in the gray that was a darker gray than the sky, two lights, moving. She said, "Is this where you used to bring in liquor from Canada?"

"Me?"

"During Prohibition."

"How old you think I am? No, that was mostly the Jews, the Fleisher brothers and Beeny Bernstein, the Purple Gang. Before my time."

She turned from the glass and sat down with him, the slate table between them. She said, "What's the catch?"

"What're you talking about?"

He reminded her of Ben Gazzara, maybe a bit older and heavier, but that type. She said, "What do I have to do?"

"Oh, you think I want to have sex with you. Pop a few Viagras, listen to Frank Sinatra while we give the pills time to kick in. And you know what? I think it'd be terrific, even with Clara upstairs saying her beads." He said, "Are you fucking the priest?"

Out of nowhere.

Like a heckler in a comedy club, something she could handle. She said, "No, are you? Does he get the check or not?"

Tony brought it out of his inside coat pocket and looked at it, a pale-green check. He said, reading it, "Pay to the order of The Orphans of Rwanda Fund," looked straight at Debbie and tore the check in half.

She said, "Well, that's that. You've got your picture and you'll come off looking great in the paper. I should've known."

"You should've known what?"

She said, "Considering how you make your money."

"You don't know what I do."

"I'm following your trial."

"The feds don't know half of it. I don't talk about what I do, I don't advertise. I don't put on a show. You see these pro backs, these jitterbugs, they score a touchdown and do their dance, the funky chicken? Larry Czonka, one of the greats, said if he ever did that in his time, Howie Long, another one of the greats'd punch him in the head. That's my style, do the job without calling attention to yourself. You say you should've known, like you know what you're talking about. What do you do? You work for lawyers, right? Personal injury stuff, but you want to do comedy. That's what Ed tells me. He says you're funny. He's never seen your act but that's what he says. Are you funny?"

"I'm working on it."

"How serious are you?"

"I'm trying seriously to do comedy. How's that?"

"I touched a nerve there. Maybe you have trouble making up your mind what you want. Or how you want to do it. I don't think you have to be that funny to get by. Most of the clowns doing comedy these days're stupid. They come on the stage like they got shot out of a fuckin cannon, and that's as good as it gets. Who's your all-time favorite comic?"

"Richard Pryor."

"Jesus Christ, the jig with the filthy mouth. What about Red Skelton? You ever see him do the Guzzler's gin skit?"

"Gimme a break."

"You don't like Red Skelton?"

"I put him right up there with Milton Berle."

"Now you're the tough kid, uh? On your own turf."

"You have your style," Debbie said, "and I have mine. If I make it, it'll be on my terms."

"Do whatever you have to, uh?"

"Whatever."

"You know I can help you."

She said, "How, write my material?"

Tony smiled at her. "You take chances, don't you?" He got up from his chair saying, "Don't move," walked over to his desk, brought something out of a file folder and came back with it. A check. This one a pale blue. He handed it to Debbie and sat down again.

"What's the amount?"

"Two hundred fifty thousand."

"Made out to?"

"Cash."

"You notice," Tony said, "it's a cashier's check, not like the other one for the newspaper picture. This one's good the minute you put it in the bank or you cash it. You don't have to wait for it to clear."

She looked up at him. "You're giving this to me?"

"It's all yours."

"Why? Is this like a test?"

"You mean see if you do the right thing? Sweetheart, there isn't any right or wrong about it. I'm giving it to you 'cause I don't care one way or the other about the mick priest and his orphans. There's always orphans around, it's the way it is."

She said, "But the whole idea, what we talked about, you know, his mission—"

"I make the deals," Tony said. "I say it's your money, it's yours, nobody else's."

Debbie was looking at the check again.

She said, "Really?"

"And if you're worried about seeing the priest again, forget about it," Tony said. "I'm sending him back to Africa."

26

TERRY WANTED TO RIDE IN front with Vito Genoa, maybe this time mention the cigarette business, try to get next to the guy and find out what was going on. Were they getting the check or not? But Vito said no, he had to ride in back. After that Vito pretty much kept his mouth shut. Terry did mention the cigarette business, but all Vito said was, "Yeah?" It was a quiet ride along the freeways, nothing to see.

Once they got to Fran's house it was a different story. Vito got out of the car to tell him face-to-face, "You gonna leave tomorrow, Father. I pick you up at nine and we go out to Metro. That means you gonna be right here."

"I told you," Terry said, "I don't have return flights."

"It's taken care of," Vito said.

"Do I leave without the check?"

"Don't worry about it."

"Does Debbie have it, Miss Dewey?"

"It's none of my business," Vito said. "I see you at nine."

"That won't give us time to deposit the check."

And Vito said it again, "Don't worry about it."

Fran let him in, Fran asking questions from the moment Terry stepped inside, and Terry said, "Let me get something to eat, okay? I'm starving." Almost nine-thirty and he hadn't eaten anything since lunch, one of Mary Pat's famous minced ham sandwiches. Mary Pat was on the phone in the library talking to her mother, talking to her for the past hour. Fran said they talked two or three times every day; how could they have that much to say to each other? Terry had another minced ham sandwich, potato chips and a beer while he answered Fran's questions up to and including the photo session with Anthony Amilia and Debbie having to stay; he didn't mention being picked up tomorrow at nine. Maybe he wouldn't be here.

While they were talking two things happened at the same time: the front doorbell rang, and Mary Pat came in with the girls to say good night to Uncle Terry.

The door opened and the Mutt said, "I'm looking for Fr. Dunn. You his brother?"

This kind of porky fella said yes he was and asked, "Is he expecting you?" Like he wasn't going to let him in otherwise.

"Yeah, I'm suppose to see him."

The porky fella hesitated like maybe he didn't believe him. He said, "By any chance did Mr. Amilia send you?"

The Mutt felt the right answer would get him in and he said, "Yes, sir, he did."

It opened the door all the way. The porky fella motioned, this way, and the Mutt followed him out to the kitchen. There was the priest in his black suit turning to look this way, and a woman and two cute little girls, the Mutt thinking, Shit. Now what'm I suppose to do?

The porky brother said, "This gentleman has something for you, Terry, from Tony Amilia."

This gentleman—the Mutt had never heard that one before. He just nodded.

The woman, their mom, was telling the little girls now to leave the pictures where they were—a bunch of photos they were looking at on the high kitchen table—and kiss Uncle Terry good night. She said to the Mutt, "We'll get out of your way."

He said, "Much obliged." But shit, those little girls were going to make it hard for him to do the job he'd come for; he sure didn't want to have to shoot the mom and dad and their little girls. The priest got down so they could hug and kiss him. Then they ran out of the kitchen, their mom and dad shooing them and also leaving. It was the priest that spoke first.

Saying, "I want to thank you for helping me catch my breath the other night. I had all the wind knocked out of me."

"Yeah, you took a shot, didn't you?"

The Mutt could hear the little girls talking loud to their mom and dad, wanting something, their little voices saying please please please. Shit. He didn't need that. The priest was finishing a sandwich, taking the last bite and wiping his mouth with a paper napkin.

This was when the phone rang. It rang twice and stopped in the middle of a ring, somebody in another room picking up a receiver.

The priest said, "You have something from Mr. Amilia? It wouldn't be a check by any chance."

"No, I don't have any check."

"Okay, then what's it about?"

The Mutt saw the priest looking past him and turned to see the porky brother in the doorway. He said, "It's for you."

"Debbie?"

"Your friend. He sounds like he's out of breath. Said he's been trying to get you but the line's been busy."

His friend, which gave the Mutt an idea who it was. He said, "Is that Johnny?"

The porky brother said, "Yeah, you know him?"

"I met him a couple times."

The brother left and the Mutt turned to see the priest with the wall phone, standing there facing the cabinets listening, like he didn't dare look this way. Well, there wouldn't be any surprise now, the priest getting the word from that son of a bitch Johnny, the priest acting like it was just any phone call from a friend, saying, "Uh-huh," saying, "No, uh-unh," putting on an act. The Mutt slipped his hand into his leather coat to take hold of the Glock. He wondered if the priest would piss his pants when he saw it. Now the Mutt glanced at the pictures the little girls had been looking at. He saw a bunch of little nigger kids playing on hardpack. Some others digging what looked like yams. They'd have to be the orphans over there, the ones the money was suppose to go to help.

He was hanging up the phone now, taking his time to look this way.

The Mutt said, "I'll tell you something I don't understand. You see pictures of skin'n bones starving nigger kids, they always have flies all over 'em. Not so much these, but what're flies doing there if there's nothing to eat?"

"Dead people," the priest said, "attract the flies."

He came over to where the pictures were, at one end of the high kitchen table, saying, "Let me show you," and reached into a canvas bag—the Mutt ready to draw the Glock and do it right then. But the priest's hand came out of the bag with a stack of pictures wrapped with green rubber bands he took off and then laid the pictures out on the table with the others, saying, "Over a half-million people were murdered while I was there." The Mutt looked and saw dead bodies, skeletons, some that looked like old dried-up pieces of leather, bits of cloth stuck to bones, all of 'em laid out flat on a concrete floor. He had never seen anything like this in his life, but for some reason it reminded him of prison, Southern Ohio Correctional. He heard the priest say, "I was there. I saw these people and about thirty more in the church that day. I saw them murdered, most of them hacked to death with machetes, like this one."

The Mutt looked up, saw the priest turn from the counter behind him holding a big goddamn machete, raising it and saying now, "This was used to kill some of them." He held it to one side like he was ready to slash with it and the Mutt wasn't sure he could get his gun out in time. Go to shoot somebody and get your goddamn head cut off. The priest surprised him then.

He said, "Tell me something. You're supposed to be a hit man— how many people have you killed?"

The Mutt, still holding on tight to the gun in his coat pocket, said, "I've shot three . . . no, four. And I shanked one."

"That must've been in prison."

"Yes, it was."

"Well, I shot four Hutus with a Russian pistol," the priest said, "one right after the other, like ducks at a shooting gallery."

"What're Hutus?"

"The bad guys at that time," the priest said. "I wonder if I could've done it with this, hack them to death like they did these poor people in the church. You should've heard the screams."

"I bet."

The priest started hefting the weapon like he was feeling the weight of it, getting it balanced just right in his hand, ready to swing it.

The Mutt felt his shoulders hunch.

The priest said, "You know what? I believe I could use it if I had to."

"I'd have to be good and drunk," the Mutt said, "cut a man down like a tree. Why'd they do it?"

"The same old story," the priest said. "Poor people killed the ones that weren't as poor. They got juiced up on banana beer and went crazy."

"Banana beer'll do that, huh? Southern Ohio Correctional," the Mutt said, "we made shine'd give you the worst headache you ever had, turn you mean. There was a riot while I was there? What you said reminded me. Six cons in L Block and a guard got killed, beaten to death. They set fire to anything'd burn and busted what didn't. You wonder what gets into people, don't you?"

"They killed children, too," the priest said. "These orphans're some that are left." He looked up then, placing the machete on the table, and said, "I'll tell you what happened, Mutt. I believe that's your name?"

"Yes, it is."

"I asked Tony Amilia if he'd help me feed these starving children. Look at this one, picking through a garbage dump. Tony said yeah, he'd get the money from Randy. You probably know about that."

"You're right," the Mutt said, "and Randy didn't want to give it to him."

"But Tony made him, didn't he? Randy gave him two hundred and fifty thousand dollars that was supposed to be for these children, but Tony kept it for himself. I haven't seen one nickel of it."

It caused the Mutt to frown and squint.

"You understand what I'm saying?"

"Yeah, but I already got paid."

"To get rid of Vincent Moraco, wasn't it? Johnny told me on the phone."

"No, I got half up front to hit Mr. Moraco. But it was him, Mr. Moraco, paid me to hit you."

For a moment there the priest looked confused, but said, "To keep me from getting Randy's money, right?"

"Yeah . . . ?"

"And I didn't. Tony's got it. You want to shoot somebody, go shoot Tony. You got no business with me." The priest turned to the pictures again. "Unless you want to give something to feed these poor orphans. Look at these little fellas here. Look at their eyes."

Fran and Mary Pat were on the sofa in the library watching television. They both looked up as Terry came in, Terry wearing a white shirt now and jeans. "He's gone?" Fran said.

"Yeah, he left."

Fran said, "He has to be the weirdest-looking gangster I've ever seen. What'd he want?"

"He heard about the orphan fund," Terry said, "and stopped by to make a contribution." He saw Mary Pat giving him her cool appraising eye as he held up a wad of bills. "Five thousand dollars, cash."

"He had that much in his pocket?"

"I guess he just got paid," Terry said. "You never know where it's gonna come from, do you?"

Mary Pat kept looking at him, but still didn't say anything, holding his gaze as he stood there.

Fran said, "Will you please sit down and talk to us?"

"When I get back," Terry said.

He went over and kissed Mary Pat on the cheek.

"I got to go see Debbie."

27

HE PUSHED THE BUTTON NEXT to *D. Dewey* and waited in the light over the doorway to hear her voice on the intercom or for the door to buzz open. She would know who it was. He pushed the button again and waited and then stepped back on the sidewalk to look up at the windows. But then he remembered her apartment was in back and faced the golf course and remembered looking out from the door to her balcony and seeing all that space where crops would be growing in the country he had left, seeing it that night as land going to waste. He ran around to the back of the two-story building and there was her balcony. Lights on in the apartment. He stood at the edge of the fairway looking up and called out, "Debbie!" A light came on in the apartment below hers. He called her name again and saw her at the glass door to the balcony. "It's me!" She saw him. He waved and ran around to the front and pushed her button and still had to wait for the door to buzz open. What was she doing? The door buzzed and he went up the stairs to 202.

She was wearing a pink kimono he hadn't seen before. She smiled, but in a tired way, nothing in her eyes.

"Why aren't you the happiest girl in town?"

She said, "I was in the bathroom." She turned from the door saying, "I thought you'd at least call first."

"What happened? He tried to jump you, didn't he?"

"Nothing like that. You want a drink?"

He followed her into the kitchen saying, "Are we celebrating or what? Why did he want you to stay?"

She brought an ice tray from the refrigerator and cracked it open. Her vodka and the bottle of Johnnie Walker were on the counter, left from that first night he was here, her bag with the shoulder strap lying next to the bottles. She said, "He asked me a lot of questions. He seemed to think he could help me."

"Do what?"

"Get into comedy. He thinks he can open doors, even get me on *Leno*."

"Why, because they're both Italian?"

"He said he had a connection."

"Are you all right?"

She said, "I'm tired, I'm worn out," and pushed his drink to him across the counter.

"Tell me what happened."

"He tore up the check."

Like that. No attempt to get him ready for it.

Terry had picked up his drink. He put it down again. "What do you mean he tore up the check?"

"He tore it in half."

"You're kidding."

"And then tore it again. That's what I mean when I say he tore up the check."

"The one he was handing me we're having our picture taken."

"That one."

"But he said okay. He gave us his word."

"Terry, the guy's a fucking gangster."

"Did you happen to, in some way, piss him off?"

"He asked who my favorite comic was and I said Richard Pryor. His is Red Skelton."

"You didn't hit it off like you thought."

"Oh—and when he said he could help me? I go, 'What're you gonna do, write my material?'"

"Really? You said that to the boss of the mob, the mob boss? 'What're you gonna do, write my material?'" Terry paused as he saw Lauren Bacall delivering the line and his mind picked up one of her lines, his favorite, and changed it to, You know how to write, don't you, Tony? You put your pen in your hand and . . . He said, "It's a good line except for your timing, the occasion. What did he say?"

She came close to Tony's low voice saying, "'You take chances, don't you, kid?' No, he didn't say 'kid,' just that I take chances."

"And you took one and it didn't work."

"Actually I think he liked it, the line."

"Then why'd he tear up the check?"

She said, "If he ever meant to give it to us in the first place. I don't know . . . He's very matter of fact. He asked if I wanted a drink. I said, 'If you're having one.' He said, 'I'm not, so you don't get one.' Gruff, but kind of cool."

"You seeing him again?"

"No. God, no. Why would you ask me that?"

"You think he's cool."

"I thought the line was cool. He said it and right away I wondered if I could work it as a bit."

Terry picked up his glass. He looked at the Scotch and swallowed most of it.

"What'd you say when he tore it up?"

"I said I should've known."

"You weren't surprised?"

"I was, but that's what I said."

"What did he say?"

She let her eyes close and opened them again. "Terry, I'm tired, I want to go to bed."

"You want me to stay?"

She took a sip of her drink. "If you want."

"Tell me what he said."

"He said, 'You should've known what?' I said something about how he makes his money, without coming right out and saying he's a crook, and he said . . ." She paused. "He said, 'You don't know what I do.' Like no one does, because he keeps a low profile, he's not a show-off. He compared himself to that guy who used to play for the Dolphins, Larry Czonka, who said if he ever did the funky chicken after he scored—and I wondered if I could do that as a bit, how pro football players showboat. If he ever did it this other guy would punch him in the head."

"Howie Long."

"That's the one. I pictured a guy in uniform punching another guy in the helmet, and the guy saying, 'Oh, shit, my hand.' "

Terry said, "I did, too, when I heard it." He said, "So I guess the whole thing, Tony just wanted to talk to you?"

"Well, nothing came of it. If you're staying, Terr, let's go to bed."

"But he went to all that trouble—"

"I don't know . . . Come on, Terry, let's go do it." She walked away.

He heard it as if she was saying let's get it over with. Maybe she was. He thought of the morning in Fran and Mary Pat's bedroom talking about changing the sheets and Debbie saying no, they'd just sleep in the bed, they could fuck anywhere; and he remembered it, not so much as a coarse thing for her to say, but as a remark that described what she thought of making love, something you could do anywhere, nothing more than knocking one off.

Terry poured another drink, sipped it and took it with him into the bedroom, sipping it again as he watched Debbie slip off the kimono he hadn't seen before and stand looking at the clock on the bedside table in her white panties that had a tiny pink bow on one side. She rolled them off and Terry saw he'd better get ready. He watched her walk into the hall to the bathroom. She was in there a few minutes and he was in bed when she came out, turning off the bathroom light.

"I took a Seconal. I've got to get that scene out of my mind and sleep." She turned off the lamp and got in bed.

"You'll wait, though, huh, till after?"

"Don't worry, I'm up for it if you are." She reached over and grabbed him and said, "Yes, you are," and away they went, kissing and touching, making adjustments and finally getting into a slow groove, Terry looking at Africa, misty hillsides and tea plantations, houses of red adobe, bats swooping out of the eucalyptus trees to help him stay in the groove and not become frantic; but as he looked at Ah-fri-ca and the sky at dusk, a thought came to him, a question:

If he tore up the check, why is he making sure you go back?

She said, "What's wrong?"

"Nothing. No, we're fine."

And they were. They made love and finished. Debbie reached for a Kleenex and fell asleep while Terry stared at the ceiling in the dark.

Why doesn't he want you around?

You can't hurt him. You're not gonna tell on him, say the photo's a fake. No—he's doing it for her. Getting you out of her way, not his.

It wasn't even his money. Something to make grand gestures with. Tear up the check and write another one to wave in front of little Debbie. He reached over to get his drink, finished it and looked at Debbie asleep, breathing, her cute nose letting little Debbie snores slip out now and again. The guy tore it up in front of her. She said she should've known. She said he wasn't a show-off. But what was tearing up the check if it wasn't putting on a show? Part of the show. Why else go to all that trouble? He likes her and wants to impress her and makes her an offer, like the one in the movie, and she accepts it, it's only for her and she doesn't want to face you, she'll go to bed and hide. You want me to stay? If you want to. What else can she say, she has a headache? She thought you'd call first. Annoyed. She thought at least you'd call first. She didn't want to talk about it, but then wanting him to believe she's being open and honest said more than she had to.

But she didn't ask about your leaving.

They'd talked about it before going in to see Tony, told her they were making sure he went back, but now it wasn't on her mind. Or if it was she wasn't bringing it up; it would happen and he would never know what she got from Tony.

She was wearing a kimono he had never seen before and it made her look different. Or she was different and it had nothing to do with the pink kimono with a deep-red border. He didn't believe she was in the bathroom when he buzzed. He didn't believe it because she told him she was in the bathroom. Picture it. She hears a buzzer she doesn't expect. Then another buzz. She decides to wait it out. But then hears him call her name and looks out—a mistake, but too late, she knows you saw her and if you're coming up she wants to get whatever Tony gave her out of sight, if it isn't already. He buzzes again and has to wait before she lets him in. She's putting it somewhere, whatever it is. I thought you'd at least call first—not sounding happy to see him, not sounding much like his love, his little schemer, his ex-con con-artist girlfriend of what, five days?

Ain't love grand—

She goes to sleep because she wants it to be over, behind her, what she's doing to you. She does like you. He believed that. But does she like you enough to trust you?

She said she was in the bathroom when he buzzed.

Maybe she went in after he buzzed.

She went in the bathroom for a Seconal and turned the light off when she came out. The first night he was here she left it on, so they could see each other while they made love.

He stared at the ceiling.

Did she hide it?

Or does she trust you, Fr. Dunn, to remain innocent and believe her?

Where does she hide things?

Didn't she tell you one time . . . ?

He stared at the ceiling.

He listened to her peaceful breathing.

He slipped out of bed . . .

Debbie woke up a little dopey but knew enough to turn her head on the pillow, see if he was still there. Nope. She sat up before looking the other way, at the clock: 9:25. She wanted to brush her teeth, yuk, get the sticky taste out of her mouth, but decided to make the call first. She expected Mary Pat to answer and she did.

"Hi, it's Debbie. Did Terry get off all right?"

"He was picked up, if that's what you mean. There were two of them."

"They're reliable," Debbie said. "I mean there's nothing to worry about, really." She said, "I don't know how much he told you . . ." and paused to see if Mary Pat would tell her.

Mary Pat said, "Well, Terry didn't seem worried, so I don't think I will."

Debbie said, "Oh." And said, "Okay then. Nice talking to you, Mary Pat."

She tried to imagine Terry's frame of mind as she walked in the bathroom to brush her teeth, walked in and saw fresh rolls of toilet paper, nine of them, stacked on her makeup counter, the plastic bag they came in lying on the floor. The sight came as a shock and postponed brushing her teeth for several more minutes.

It meant he didn't believe her. Her buddy, her partner, didn't fucking believe her. He looked for it but couldn't possibly know what he was looking for. He looked here because, shit, she must've told him about Randy snooping in her bathroom.

But she didn't hide it here. She didn't hide it anywhere. She had thought about it in a panic between door buzzes and thought, Wait. Why? It's Terry. What reason would he have to snoop around?

No, she left it in her bag, in the kitchen. She went in there and that's where the bag was, on the counter, the check in a plain white envelope inside . . .

But it wasn't.

28

RIGHT AFTER THE TRIO FINISHED their set the piano player would say into the mike, "And now, to tickle your funnybone and your fancy, here is that rising star of comedy, Detroit's own Debbie Dewey."

It reminded Debbie of the bored voice on the PA system in *M*A*S*H* announcing the movie for that evening and what it was about. She said to the piano player after the first time he brought her on, "Carlyle, I don't tickle funnybones."

Carlyle said, "I know you don't, girl. But this is the only game in town for us, you dig? The man, dumb as he is, tells me what to say, I say it."

That fucking Randy. She said, "Well, could you not sound so bored?"

"The man say keep it gentrified, meaning to him low-key. Meaning to us, you right, bo-ring."

The meeting that made it happen—Vito Genoa giving Randy the word—reminded Debbie of a sentencing hearing.

"Tony wants her to work your room three nights a week."

Randy, in his manner, said, "I don't run a comedy club. This is a four-star restaurant."

Vito said, "You pay her five gees a week, guaranteed ten weeks. After that you can do what you want."

"Pay her fifty thousand," Randy said, "on top of what I've already given her?"

"Five gees a week," Vito said, "you can write off. Also during the ten weeks you don't have to pay the commission on the ladies. Tony's giving you a break."

Randy said, "I'd love to know what she's giving him."

Debbie spoke up. "What if I don't want to perform?"

Vito looked over at her sitting in the chair under Soupy Sales. He said, "You're smart you'll keep your mouth shut till you have something funny to say," and turned to Randy again. "Where's the Mutt?"

"I haven't seen him. He must've quit."

"They find your car?"

"Not yet."

"I think he did Vincent and took off in your Cadillac. What do you think?"

"I've learned not to speculate about him," Randy said. "Where the Mutt's concerned, anything is possible."

The Mutt had called Randy from Ohio saying, "You know who this is? It's me. I don't want to say too much over the phone. I did the one but not the other, since he never got your money. And I didn't come by to collect you know what as I decided to keep the car instead."

"But it's worth three times what I owe you," Randy said.

"That's okay, you have in-surance, don't you? What I need is the title, so when I go to sell it I can. Send it to the amusement park at Cedar Point, where I'll be working for a while. Man, they got some rides here. They got the Raptor, the Mantis, the Mean Streak. They got the Iron Dragon, the Demon Drop . . ."

When Debbie called Tony, and told him, sniffling, what happened, she said, "I had it in my hand, the chance of a lifetime, and he ripped me off—a priest."

"I think what you mean to say," Tony said, "you tried to fuck him over; only the mick priest knows you better than you know him and he taught you a lesson. You weren't paying attention."

"Aren't you gonna do anything?"

"Like what, send one of my guys to Africa? It's your money, kid, not mine."

"Tony, he's not in Africa. Just because you bought him a ticket . . . That's the last place he'd go. I wouldn't be surprised if I got a call from like Paris or the South of France, a familiar voice on the phone—"

"Don't tell me," Tony said, "you talked him into leaving the Church, or he wasn't a priest to begin with."

She didn't say anything.

"I don't want to hear that, you understand? I don't want you telling me anything like that."

Debbie said in a quiet, contrite voice she kept handy, "I was just, you know, talking. I held out on him, he found the check and I got what I deserved." She made herself say, "At least he'll use it for the orphans."

"So you were slandering him 'cause you're mad, you hate to lose. Is that it?"

"I'm sorry, I really am."

"You want to chase after him? Go to Africa and come down with some fuckin disease you never heard of?"

"I'll get over it."

"Maybe it would help," Tony said, "you had a ten-week engagement at, say, five grand a week. Get some of it back."

"I don't have the name to demand anywhere near that much."

"I do," Tony said.

She stopped sniffling. "You could make that happen?"

"Would I say it if I couldn't?"

She didn't ask if there was a catch.

The piano player from the trio said into his mike, "And now, to tickle your funnybone and your fancy"—giving it a little more punch—"here's that rising star of cool comedy, Detroit's own Debbie Dewey!"

She came out from the back hall and stepped up on the bandstand in her oversized prison dress and shitkickers. She looked out at white tablecloths and patrons who could afford Randy's prices, a polite audience, patient.

Okay, go.

"I'd like a show of hands, please. How many of you have ever done time? I don't mean a night in jail on a DUI, I'm talking about serious prison time." Debbie put her hand flat above her eyes as she looked over the room. "No one here has been caught out at Metro with dope? Fly home from some groovy spot, you see that little dog, Snoopy, checking out your bags and you hope to God the fink dog doesn't rat you out?"

They liked it, wanting her to know they were hip.

"I guess I'm the only one in the room who's been down. I did most of three years for aggravated assault with a deadly weapon."

Debbie looked over at Randy standing at the bar and offered the next line to him.

"I was visiting my mom in Florida and happened to run into my former boyfriend . . . with a Ford Escort. Not what you think of as a deadly weapon, but it did the job, put him in traction for a few months."

She turned to the audience again, the white tablecloths and the faces, some smiling.

"When I tell you what a snake this guy was, you'll understand why I wished I was driving an eighteen-wheeler loaded with scrap metal. Listen, ladies? If a guy who has a pet bat, and sometimes poses as a priest, ever asks you for a date? Tell him you're busy. The first thing he said to me, at a fancy wedding reception I found out later he wasn't invited to . . ."

Chantelle watched through the screen door: Laurent the RPA officer, beret under his arm, and Terry, his hands in the pockets of his khaki shorts, in the yard talking, moving from one foot to the other, looking at the empty church and talking, looking in the distance to the tea plantation, the green slope dark at this hour of the day, time for Mr. Walker but still talking, Terry not calling to the house to bring it out, please, for our guest. They would be speaking as gentlemen as each wondered what the other was doing here. It was like watching a film without sound, but having an idea what they were saying, each telling the other it was good to see him again. No, nothing new has happened. Yes, the ones from the church have been buried . . . She waited until Laurent shook Terry's hand again, put on his beret, walked to his Land Cruiser, waved and drove away. Now she pushed the screen door open with her foot and came outside with the tray of glasses and the bowl of ice, the bottle of Johnnie Walker pressed beneath the stump of her arm. She believed it was good for the muscle to be used this way, squeezing the bottle, and believed she would be using it again and again and again, the woman knowing things the man didn't seem to know.

"Why didn't you bring it out while he was here?"

"Why didn't you tell me to?"

She placed the tray and then the bottle on the warped table and put ice in the glasses.

"I thought we were celebrating, having the black."

"One day I dropped it on the floor and it broke."

"It doesn't matter. Did you have any of the bourbon?"

"Yes, I like the taste of it."

"Has Laurent been around much?"

She handed him his Scotch full of ice. "You know how long you been gone? Eleven and a half days. Tell me what you mean by 'much.'"

"Has he?"

"He likes me. He comes to see am I all right, being alone here. He has his wife from Kampala living with him now."

"You go from a priest to a married man—"

She said, "Let me think. Do I go to them, or they come to me? Don't concern yourself with Laurent." She turned with her drink and sat down next to him in this quiet time before the insects began making their noise, looking to attract insects like them to have sex with and make millions of more insects. "You say you came back to take care of children. But you not a priest anymore."

"I told you, I never was."

"What are you now, a Seven Day Adventist? They take care of

children. Are you going to hear Confession? It was something you like to do."

"I'll talk to people, try to help them. Even do it like Confession if they want."

"Yes, and you give penance?"

"Can't do that anymore."

"Did you tell Laurent?"

"I will the next time, when he realizes I'm here and not visiting or happened to be passing by—the reason he told me he stopped. But if you happen to be passing by, where are you going? The road ends here. He asked if I knew I was coming back."

"What did you tell him?"

"I said, 'Not until I got here.' "

"With practice," Chantelle said, "you could become a visionary, tell people what the Blessed Mother says to you, good things that will happen in the future. People would like that very much and reward you, bring you chickens, tomatoes, a bushel of corn—"

"Banana beer?"

"You said you don't like it."

"I said I've never tried it. Do you know who you sound like?"

"Let me think," Chantelle said. "It must be the woman you robbed and you believe is the reason you left her."

Terry looked at Chantelle and smiled and shook his head in a good way, appreciating her. He rose and, leaning over her chair, kissed her on the mouth, a long kiss but tender.

He said, "You're the visionary. Tell me my future."

She said, "You mean, what you'll be when you grow up, or when your money runs out?"

He said, "I can always get more."